Bones of Evidence

Clea Koff is a forensic anthropologist and author. Born in London and raised in England, East Africa and the US, she was a member of the first international forensic team brought together by the UN in 1996 to investigate evidence of war crimes and crimes against humanity, commencing in Rwanda after the 1994 genocide. She subsequently worked for the UN International Criminal Tribunal for the former Yugoslavia in Bosnia, Croatia and Kosovo. *The Bone Woman* (2004), her memoir about this work, was published in the UK, US, Australia and Canada and sold in translation to ten languages worldwide.

cleakoff.com
thebonewoman.com

By the same author

The Bone Woman
Silent Evidence
Deadly Evidence

Bones of Evidence

Clea Koff

avon.

Published by AVON
A division of HarperCollins*Publishers* Ltd
1 London Bridge Street
London SE1 9GF

www.harpercollins.co.uk

HarperCollins*Publishers*
Macken House, 39/40 Mayor Street Upper
Dublin 1, D01 C9W8, Ireland

A Paperback Original 2026
1

Copyright © Clea Koff 2026

Clea Koff asserts the moral right to be identified as the author of this work.

A catalogue record for this book is available from the British Library.

ISBN: 978-0-00-868782-3

This novel is entirely a work of fiction. The names, characters and incidents portrayed in it are the work of the author's imagination. Any resemblance to actual persons, living or dead, events or localities is entirely coincidental.

Set in Sabon LT Std by HarperCollins*Publishers* India

Printed and bound in the UK using 100%
Renewable Electricity at CPI Group (UK) Ltd

All rights reserved. No part of this publication may be reproduced, stored in a retrieval system, or transmitted, in any form or by any means, electronic, mechanical, photocopying, recording or otherwise, without the prior written permission of the publishers.

Without limiting the author's and publisher's exclusive rights, any unauthorised use of this publication to train generative artificial intelligence (AI) technologies is expressly prohibited. HarperCollins also exercise their rights under Article 4(3) of the Digital Single Market Directive 2019/790 and expressly reserve this publication from the text and data mining exception.

For my mom, Msindo

A note for the reader

Although Agency 32/1 does not exist, it should.

It is based on the Missing Persons Identification Resource Center, a California non-profit founded by the author in 2004 to link families of missing persons with coroners holding thousands of unidentified bodies across the United States. MPID has since closed.

- The plot and characters of this book are fictional.
- The statistics on unidentified bodies are fact.
- Forensic profiles of missing persons are hope.

Prologue

April 2005 – Atlanta, Georgia

King kept his eye on the digital camera's screen as he deepened the focus past the fern fronds fluttering in the evening's soft rain, past the window frame thick with layers of white paint and on through the glass. It amazed him that people didn't close their curtains at dusk – that people didn't think anyone was watching. Granted, he'd had to use a long lens from across the street to get a visual this deep into the townhouse.

What he could see was augmented by what he could hear. He'd planted the microphone in the window box, right among the ferns, and it was picking up the murmurs from the bedroom at the back. He thought 'boudoir' would be a better description. The wallpaper was golden, the four-poster draped in jewel-toned silk and the bedding . . . well, there wasn't much of that left on the bed at this point, which was interesting because he'd watched the homeowner prepare every pillow and every rose petal as she'd awaited her bedmate.

And wasn't Special Adversary Houston making straight men look good, the way he was giving Callista an extensive massage. King took another photograph. He hadn't decided how he'd use these photos but they would provide ammunition if Plan A wasn't lethal enough.

He turned down the volume on his headphones; he could not stand this woman's giggle and, frankly, didn't know how his adversary could stand it either. Then again, he'd noticed that Special Adversary Houston wasn't spending much time with Callista anymore, nor did he respond whenever she said, 'I love you,' which was often, as though repetition would eventually generate an answering 'And I love *you*.'

King wondered if his adversary would stay the night like he used to. Or would he leave soon, as he had lately, showered and already dialing his favorite companion? Now, *those* conversations were interesting. King could only hear one side, of course, and only when he was close enough to point a directional mic without being noticed. But those times had been enough to reveal that his adversary was more than a venal robot. Not that that changed anything; he would take him down regardless. Oh no, that giggle again. But what was this? King focused the lens and turned up the volume.

His adversary was stretching for his BlackBerry on the bedside table, six-pack on full display. Now he was sitting, feet on the floor. Now standing. Oh dear. The lady had put her hands on her hips, perched on the bed. King couldn't see her face but imagined a pout because her tone was . . . special: 'You have to go? *Now?*' King softly tut-tutted his adversary. Hadn't he noticed that his lady had had dinner delivered, had set the fussy table for two under the candelabra in the front room?

When the couple came out from the bedroom, the lady was still naked. His adversary turned to face her: 'Callista . . .' King saw her smile and reach for him with confidence: 'Yesss?' Her tone was a slice of sultry Southern nights but his adversary just covered his gun with one hand, disengaged her with the other and indicated the window with a tilt of the head: 'You should close the shades.'

As she came to the window, right toward the hidden camera, her face betrayed her annoyance. But her body was breathtaking – by mainstream standards. It didn't do anything for King. He snapped a photo as she reached for the curtains.

And then the front door opened to emit Special Adversary Houston, glancing up at the drizzle as he trotted down the wet porch steps. The light of the vintage streetlamp picked out the FBI shield on his belt and the phone in his hand. No guesses needed as to whom he was dialing but the surveillance mic clinched it: 'Jayne. I'm so glad you called. How's the weather in LA?' Then his adversary was closing the door to the Bureau Suburban and the engine was roaring to life.

King aimed the camera back at the townhouse window. Callista had reopened the curtains and was watching the vehicle accelerate away, twirling the ring on her left hand. He took a photo of that. *Click.*

Four Months Later

DAY 1

Monday

1

Jayne woke up in her berth and could immediately tell that the mobile unit was parked. She checked her cell phone: 5:27AM Central Time. The convoy must have driven through the night and she was three minutes ahead of her alarm. She cancelled it. Pulling back her window curtain, she discovered there was enough daylight to see that they'd arrived at their Louisiana base camp, a graveled highway rest area surrounded by trees. The other Federal Bureau of Investigation RVs were there too, parked in a semi-circle.

Jayne tensed. There had been a sudden movement just below her window. She stared hard, trying to see more. A man wearing dark clothing and a cap. Then he made an about-face and she spotted his badge. He was a police trooper, not the man who had attacked her and Steelie just months ago, the man who had been their friend – no, their trusted colleague – on a United Nations forensic mission to Rwanda. The man who'd kissed her once. It was not Gene.

She got up and dressed quietly since Steelie hadn't emerged from behind the fabric panel that provided a measure of privacy and road safety to each berth. Special Agent Angela Nicks' panel was open, however, her bedding pulled neatly over the pillow. Jayne had been glad of Angie's presence last night when the convoy had left Atlanta. As the agent had rolled into her berth wearing a blue T-shirt with 'FBI' emblazoned in yellow across the chest, she'd said, 'I sleep lightly. But my Glock? It never sleeps.' That had helped Jayne to rest even as the bus hurtled through the darkness, taking her ever closer to Gene.

The moment Jayne opened the door from the sleeping compartment, she smelled coffee. Angie was working at a laptop in a pool of light at the dining booth, a cup set off to the side next to a half-consumed energy bar. She was wearing a navy-blue collared T-shirt, the FBI insignia on the left side of her chest. Her braids were pulled into her trademark high ponytail and a gleam of gloss on her lips was her only nod to make-up.

She looked up. 'Hey, Jayne. Coffee? I made a pot.'

Jayne returned the greeting and found a mug in the kitchenette.

'If you need a snack, we've got some stuff in the fridge, but otherwise . . .' Angie paused as she looked at her watch. 'It's exactly twelve minutes until breakfast. Not that I'm counting.'

Jayne poured herself a coffee and added a splash of cream plus a packet of sugar. Stirring the steaming concoction, she slid into the booth across from Angie, who indicated her laptop.

'Just reading through the antemortem data you and Steelie gathered from the families. This is good. You got a lot of material we didn't have from the missing person reports.'

'We wouldn't need this much antemortem data if more

families were willing to give DNA samples. But you know how it is.'

'That I do. They're worried the Bureau is going to run their DNA through every law enforcement database in a wild attempt to solve cold cases.'

'Angie, some of them think they're going to be fitted up for those cases.'

The agent grimaced and closed the laptop. 'Maybe your meetings with them will have changed their minds.'

'I think that getting some IDs will change their minds. Not to pile any more pressure on all of us.' Jayne sipped her coffee and then lifted her mug toward Angie. 'Thanks for this.'

The door from the sleeping compartment opened and Steelie emerged. Like Jayne, she was dressed in a long-sleeved shirt over a sleeveless vest and cargo pants, but her hair was wet at the edges from where she'd splashed water around liberally when washing her face. The silver strands that had appeared above her ears in college and led to the nickname of 'Steelie' weren't as bright when her blonde hair was damp like this.

Steelie sniffed the air in an exaggerated manner. 'Where there is coffee, there must be donuts and yet I detect only coffee. Jayne, what kind of lawyer would I be if I let us sign a Memorandum of Understanding that didn't predicate our involvement on the presence of donuts?'

Jayne pretended to give this some thought, then said, 'I have yet to see a donut clause in a government MOU.'

Angie left the booth with her laptop, her noticeable biceps moving with the action. 'Take a pew, Steelie. I'll go see if the local cops can rustle up something deep-fried.'

As Angie stepped down to the RV's door, Steelie called after her. 'My preference is lemon-filled, regular glazed and jam-filled – and in that order!'

'Ten-four, Ms. Lander.' Angie chuckled and closed the door behind her.

Steelie poured herself a half-cup of coffee, added creamer and sugar and sat at the table, filching Jayne's spoon to stir her drink. 'How long have you been up?'

'Not much before you.'

'Have you seen your man?'

Jayne was about to issue her usual rebuttal that Scott was not 'her man' before she realized that, at this point, he actually was. They'd been as good as living together for the past two months; only parted by her working in Atlanta last week. 'Not yet,' she replied.

Steelie cranked open the blinds and looked out the window as she sipped her coffee. 'I see some Critters and a load of cops. They haven't brought Gene yet, have they?'

'I don't think so.' Jayne was glad Steelie was betraying a measure of anxiety as well. 'I'm not sure I'm ready to see him.'

'Maybe breakfast will help,' Steelie ventured.

'If it stays down.'

Steelie made a noise like *yech*.

After a few minutes, they headed out. The trooper on the door of their RV glanced at their FBI adjunct badges and nodded at them.

Gravel crunched underfoot as Jayne walked with Steelie across to the mess, which was housed in a massive fifth-wheel trailer with slide-outs attached to a heavy-duty double-cab pick-up truck. The trooper outside inspected their badges and then opened the door for them.

They were immediately assailed by the noise of talking and laughter coming from a large group of people already serving themselves breakfast. Buffet tables were laden with large foil trays of pancakes, bacon, scrambled eggs and grits. Flanking the food were urns of coffee and hot water.

Angie's voice called out over the din: 'Steelie. Got your donuts over here.' She lifted a bulging paper bag high in the air.

'Angie, you are a goddess,' Steelie called back as she and Jayne joined the queue for food.

Jayne looked around, taking in the room and hoping to see Scott. Folding tables were set up in a single row down the middle of the trailer, chairs on either side, and there were a number of people she didn't recognize. It was when one of them moved to the side that Jayne finally saw Scott, in conversation with them. His green eyes were focused on his interlocutor and his dark blond hair looked as though he'd just had it cut. His arms were comfortably crossed over the same Bureau-issued shirt as Angie's but his beige cargo pants were punctuated by a black gun holster at the thigh rather than the waist. He looked in his element: engaged, determined, purposeful.

Then Jayne spotted Eric approaching Scott. Eric's warm brown eyes were fixed on his partner and his dark hair shone along the side part as always. He was dressed in the same uniform as Scott but he was even more muscular than his partner, into whose ear he was now whispering. Scott immediately looked up, eyes alight, found Jayne and smiled. *Oh my God,* Jayne thought, *he makes me feel alive.*

She smiled back and Scott resumed his conversation. Jayne barely paid attention to what food she selected at the buffet. All she could think about was how she would handle four days of being this close to Scott without touching him.

Once everyone had been seated for a few minutes amid a buzz of conversation, Scott stood up at the far end of the table, pushing his plate to the side in favor of a notebook he had open in front of him.

'Okay, folks, most of us know each other but we're going to do a few introductions anyway.' The room fell quiet. 'I'm Special Agent Scott Houston out of Los Angeles. I've been assigned to lead this mobile operation to recover the remains of Atlanta victims of convicted serial killer Eugene Frederick King. This is my partner, SA Eric Ramos. We had the lead on the federal investigation into the disappearances of these thirteen women when we were posted in Atlanta earlier this year. If I am out of commission for any reason, Agent Ramos here is your go-to for anything umbrella-level. We have the same knowledge, the same clearances.'

Eric nodded at everyone around the table and then smiled at Jayne and Steelie, who smiled back.

Scott continued, 'The four bodybuilders currently getting a second helping of pancakes are the Bureau's Western Region Critical Stabilization and Recovery Unit, AKA the Critters: Special Agents Tony Lee, Steve Weiss, Duane Sparks and Xavier Tollen.'

The four men, all in their thirties, had turned around

while Scott was speaking, holding their plates and inclining their heads as their names were called.

'They'll be doing evidence collection, processing, photography – all the crime scene stuff. The laboratory RV is their domain, so if you want to get in there, talk to them. From Atlanta here on my right, we have SAs Angela Nicks and Mark Wilson. They helped break the King case and aided in his capture. Agent Nicks is also our liaison to Atlanta PD's Missing Persons Squad. She's their sole point of contact with us as we deal with recoveries and, hopefully, identifications. So, no personal phone calls to anyone you know in APD Missings.'

People nodded, faces serious. Scott took a sip of his drink and the Critters slipped back to their seats in that break, quietly dressing their food with condiments.

'At the other end of the table, the three light blue shirts are our Bureau logistics team. Nate Heller, Sara Young and Joe Thompson. You will recognize them as the drivers for the men and women's accommodation units and this mess trailer respectively. They are doing site set-up, breakdown and any logs issues. If your shower isn't hot enough, they're who you complain to.' He winked at them.

Someone called out, 'Where *is* the complaints box? I couldn't find it this morning.'

Everyone laughed and the logistics folks rolled their eyes.

Scott continued. 'In the white shirt is John Taylor, our IT guy, out of the Atlanta Bureau office. He's here to support the evidence team so don't ask him how to set up your voicemail or any other trivial shit.'

John gave Scott a loose salute.

'On my left here,' Scott said, 'we have our two civilians: Jayne Hall and Steelie Lander. They're forensic anthropologists who run the LA-based non-profit, Agency 32/1, which IDs John and Jane Does using forensic profiles of missing persons. Let me be clear: Thirty-Two One is not here on a field trip. They have a Bureau MOU – that's Memorandum of Understanding for those of you who don't know – that is specific to the recovery of these remains. They have prior involvement in this case and the families of the missing women would only work with the Bureau if Thirty-Two One was involved. Let me flip that around: none of the families – none – would provide DNA samples to the Bureau on our request but said they'd consider it if Thirty-Two One was on board.'

There were murmurs so Scott spoke louder, his eyes moving across the people who were talking. 'We have high-quality antemortem data only because Hall and Lander spent the past week in Atlanta doing one-on-ones with the families. Now. We can likely make some IDs with what we have but the intel we have from Thirty-Two One is that even presumptive identifications will improve family cooperation on DNA for the rest of the remains.'

John, the IT technician, was looking at Jayne and Steelie with frank curiosity. 'So you guys soften up the families.'

But Scott addressed him. 'The word is "liaise", John, and it works. And it matters here because the remains on this operation will not be whole bodies. It might be as bad as a single bone here or there. It's going to be tough. I'll get to recovery protocols in a minute.'

Scott glanced down at his notebook. 'First, security. Federal Corrections will be transporting King in and out of the sites each day. King's coming in person as part of a deal, the details of which I won't go into here, but without him, we do not have enough info to locate these remains without wasting huge amounts of money and manpower. Corrections is responsible for keeping him cuffed, ankle-shackled and whatever else they do with him. This is key because he's already posed a critical threat to both Thirty-Two One and Atlanta-based Bureau staff.'

He looked around the room, ensuring he had everyone's attention.

'Now, we do not consider him dangerous while Corrections is doing its job. However, Thirty-Two One is under our protection for this entire operation. Unlike King, they *are* our responsibility. If you are weapons-trained and have a weapon on you, you are locked and loaded whenever King is present with an eye to the security of Thirty-Two One. That is coming straight from Supervisory Special Agent Turner in Los Angeles. It is in their contract with the Bureau.'

Scott let that sink in before continuing. 'Let me give you a scenario: we have the highway cordoned off around a recovery site, and a car plows through the perimeter tape. You do not preserve the site. You preserve Thirty-Two One.'

'Roger that,' Angie said.

Scott acknowledged her remark with a nod. Then he looked around the table. 'Do not engage with King on anything. At all times remember that he used to be FBI. He worked in our lab in DC. He may even know your name. Don't respond to him if he speaks to you even if he just asks you what time it is or what day it is. Am I understood?'

There were nods and murmurs around the table.

Scott checked his BlackBerry. 'Okay, last thing for this morning.' He turned to a whiteboard onto which was taped a map. 'Where we are today, east of New Orleans, is simply the first recovery site when moving out from Atlanta.'

He pointed to a location marked with a blue magnet. 'As most of you learned when you were selected for this team, we are moving westward along the highways as King attested he did when he dumped the frozen body parts of the women he kidnapped and killed in Atlanta. The map shows the locations of our stop points, so after today, presuming we complete the recovery, our convoy rolls overnight to San Antonio, Texas, where we have two sites. Then we move on to Lordsburg, New Mexico. Last recovery location is Phoenix, Arizona, with three sites. These are not the exact site locations. We need King for that.'

He turned back to the room and used his pen to indicate a person Jayne knew already. 'Special Agent Mark Wilson will move the lab vehicle as needed. Logs will take care of the other mobile units. Some people may need to work on the road; some will be in downtime. Don't worry about who's doing what. Mark here will be doing head counts, but watch yourselves: if you get left behind, we will not be coming back for you, not least because our drivers have told me that this trailer can't be turned around.'

People laughed.

He glanced at his watch. 'Okay, we have ten minutes for

people to make themselves beautiful. If you're deploying to the site with the scientists, you'll find protective gear and anything else you need set up on tables by the lab. Mark will ensure you know when it's chowtime. Are we good? Any questions?'

People shook their heads in the negative. Scott twirled a finger in the air to indicate they were moving out and everyone rose, chairs scraping along the floor as they were folded amidst the noise of talking, jockeying to throw away trash and leaving the trailer. Jayne and Steelie were swept out with everyone else.

Back at their RV, Angie was already inside, taking a last bathroom break. Jayne and Steelie followed her lead, coming out to find that Angie had waited for them.

She said, 'I noticed neither of you drank much at breakfast but it's going to be hot when you're out looking for the site. It's a plain stretch of Louisiana highway so make sure you hydrate.'

Steelie said, 'We try to balance hydration against needing a bathroom where there isn't one.'

It was only a beat before Angie got it. 'Oh yeah. The men can just turn their backs and go in the bushes but you'd have to drop your pants.'

Steelie smirked. 'Hey presto: not "one of the guys" anymore. Though we could do what we used to do overseas, Jayne?'

Angie asked, 'Adult diapers?'

Jayne laughed but Steelie said, 'That's not a bad idea! No, we went in pairs: one woman to pee, another to hold the privacy shield.'

Angie looked incredulous. '*Two* women had to down tools at the same time?'

Jayne said, 'Learned that on our first UN mission when a delay in getting portable toilets to our site in the middle of nowhere meant we had to pee without vegetation for cover.'

'What about, y'know, that time of the month?'

Steelie whistled. 'Don't ask. Seriously, Agent Nicks, do not ask.'

Jayne gave Angie a smile. 'All that being said, we will drink water – the second we start sweating.'

Angie said, 'So your system will be balanced. Got it.'

They left the RV but Angie paused before they parted ways. 'I wanted to say: try to remember that the last time you saw King, he was free, running surveillance on you and setting traps. But now he's an inmate. I know because I interrogated him myself. He's going to be cuffed, monitored, watched – the whole nine yards.' She gave Jayne an appraising look. 'Good to go?'

Jayne inhaled deeply, let it out and nodded.

'I notice that no one asks me if I'm good to go,' Steelie grumbled.

Angie raised an amused eyebrow. 'That's because all your problems are solved by donuts.'

Steelie shrugged. 'This is true.'

2

'Ladies,' Agent Tony Lee said when Jayne and Steelie walked up to the laboratory RV. The three other Critters paused in the act of putting on their protective scene gear and there were enthusiastic greetings between everyone.

'We have to stop meeting like this,' Duane Sparks said as he put a hand out to Steelie.

She exclaimed, 'Sparky, it's been, like, two months since we last saw you!'

'Almost exactly two months,' Xavier Tollen added. 'We were at UCLA. The Hart exhumation.'

Tony gave Jayne an apologetic look as he shook her hand. 'I don't think they've forgotten, Xavier.'

'Definitely didn't forget,' Jayne said, turning to get a coverall. 'But that was a good day. Hard, but good.'

'Speaking of hard days,' Steve Weiss said as he zipped up his coverall and tried to settle his broad shoulders in the fabric, 'what was that at the briefing about King being a critical threat to you two? That was the first I'd heard about it.'

Steelie said, 'You only heard about that today? I thought news traveled fast in the Bureau.'

Duane interrupted, waggling his index finger. 'That's only for who's dating who.'

'Whom, surely?' Steelie grinned at him.

Steve ignored them. 'I was just thinking it had to be from Atlanta because I'd have heard about it if it was in LA.' He turned to look at a sedan with tinted windows that was rolling slowly into the rest area.

Jayne felt an anxious knot forming in her stomach; Gene had to be in the car. He was the only one not here yet. She said, 'It's kind of a long story, Steve.'

Tony came to stand next to her. 'I can make it short; Mark gave me the low-down.' He opened the box of gloves labeled MEDIUM and pushed it toward her. 'Okay with that?'

Jayne nodded as they stood almost shoulder-to-shoulder, each double-gloving.

Tony said, 'Thirty-Two One did the forensic consult on the King case in Atlanta, nice and easy, and they were set to fly back to LA. The Bureau determined King was on the run, being a wanted man and all, but he'd actually stayed in Atlanta. He kept Thirty-Two One under surveillance and ambushed them at a time of his convenience. However, Jayne here,' he patted her on the back, 'gave him a concussion.'

'Not before he'd attacked Steelie,' Jayne said, watching the sedan execute a wide U-turn on the gravel.

Steve jutted his chin out toward Tony. 'How come the rest of us are only hearing about this now?'

'Mark said Scott wanted it kept under wraps. It was advantage King at the time.'

'Well, not anymore,' Duane said, gesturing at the sedan, which had parked at a point equidistant from both the frontage road leading back to I-10 and the boundary fence leading to acres of woodland.

The sedan's back door opened and Jayne felt the knot

in her stomach twinge, but the man who emerged wasn't Gene. He was tall and lean like Gene but his hair was dark, not fair. Then she saw that he was wearing the uniform of a Corrections officer. He kept the back door open as a woman in the same uniform emerged from the driver's door. She was stocky, brown-skinned and wearing her afro in a short fade style that was sensible for a woman in Corrections who didn't want her head pulled back by a ponytail if that chance presented itself to a detainee. Both officers had a stiff and serious demeanor, each with a hand resting on a sidearm. Jayne watched Scott confer with them before the male officer leaned into the sedan's backseat to bring out their charge.

Jayne heard Steelie's intake of breath. She was equally shocked. It was indeed the man they'd known for almost a decade but the usual air of superiority Gene gained from his remarkable height was undercut by a stoop from a chain linking his handcuffs to his ankles. His yellow Corrections jumpsuit made his sallow complexion look almost sickly. His demeanor was subdued and docile – until the officers removed the linking chain. Then he straightened, pulling his shoulders back as if to stretch and tilting his face to the sun. Next, he took in his surroundings. His pale eyes quickly passed over everything in the rest area – Jayne was relieved that she and Steelie were unrecognizable at this distance, completely covered as they were in protective gear – and then settled on Eric, who was walking toward him. Scott indicated that they should get moving.

The Critters, Jayne and Steelie picked up their toolkits to come up behind Scott and Eric. Everyone was walking in single file except for Gene at the front where the two

Corrections officers flanked him as he moved at a slow pace. The group entered the shoulder of the interstate where Louisiana State Police had blocked off the nearside lane with orange cones and yellow tape emblazoned with the word CAUTION. At the top end where traffic was filing past, a single State Police vehicle was parked on the shoulder facing oncoming traffic with its rooftop lightbar activated.

Gene reached a highway emergency telephone and stopped. 'About here.'

Scott gestured for Jayne, Steelie and the Critters to come forward. That's when Jayne heard Gene's voice again. She felt it like a slap across the face.

'Well, well, if it isn't—'

Scott cut him off. 'Don't talk to them, King. Talk to me. And get on with it. We don't have all day.'

Gene still took a long, exultant look at Steelie and Jayne but then he pointed with his cuffed hands to the vegetation running out from the edge of the tarmac. 'I left them pretty near to this phone, trying to make it easy for someone to find. But there's no accounting for people's lack of observation. Or maybe animals took them—'

'Enough,' Scott interrupted. Then he nodded at the Corrections officers, who started to walk Gene back to the rest area.

Scott gestured at Tony, who was making adjustments to a video recorder. 'Let us know when you're ready, Tony.'

Then Scott walked over to Jayne and Steelie. He shook their hands in turn, saying, 'I'm really glad to see you both.'

Jayne felt the extra squeeze he gave her hand and she squeezed back.

Tony gave a thumbs-up once he was recording so Jayne and Steelie joined him, each holding a probe, while Steve, Duane and Xavier held grass beaters that looked like elongated tennis rackets. With Tony filming their actions, they moved into the vegetation, probing among the grass and shrubs. It took less than fifteen minutes to find the remains: dismembered ankle bones as well as long bones, either decomposing or partially skeletonized. All showed marks of animal scavenging and had been shifted from their original location. Jayne and Steelie fell back for Tony to switch from video to a still camera and then Scott and Eric came forward.

'More than one person?' Scott said.

'Can't tell yet but you're right that it's human,' Steelie said.

Jayne said, 'I think we need to do an extensive search for additional foot bones.'

Scott looked at her. 'You don't think King dismembered them and took them elsewhere?'

Jayne shook her head. 'No. From what I can see, everything's been separated by decomposition and animal activity. We want as many foot bones as we can find because we have at least one misper with a foot injury we could use for an ID.'

Steelie raised her gloved hand, extending the index and middle fingers. 'Two. Two with foot injuries.'

Scott nodded. 'Got it. Okay, I'll have Tony and Duane go back with you two and this material. Steve and Xavier will work on additional recovery and they'll bring you whatever they find.'

The Critters documented the bones in situ and put them into separate body bags. The black polyethylene retained its pleats from where it had been folded and the scent of warm plastic mingled with the scent of decomposition. Tony took the stretcher's front handles while Duane took the other end and they proceeded back to the highway with Jayne and Steelie bringing up the rear.

As they walked along the shoulder, cars in the fast lane slowed to a crawl to look at them, passengers holding up cell phones, apparently taking photos or video of the stretcher. Jayne wondered if they would be as fascinated if they knew the body bags held the remains of women who had crossed paths with a man who valued their lives not at all; who had deprived their families of their presence, their love; who had deprived children of their mothers, parents of their children. The deep anguish of those families was still fresh in her mind from the interviews in Atlanta. The mere thought of them was enough to put her on the verge of tears but she was wearing dirty surgical gloves and wouldn't be able to wipe them away. She had to refocus. Exhaling, she looked back at the body bags but in a new way: this was the beginning of the journey home for someone, maybe even more than one person. *That* was what mattered and *this* was where she could make a difference. She elongated her stride and felt her strength returning.

When they entered the rest area, the Corrections sedan was still in the center of the space, its engine running and driver's window down but all doors closed. Jayne and Steelie stopped at the lab to strip off their protective suits, which were now studded with grass and burrs, aware that Tony and Duane would have to document the remains before their anthropological analysis could commence. They had a wait of half an hour or more.

Jayne went to the women's RV and found that someone was emerging from one of the bathrooms at the back. It turned out to be the female Corrections officer. She was holding her weapons belt in one hand as she advanced. They nodded to each other, the other woman murmuring, 'How ya doin',' as she squeezed past Jayne in the aisle, close enough for Jayne to read the name on her identification badge: *Harrison, L.*

Jayne used the toilet and then splashed tap water on her face to cool down. When she opened the RV's door, she noticed that the Corrections sedan had reversed to come closer, apparently to save Officer Harrison the long, hot walk across the rest area. The male officer had the back door open, doing something to Gene's restraints, and Gene was openly staring at Jayne. She felt exposed and wished she hadn't opened the door just then, wished her eyes hadn't gone to find him, like he was what mattered most to her, and yet she didn't want to immediately look away for fear of seeming weak.

Then Gene's gaze shifted to take in the RV itself, his eyes traveling the full length to the end and back again, back to her, and he winked. Jayne almost retreated in an effort to get away from him but forced herself to walk on. She felt sure Gene was staring at her back. Finally, she heard the sedan's tires roll over the gravel. It was leaving the rest area and taking Gene with it. Only when she heard the sedan accelerate for the highway did Jayne feel some tension leave her body.

*

When Jayne and Steelie had suited up in fresh protective gear, they entered the mobile lab. Angie greeted them from her workstation. Behind a clear plastic barrier that ran from floor to ceiling, Tony was watching Duane place a forensic ruler and a photo board at the head of a table on which rested one of the two humeri they had recovered. There was a central fume extractor removing the scent of decomposition so the air at Angie's end of the RV would stay fresh.

Duane called over. 'Hey, Thirty-Two One. We're just about ready for you.'

Tony said, 'Sparky, the photoboard needs to come in more.' His voice was muffled behind his mask, his eyes still on the digital camera on its tripod.

Duane made the adjustment and glanced at Tony, who nodded and took his shot.

Looking at Jayne and Steelie, Duane said, 'You mentioned you've got ID info for feet or legs?'

Steelie nodded.

Duane gestured to where the two legs were set up on separate workstations that had been folded down from the wall. Each leg was loosely connected by tissue to ankle or foot bones and was resting on a sheet.

He said, 'So because of that, I thought you might want to start with your externals over here. They're fully documented, processed and good to go. The equipment you requested is here on the cart.'

He indicated a multi-shelved unit holding an array of osteological analysis tools. 'Anything else you need, just say the word. And when you're ready for radiography, Tony will set it up. DNA sampling will be done when everyone else is done.'

They thanked him and got to work, each examining a different leg, first using scalpels to expose any bone still covered with tissue, then cleaning the bones with dry brushes of different sizes, examining them and wet-cleaning them. Next came the osteological analyses to estimate age, sex, stature and ancestry, with each anthropologist making her own notes while Tony and Duane took a break with Angie.

Eventually, Jayne addressed Steelie. 'I've got the right leg of a probable female, over nineteen, probably Caucasoid based on tissue but I wouldn't bank on that, so stature is a going wide with . . .' She converted the centimeters to inches on the side of her paper. 'Five foot one to five foot four.'

'Okay, we've got different people then.' Steelie pointed at the leg on her table. 'This is a left leg, female – no question. Over nineteen like yours. I don't have enough for ancestry so I'm ball-parking five foot four to five foot six for stature. No pathology.'

'Well, I've got path.'

Steelie's eyes widened and she came over to see the pathology for herself, putting her gloved hands behind her back so she wouldn't touch Jayne's table.

Jayne pointed with a chopstick. 'On the proximal ends of those metatarsals.'

'I see it.' Steelie straightened up. 'We absolutely need the rest of the foot.' She called over to the Critters, projecting her voice loud enough to be heard through her mask, over the noise of the fume hood and past the somewhat muffling nature of the plastic barrier. 'Tony or Sparky, is there word yet on whether any more foot bones have been recovered?'

Angie pointed at herself. She pressed a button on the radio on her desk. 'Base to Kilo Alpha, Base to Kilo Alpha.'

They waited.

Then they heard Scott's voice. 'Go for Kilo Alpha.'

'Any more packages? Over.'

'Wait one.'

Angie looked over at Jayne and Steelie. 'He'll be checking with the boys.'

The air conditioning hummed down to a slower speed and the room fell silent.

'Kilo Alpha to Base.'

Angie clicked the button. 'Go ahead, Kilo Alpha.'

'Multiple packages en route. Requesting input on arrival regarding whether packages are complete. Kilo Alpha out.'

'Base out.' Angie lifted her finger from the radio button and swiveled in her chair to look at Jayne and Steelie. 'You got that?'

They nodded. Steelie said to Jayne, 'I'll go ahead and pull up the database.'

The Bureau laptop they'd been using for the past week was open on a standing workstation nearby. Jayne came to look over Steelie's shoulder while she searched 'Right Leg' under the subheading of 'Trauma'. Nothing came up. Then Steelie adjusted the search to 'Right Foot' and a record filled the screen: COLLINS, Ellen (Ellie).

3

Jayne and Steelie reviewed Ellen Collins' X-rays that had been provided by her father when Thirty-Two One interviewed the Atlanta families. The interviews had really been free-flowing retellings of family stories, during which Jayne had posed benign-sounding questions designed to elicit the kind of information she and Steelie could use to build what they called forensic profiles of the missing.

Their profile was distinct from a police missing person report, which prioritized the clothing someone was last seen wearing or where they were last sighted, since police were looking for living people. Thirty-Two One profiles, on the other hand, described intrinsic physical characteristics that could enable postmortem identification if a missing person was found dead, regardless of how decomposed their body had become. So, where a police missing person report noted the presence of a scar, a Thirty-Two One profile canvassed the injury that had led to the scar – and included X-rays of the underlying bone.

Steelie had digitized all the X-rays they'd received in Atlanta, just as she would if they were at their office in LA, and dropped them into the database before the mobile operation had commenced. The X-rays for Ellen showed different angles on a right foot injury and one X-ray of the foot after surgery.

It was while Jayne and Steelie were re-familiarizing themselves with the films that the lab door opened, bringing in a wave of humid heat and Agent Xavier Tollen's head.

'Guys, got a couple of bags for you.'

Duane and Tony gloved up and took custody of the body bags. They then did photography and evidence collection on what appeared to be copious foot bones that included ankle elements. But when the Critters gave Jayne and Steelie access to the tables, the two anthropologists struggled to allocate the foot bones to either of the existing legs. Many were the same bony element and were also from the same side of the body, which meant they represented more than one person. However, a right calcaneus exhibited healed pathological changes: in short, a foot injury.

Jayne called to Tony. 'We'll need radiography on this one. Might need X-ray for others, but for the sake of expediency, let's start here.'

Steelie added, 'Can you get shots like they'd have been able to get when the person was alive? Like, lateral, posterior, anterior?'

'You got it.' He moved to prepare the portable X-ray machine, pulling it out of its alcove and programming the digital photography software.

The door to the RV opened again and Xavier, Steve, Scott and Eric climbed up. It was obvious they had all showered. They looked over at the machine expectantly.

Jayne walked up to the plastic barrier so she could lower her mask to talk. 'Nice work on locating the foot bones.' It felt good to be part of a team. It made her feel hopeful.

Steve and Xavier gave thumbs-up symbols.

Scott looked like he'd caught the sun. 'Are you getting anything so far?'

'We might get a presumptive ID depending on what Tony finds.'

Eric was looking over Jayne's shoulder. 'What's it off of?'

'Pathology on a right foot bone.'

'Who's it for?' Scott asked.

'Ellen Collins.'

Jayne caught Scott's grimace but he was looking at Eric. Eric pursed his lips, his expression serious, and she realized that the two of them had actually known Ellen from when they were working the case in Atlanta.

After a beat, Xavier said, 'What kind of pathology did you see?'

'Healed trauma,' Jayne said. 'Her father told us that Ellen had been in a car accident about a year before her disappearance. It caused a foot injury that didn't heal well. Mr. Collins blamed it for everything going wrong.'

The X-ray machine emitted a series of beeps and they all turned to watch Tony.

'What was the deal?' Steve said in the ensuing silence. 'Was she a sex worker or . . .?'

'Not at first,' Jayne said, still watching Tony. 'She was a trainee forklift driver in a warehouse, but after the car accident, her employer could see she wouldn't be able to pass the fitness test and she lost the job. Her car had been totaled and she had medical bills that weren't covered by her insurance, so she got a job as a cashier but that exacerbated her injury. She'd applied for disability, been rejected once and was applying again when she turned to sex work to help meet her medical bills.' She looked at Steve. 'Her father told us he'd been trying to help her pay off the bills. Had no idea what she'd been doing to make some extra money.'

Scott said, 'Ellie didn't want her family to know.'

Jayne looked at him. He'd called Ellen 'Ellie' the same way her father had.

Scott continued, looking preoccupied. 'They just thought she worked at a grocery store. And she didn't do the sex work every day. Just enough to get rid of the debt. Or try to.'

Tony called out, 'Okay, folks, I need you to stay over there until my say-so.' He was now wearing a lead vest and he turned to take the radiographic images as Duane, also in a protective vest, made adjustments to the angles.

Unsure of how difficult it was for Scott to talk about someone he'd actually known, Jayne spoke gently. 'Scott, did she walk with an uneven gait?'

He nodded and at first Jayne didn't think he was going to speak. Then he added, 'A limp.'

'Okay. So that's why we'd expected bony changes around the right foot, but what we were really hoping to find was the surgical pin in her foot – because we do have an antemortem X-ray of that.'

Tony called out, 'Thirty-Two One, you're up.'

Jayne and Steelie walked over to where Tony had displayed the radiograph on a wall-mounted screen. Steelie pulled up the X-ray from Ellen Collins' foot surgery that her father had provided.

Even though Jayne had hoped for a possible match, to

see it left her speechless. They had actually found one of Gene's victims.

Steelie murmured, 'I think we have a winner.'

Jayne could only nod, so Steelie called to the others. 'This is a presumptive ID for Ellen Collins.'

The Critters immediately high-fived each other and Angie said, 'Wow.'

Steelie held her hands up in a gesture of caution. 'Just a reminder that the presumptive ID only extends to this foot bone. To ID the rest of this material, you're going to need to go straight to DNA.'

'I'll contact Missing Persons,' Angie said as she turned back to her desk.

Steve and Xavier headed for the door, making bets on whether dinner would be crab cakes or gumbo since they were in Louisiana and the team had been promised locally-themed meals at each stop. Meanwhile, Tony and Duane began bagging the remains for storage.

Eric said, 'Good work, Thirty-Two One.' He nudged Scott, who Jayne had noticed was in some kind of reverie. She wondered what he was thinking.

Scott came to. 'Thanks, you guys. All of you,' he said before going to look over Angie's shoulder where she was scribbling notes while talking on the phone.

Scott's body language suggested he wished the call was on speaker, but Angie was making him hover. He didn't notice when Jayne and Steelie headed out of the trailer but Eric gave them a parting wave.

By the time the two women arrived at the mess for dinner, they had both showered and built up a strong appetite. The logistics team had done everyone proud, procuring their meal from a local barbeque place: rib meat off the bone – Angie explained that this had been Sara's idea because she thought some team members might not want to rip flesh from bone after doing that to human remains all day. There was a vegetarian pot pie for Steelie, and lots of sides: collard greens, scalloped potatoes with a cheese sauce, green beans and fresh bread rolls with copious foil-wrapped pats of butter sitting in a bowl of ice.

Steelie was having dessert first, a slice of apple pie with whipped cream from a spray can, smacking her lips over the deliciousness of it while pointing out that she had to have dessert first because certain team members weren't at dinner yet and she knew they would eat it all. She was referring to Duane, Scott and Eric, who then arrived.

The first thing Jayne noticed was that Scott's mood had been transformed. He wore a proud smile.

He got the attention of the room, then announced, 'Positive ID on Ellie Collins, folks.'

The news was met with shouts and whoops and then it was high-fives all round. When Scott made his way over to Jayne, they shook hands. She savored smiling at him without a mask on and then he moved away, doing some kind of multi-part handshake with Angie that she'd seen them do before. She overheard him saying that he had to call his boss and then watched as he placed his call, aware that there was a duality to her feelings for him at times like this. She loved him as a person but she also loved him for the work he did, for the things he made possible in the lives of others – including her own, since doing this kind of recovery work made her feel incredibly good. Doing it alongside him had added another layer: she felt connected to him on a metaphysical level. She watched as he used a hand to cover his other ear, clearly trying to hear his phone over the jubilant hubbub around him, and then he slipped out the door.

*

When Scott hadn't returned to the mess by the time Jayne had finished dinner, she realized that the Collins identification had probably led to other work for him and he would eat later. Since Steelie was engaged in an arm-wrestling competition with Angie and two Critters, Jayne went back to the RV. As she walked over, she was aware of the logistics team readying all the vehicles for departure. According to Mark's update at dinner, they were due to convoy to a stop point a few hours away along I-10 where they would gas up before the overnight drive to Texas. Team members could get to their berths now or at the stop point, their choice. She'd made hers.

Jayne was changing into her sweatpants in the sleeping compartment when she heard the RV's engine start up. The lights dimmed, then strengthened, and Jayne listened for a moment, realizing that the vehicles would get into convoy formation soon. She was about to climb up to her berth when she heard the RVs open and close. No one came through to the sleeping compartment so she peeked out and was taken aback to see Scott climbing up the steps.

He grinned. 'Hey.' He started to cross the room but had to find his footing when the vehicle lurched forward.

Jayne took hold of the doorjamb, only able to smile at Scott as he made his way to her despite the RV rolling over uneven ground. He grabbed onto the lintel above her head and tried to kiss her but the motion parted their bodies just before their lips met – twice.

He laughed. 'Should I tell Sara that her driving makes for amazing foreplay?'

'We can't—' Jayne stopped as it dawned upon her that the convoy was on the move, so they would be alone for . . . she couldn't do the math.

'We can,' he said.

With a loud engine noise, the RV finally gained smooth road, which allowed Jayne to kiss Scott, and it was like a starting gun had gone off. He quickly wrapped his arms around her, pulling her close as his tongue sought hers. Moving into the sleeping compartment, they didn't fully undress and their lovemaking was physical, urgent and breathless, lent a desperate quality by the unpredictable bucking and swaying of the vehicle on the highway before it reached its cruising speed.

*

Scott lay on his side in Jayne's berth, the RV's motion rocking them gently as it ate up the road. He'd been trying to touch her lightly the same way she'd been touching him, enjoying looking at her in the glow of the reading lamp where it was illuminating the top of her forehead, her cheekbones and the line of her nose.

'I missed you so much last week,' he said softly. 'LA felt empty without you in it.' He wanted to tell her that he had felt empty too but held back. He stroked her cheek and she turned her face to kiss his palm.

She said, 'Isn't it interesting how it wasn't enough to talk on the phone every day? We used to be almost satisfied with that.' She ran her fingertips down his chest hair, all the way to his stomach.

Scott didn't want to remember those days. 'I was never satisfied with just that.'

She looked up at him. 'Neither was I. But I told myself that I was.'

'Don't get me wrong,' he said. 'I love talking with you, but . . . being able to do that *and* this is better.'

Resting his hand on her hip, he kissed the beauty mark at the base of her throat, that little dot of chocolate in the honeyed sea of her skin that always drew his eye, and she trembled. He was fascinated by how his smallest touch made her react. It was what made him hope that, even when they were working together as on this operation, Jayne would feel that electric charge despite only being able to shake hands with him; that she would know how much he cared about her, how much he wanted her. And then she began to move on top of him. Scott felt his heart pounding as he eased himself flat beneath her. It wasn't long before he knew he couldn't hold out.

'Stop, stop, stop,' he whispered.

She slowed her movement but didn't stop – as though she couldn't bear to stop. As much as he loved that, he really needed her to stop so this would last longer. He stilled her hips with his hands and she laid her body along his, her face turned to the side. He tried to slow his breathing and put a hand on her head, twirling her hair until the waves curled around his fingers, something he loved to do when they were in bed together. Jayne had told him that she, in turn, loved him doing it, asking only that he not leave her looking like she had antennae. Sometimes she even pulled his hands into her hair, inviting his touch.

He stopped making curls now and smoothed out the ones he'd made. Then he caressed her head, wondering, not for the first time, what he was going to do about the fact that the only time he felt at peace was when he was with this woman. Well, he had one idea of what to do, but this wasn't the right time.

He whispered, 'I love you.'

Jayne turned her head to look at him, her face holding that look of blushing surprise that made her catch her lower lip in her teeth.

Then she smiled. 'I love you, too.'

He lifted his head to reach her lips as he moved again. She responded instantly, latching her mouth onto his, and the guttural moan deep in his throat was both of theirs combined.

DAY 2

Tuesday

4

Scott watched King acting like he couldn't remember where exactly he'd left the body parts in the vicinity of this truck stop on the outskirts of San Antonio, Texas. It was a huge complex. The large building didn't just anchor the gas station, it also held a full restaurant, bathrooms with shower facilities, a souvenir shop and games room, while the parking lot extended for a long distance to accommodate parking for big rigs. There was even a stall that housed an automated truck wash. The back end of the complex met dry scrubland punctuated by shrubs and small trees, everything baking in Texas morning heat that Scott remembered well from being stationed in Dallas for two years.

Despite all of this, Scott remained aware that King was milking the situation after yesterday, when he'd been returned to a holding cell so soon after being removed from one. He'd clearly not expected anyone with expertise like Jayne and Steelie, or the Critters for that matter, to be part of this exercise to locate the body parts he'd dumped along the interstate highways.

Scott looked over to where Jayne was standing near the perimeter fence, assessing the truck stop as she put down her toolkit. His desire to be near her was not sated after being with her the night before. It was as though those two hours had only topped up a level that had been dropping each day she'd been in Atlanta while he was back in LA. The level had been dropping again through the night while he'd lain in his own berth, thinking about being in hers.

Their connection was about more than the sex, he was sure of that after having been temporarily worried that sex had become the glue holding them together – and it had been a worry because he'd done that with other women. But his closeness with Jayne was because they had spent almost all their free time together over the past few months. He felt like it had been quality time.

He wished that he had figured out how to be with her sooner; that he hadn't squandered years only talking with her on the phone while pretending to live life with someone else. He'd had it backwards, had his life backwards. And then there was King. It bothered Scott that he effectively had King to thank for getting him to Jayne's city. If King hadn't attempted to get him fired, he wouldn't have been transferred to LA in the summer; it was as simple as that. He glanced at King again. The man was outwardly staring at Jayne and Steelie. Scott felt his anger rise and he called to Eric.

Eric came over. 'This is bullshit. We're going to get heatstroke if we stand around here any longer.'

'I know. I'll go turn the heat up on King.'

Eric used his hand as if to say, *Be my guest*.

Scott walked up to the Corrections officers. 'Harrison. Mercier. You can take the inmate back to the cell.'

King's head snapped around, blue eyes flashing. 'But I haven't told you where I dumped them.'

'We're done waiting on you.' Scott turned to Eric. 'We'll need to notify HQ that he's reneged on the terms of his deal.'

'Ten-four,' Eric said, pulling out his cell phone.

'Wait.' King's eyes flicked quickly from Eric's phone to Scott's face.

Scott looked back at him with feigned disinterest.

'I'll show you where I put them,' King mumbled as he started walking toward the trailer truck parking bays, his hands cuffed in front of him while the Corrections officers kept hold of his arms.

They followed King to the rear of the truck stop. He stopped by the doors to the men's restrooms and faced the low perimeter fence.

He gestured with his head like he didn't want to call attention to his cuffed hands by trying to point with them. 'By those trees.' His voice was almost inaudible.

Scott knew King was trying to prolong his freedom even for the thirty seconds it would take for someone to ask him to repeat what he said. Scott shook his head in astonishment. He'd just shown King which of them was wearing the choke chain. Did he have to do it again? Scott turned to his team. 'You heard him?'

Tony nodded, activating his video camera and starting forward with Jayne and Steelie following. The remaining Critters fell in behind them. Scott watched them climb over the fence and approach the trees, saw them using probes, but then there was something that got them all focused on one place. Jayne and Steelie both crouched down. When they stood up, Tony lowered the camera and they all walked back to the truck stop in single file, stepping carefully in each other's footsteps. Scott knew what that meant.

Apparently so did King. He'd straightened up, his entire posture alert. 'Hoo-hoo-hoo-hoooo,' he said in a singsong tone. 'I think there's something there besides my little treats for you, Mr. Special Agent. Have fun!'

Feeling like King had turned the tables yet again, Scott locked eyes with the Corrections officers. 'Get him out of here.' They didn't hesitate and turned King toward the parking lot.

Scott tried to read Jayne's face as she came toward him from where she was first in the line, but it was impossible to see much between the protective gear and the mask.

'What's over there?' he said when she was close enough.

She pulled down her mask. 'Two bodies – fresh – in addition to the body dump material,' she said.

'Fresh?' Scott had been able to tell from how the team had reacted that there were other, unrelated human remains but he hadn't expected overlapping crime scenes. This was going to be an unholy mess.

'Probably been there less than a day,' Tony said. 'Clearly not attributable to King since he's been in custody for months.'

Steve added, 'One male, one female.'

Scott was doing damage control in his mind. He squinted over at the trees. 'Where are they in relation to the material we have to recover? Can we recover ours separately from whatever San Antonio Homicide's going to have to do?' He glanced at Eric, aware that his partner wouldn't approve of an unorthodox approach to any crime scene, even an adjacent one.

But Eric showed that he had guessed at Scott's real concern. 'You're thinking we could be here all day?'

'I'm trying not to be here all week.'

Jayne said, 'The dismembered remains are close enough to the bodies that the coroner's office will want to at least photograph them in situ if not check them for trace – or have you check.'

'But,' Steelie raised an index finger, 'the FBI has both testimony and evidence that its material couldn't have been placed here, like, yesterday, so there's likely no argument for relevance once the locals do their documentation. What say you?' She was looking at Scott.

He was impressed. 'I say you should be on the call to our boss.' He gave her a rueful smile and turned away with his phone.

Scott made several calls, including to his supervisor, and then reported the discovery to a San Antonio Police Department homicide lieutenant, who responded that he would dispatch a detective as well as notify the county medical examiner's office. The lieutenant couldn't say how long the ME would take, emphasizing that he had no control over them.

Scott came back to the group. 'Okay, I'm going to split the teams so that we can get started on the second site. If we wait until Homicide's done here, we'll be too late to get over there in decent light and that'll put the operation a day behind. Team A – that'll be Steelie, Sparky and Xavier – you're here with me because now I'm the point of contact for San Antonio Homicide.'

He put his hand on Steelie's shoulder. 'Steelie, I also

want you here for any legal lingo that gets thrown around. I want us extracting our remains and leaving tonight come hell or high water.'

He addressed the others. 'Team B will deploy with Eric to the second site – that's Jayne, Steve and Tony. Steve, use the lab vehicle to drive there. Watch yourselves with King. Everyone copy?'

As the teams split up, Scott caught hold of his partner's arm. Eric looked back at him.

Scott dropped his voice. 'Don't let Jayne out of your sight.'

Eric nodded and carried on after her.

*

Jayne alighted from the mobile lab and stepped down onto the shoulder of the highway. The heat of the tarmac seeped through the soles of her boots as she looked at a small forest of trees growing down a slope and sending up a noticeable insect noise. A little further along the road, there was the same kind of emergency telephone that had marked the recovery site in Louisiana. Local cops were milling around, ensuring that the tape line was holding fast where Texas State troopers had attached it to orange cones to block off the slow lane. Tony and Steve were adjusting their protective gear while Gene was with his minders at the edge of the trees. Eric walked over to Jayne.

He said, 'King's saying he thinks this is the place, but there's nothing here. He says it's a couple of heads so they could've rolled down the slope. I'm going to have him descend but I want you to climb down behind him to do a recce; see if his statement is plausible. I'll have Tony and Steve flanking you. Okay with that?'

Jayne nodded. She was finding that tapping into the motivation of finding the remains was helping her keep Gene in perspective. She knew what she was doing here and her role outweighed the disruption that Gene was trying to produce. She belonged here, doing her job, undoing his deeds. Being with Scott the night before had played a role too; she'd felt bold, unafraid, home.

As of this morning, instead of looking at Gene like he was capable of anything, she saw an undeniable fact: he literally couldn't touch her.

Feeling confident, Jayne kept her mask down and goggles off as she moved down the slope behind the others. She had to focus on keeping a foothold in the surprisingly soft earth and a handhold on the trees as she scanned the vegetation for cranial material. As they moved in further, the temperature dropped a little but the insect noise increased.

Suddenly, the ground shifted under her feet – a lot. She had nothing to get purchase on and landed on her backside as the soil started running down the hill. She saw Gene being pulled down by the landslip and how the two Corrections officers were unable to keep hold of him as they too were pulled down the slope. Tony and Steve were in the same mess. Jayne scrabbled for a handhold and managed to grasp onto a tree root. Hearing a grunt, she looked over: Gene, still handcuffed, had collided with a tree stump near her. Then she heard Eric calling down to her from the road above.

'Jayne, you okay?'

She shouted up to him. 'Yeah!'

'We're coming to you.'

She got a better hold of the root and listened to the noise of the others making their way toward them from above and below. Then she realized Gene was softly calling her name. Without thinking, she looked at him.

He said, 'I know you and Scott were playing house in a Bureau mobile unit last night, tut-tut. But if you want to play house with him in the real world, you should really find out if Callista's still wearing his ring.'

Jayne just stopped herself from hissing, '*What?*' but she couldn't prevent her body from reacting. She felt like her heart was hovering between beats and she lost all hearing. Not even the sound of the insects reached her as she stared helplessly at Gene, whose lips were curved into a satisfied smile.

Jayne finally, consciously, told herself to breathe, and sound began to return. She was still on the hillside and Gene was still talking.

'I only tell you this this because I care.' His face had taken on a look of exaggerated concern but his eyes were dancing.

Jayne felt Gene had the upper hand, just like he'd had in Atlanta that summer. He'd known things about her life then but he hadn't even been *in* her life. It hadn't made sense until he revealed that he'd had her under surveillance. Now it turned out he knew things about Scott too. Things she didn't know. A woman, a ring . . . a wife? Seen on a surveillance tape? Jayne felt tears prickling in her eyes. She wanted to get away from Gene but she couldn't move without slipping again. Then she realized she could just turn her head the other way. Easy.

But it wasn't that easy. The action dislodged dirt and leaves just above her head and she had to close her eyes as she turned her face. When she opened her eyes, she was looking almost directly into the mouth of a skull, the mandible hanging on by a sinew. Her mental assessment of it was automatic and unstoppable: *Human, adult, female, African ancestry, left mandibular molar restoration—* She felt hands on her waist.

'You okay?' Eric was leaning over her, holding her steady as he tried to see her face.

'Look.' Jayne tilted her head toward the skull.

Eric said, 'Oh!' Then he called out, 'Tony, Steve.' He pulled Jayne to her feet. 'Lean on me.'

Jayne stood, allowing Eric to support her, and then she looked toward Gene. The Corrections officers were getting him to his feet; all three of them were covered in dirt and leaf litter. Gene didn't look back at her as they helped him move up the slope. It was slow progress as the climb needed one's hands as well as one's feet, but they apparently didn't want to risk taking off his cuffs.

Tony and Steve arrived, half-climbing and half-slipping.

Steve took a look at the cranium. 'Looks like it rolled down just now.'

Jayne nodded. 'The dark line is where it would have been partially buried up until now. It's as good as upside down from wherever it was resting before.'

'So, no provenance for this one.' Steve looked to Tony. 'We can lift it.'

Tony was readying his still camera. 'Let's photodocument and then you can get started, Jayne. There's some dental work there, right?'

She nodded and looked back at Eric, who was regarding her with concern.

'I'm fine,' she said in response to his expression.

He looked unconvinced. 'I'm going to help you up to the road.' He put a hand to her back.

'Eric, I said I'm fine.' She didn't want him near her with his sympathetic eyes, his steadying hands. But when she tried to move, she lost her balance, so she let him assist her and he stayed with her until they reached the tarmac.

The Corrections sedan was leaving. *At least Gene's gone.* She started to take off her protective suit, which was dirty and half-shredded in places, but as she went through the motions of removing one set of gear and putting on another, her mind was already back on the name Gene had spoken so casually. She glanced surreptitiously at Eric as he hopped up into the mobile lab, wondering what he'd say if she were to ask him, *Do you know someone named Callista?*

She couldn't dismiss what Gene had said because his other words had been accurate: she and Scott had indeed been 'playing house', in a manner of speaking, in a Bureau mobile unit the night before. She felt her face burning with embarrassment. How could Gene have known about that? And if he knew, then *everyone* knew. Had everyone been looking at her at breakfast, knowing that she had been making passionate love with Scott in that RV and he was . . . what? Married? Separated? Divorcing? Involved.

She felt the heat of embarrassment turning into something else. She wanted to run, to scream, to rip off her suit. She wanted to hide, to hit.

So she turned on herself, thinking: at what point *after* Scott had moved to LA and *before* they'd launched into the intense relationship they were now having had she actually ascertained the validity of the fantasy in her head where the two of them went off into the sunset with . . . okay, maybe not kids (that was too hard to picture), but at least living together?

They had spent years flirting long-distance around an attraction that had started the day they'd met. Jayne knew what her reason had been for keeping Scott at the end of a phone line: it had allowed her to hide the recurrent trauma symptoms she'd wrangled with since working overseas. Scott being married would totally explain his reason. But hiding PTSD and hiding a wedding ring were two very different things. And she had never even asked him if he was single – a basic question at the start of a relationship.

Jayne watched Tony carry an evidence tray holding the cranium and mandible into the lab and then Eric emerged. *Eric*. Would the gentle – *gentlemanly* – Eric have just let Scott carry on with her if he knew Scott was not actually free to do so? Then Jayne rolled her eyes. What did it have to do with Eric? For all she knew, Eric had objected to what his partner was doing with Jayne but Scott had said, 'It's just an affair.' Or, 'It's just sex.' Imagining that, Jayne realized that it was more likely that Eric hadn't said anything; men don't say things to each other, don't psychoanalyze. Then again, Scott had told her many times that Eric was his conscience. *Argh*. She was going in circles. Worse, concentric circles, and they were growing larger each time she let herself think a thought, like ripples in a pond, and it was Gene who'd dropped the stone in the water. For this reason alone, she told herself to stop. *Stop. Forget. Don't think.*

She heard Tony call to her from the trailer: 'Okay, Jayne, it's set up for you.'

5

Steelie stood outside the cordon put up on the edge of the truck stop by the San Antonio Police Department. The SAPD investigators had erected a tent over the two sets of fresh remains to protect them from the sun and they were now in a dance with the coroner's medical investigator who was taking her own notes and photographs.

Scott walked over to Steelie. 'They're saying they're going to need to take shoe impressions from whoever walked over. They'll do it at the end.'

Steelie was relieved that the locals were looking to exclude only their footprints from the unknown or suspect pool. That was taking a low-key approach to the possible scene contamination. Then she thought of a snag. 'They'll have to get shoe prints off of the others you sent on with Gene.'

Scott un-kinked his neck. 'Any chance you can call that piece of shit "King", like we do?'

'Or just "Piece of Shit", like you do?' Steelie grinned at him, hoping to reduce his tension, but she'd only succeeded in making him look abashed.

'Sorry.'

'Don't apologize,' she said. 'He has acted very shittily. It's just hard to call him anything other than the name I know him by.'

Scott gently bumped her arm with his in friendly

acknowledgment. 'And yes, I told them we have a second team they'll have to process.'

Steelie decided to ask about the more worrisome thing. 'Have they said anything about wanting exclusionary DNA?' She didn't particularly want to leave a cheek swab on file with the San Antonio Police Department. Or any police department anywhere.

Scott shook his head. 'They said something about transference being unlikely because you all were suited up in protective gear.'

'Which just left our boot prints.'

'Yeah.'

Steelie peered over at the tent. People were hard at work, probably taking impressions of their shoe prints and knowing most of the work would be a waste of time because the prints belonged to a bunch of people on FBI business. 'I hope we didn't screw anything up, wading in there like we did.'

'That wasn't "wading", Steelie.'

'You know what I mean.'

'Yeah, I do, but the lead investigator isn't concerned – so far. Hmm, I see him looking for me.' Scott raised a hand to get the man's attention.

The detective, in his fifties with a long, large body over narrow legs, was wearing slacks and a short-sleeved button-down without a tie. He ducked under the scene tape then put on a massive cowboy hat as he made his way around the shrubs dotting the area. When he reached them, he tucked a small notepad into his shirt pocket and removed his sunglasses.

With a nod to Steelie, he addressed Scott, his Texan

twang wrapping a deep voice. He talked like he'd found that speaking slower worked better on hot days. 'Seems these will be yours.'

'Not possible,' Scott said promptly. 'None of our vics would be that fresh.'

'I wasn't clear.' Texas said deliberately. 'It's going to be federal.'

'Oh?' Scott's eyes flicked over the detective's shoulder to the tent. 'Why?'

'We've got an ID on the female: Canadian. Misper report has her as likely trafficked.'

Scott opened his hands in a relaxed gesture. 'Fine. You just need to call the San Antonio SAC. The local Special Agent in Charge. He'll service your scene.'

Steelie liked this. It was clean and they could get out of there. But Texas didn't respond. Steelie glanced at him. The detective was giving Scott a slightly amused look but he wasn't talking.

Scott raised his eyebrows and returned the amusement. 'What? You need their number? I don't know it offhand.'

Steelie thought, *Oooo, harsh!* She looked over at Texas. The man's poker face was unreal.

He drawled, 'Well, *you're* FBI and you're already here . . .' He shrugged, like his meaning was so obvious that he didn't need to finish the sentence. Especially not in this heat.

Steelie looked back at Scott.

Scott pointed in exasperation at his own chest. '*I'm* out of Los Angeles.' He pointed in the general direction of San Antonio. 'We're not interchangeable!' He seemed to realize he was flailing around with his arms and crossed them over his chest. He glanced at Steelie. 'Give us a minute?'

Steelie was only too glad to get away.

Seeing Duane and Xavier standing in the light shade of a small paloverde tree on the far side of the cordon, she made her way over to them.

Nodding a greeting, she said, 'I heard they have an ID. Do you know how they got it that fast?'

'Fingerprints,' Xavier said.

'Oh,' Steelie said. 'Canadian, the detective said.'

Duane elaborated, 'And Indigenous. *And* a juvenile.'

Steelie's heart sank as she stared over at the investigators working around the bodies. She was aware of the disproportionate number of missing Indigenous young women but to have the problem extend over the border was a frightening thought. It multiplied the danger faced by an already vulnerable population. 'That's . . . worrying.'

His eyes on Scott in the distance, Xavier said, 'No doubt. But it explains why San Antonio's probably trying to hand it off to us.' He murmured to Duane, 'Sparky, check out Houston.'

Steelie looked too. Scott was on the phone, looking exasperated, feet planted like the detective's.

Xavier said, 'We should be glad Jayne's on this operation. She can calm him down later.'

Duane's chuckle turned into an embarrassed cough. 'Sorry, Steelie.'

Steelie started. Not over the joke – she was used to that kind of banter – but for the fact that they knew. 'Wait, you know about them?'

Xavier shrugged, 'Well, we *were* at the Sunkist building this summer.'

Steelie remembered that day. Sure, it had been the first time Jayne and Scott had seen each other in years but it wasn't like they'd leapt into each other's arms.

Feeling like she was missing something, she said, 'What happened at the Sunkist building?'

Xavier looked at Duane as he formulated his response. 'Let's just say, we've known Scott a long time and he had a spring in his step that day.'

Duane nodded. 'And he's had it ever since.'

Steelie was stunned that they had deduced – correctly – just off of Scott's gait. These guys really knew each other. And no one had let on. Impressed, she said, 'Jeez. You're good at keeping a secret.'

Duane looked puzzled. 'Scott doesn't keep it a secret.'

'Except from SSA Turner,' Xavier corrected.

Duane said, 'Oh yeah. But that's just sensible.' He pointed an interrogatory finger at Steelie. 'You know that you and Matthew West aren't a secret either, right?'

Steelie felt her mouth open and knew she had to fill it with words or else they would know she was shocked. Quite why she had to hide her shock, she didn't know right that second; it was just habit. 'Sparky, for the record, there is no me and Matthew West.' *Case closed*, she finished in her mind.

'He'd like there to be.'

Case so not closed!

Duane smiled at her speechlessness. 'I'm just sayin'. And I can tell you wouldn't mind because you're blushing.'

Steelie recovered. 'I'm physically incapable of blushing,' she asserted. 'A congenital anomaly.'

Duane made a face. 'Oh, *now* I understand. It's the heat making your cheeks red.'

'Something like that.' But after a moment, Steelie couldn't help herself and asked, 'How'd you know about us?'

Duane pointed at her like he'd caught her out. 'I thought there was no "us"?'

'Ha ha,' Steelie said drily.

He smiled. 'It was Detective West's partner and Scott talking; I just happened to be there. Then I informed . . . well, everyone.'

Xavier raised a finger. 'Except Turner.'

'Of course,' Duane concurred placidly.

Steelie smiled thinly. 'Of course.'

'Xavier.' Duane straightened up. 'Here comes Houston. Would you say he's down to a Category 2?'

Pulling the top half of his coverall back up over his clothes, Xavier murmured, 'I think we can downgrade him to a tropical storm.'

But as Scott drew closer, Steelie saw that his expression was strained.

'Just heard from Eric,' he said. 'There was some kind of landslip over at the other site.'

'Everyone okay?' Duane and Steelie had spoken on top of each other.

'Looks like it.'

'And the scene?' Xavier asked.

'That was compromised,' Scott explained. 'But it was already a mess. Turns out Texas DOT had dumped a bunch of earth there when they expanded the shoulder near an emergency call box. That's what slid: the backfill.'

Xavier was incredulous. '*Now* they tell us?'

'Tell me about it,' Scott said with feeling. 'It may be a while before they can bring the mobile lab back to base because Tony and Steve are hunting all over the hillside looking for heads. Steelie.' He rested his hand on her shoulder. 'Mark will set up a pop-up lab for you back at base so you'll be able to do anthropology on the body parts we recover here. In the meantime . . .'

He let his hand drop as he looked over to the parking lot, where a coroner's body recovery van had pulled up next to the police and crime scene investigator vehicles.

Xavier finished the sentence. 'We can get started?'

Scott refocused on him. 'Almost. They want to get your shoe prints while the coroner's people lift the remains. *Then* we can get started.'

*

Sitting at a workstation in the mobile lab, Jayne had to continuously snap herself back to concentrating on the job at hand, which was cleaning the cranium and mandible that she'd come face to face with on the hillside. The problem was that she'd been alone since Eric had gone back outside to communicate with Tony and Steve, still searching for crania. So, while she did this initial cleaning job that didn't require much concentration, there was no one to see her shake her head whenever she heard the echo of Gene's voice. Nor could anyone hear her when she told herself to stop it.

While she cleaned the buccal surfaces of the maxillary molars and premolars, she wondered what kind of smile this Callista had, what kind of teeth. Was she an all-capped model of perfection, hurtling toward middle age with a bright white grill only rivaled by a Baleen whale or a row of new headstones? Jayne started to laugh to herself but then another thought took the smile off her face. What if Callista wasn't middle aged or even approaching it? She could be younger. Just because Scott was pushing forty, that didn't mean Callista was too. Jayne pictured that for about one second and then groaned aloud.

She pushed back from the table, retrieved a fresh toothbrush and systematically wet-cleaned all the skull's teeth. It was then that she saw something that brought all her attention firmly back to the cranium. She hadn't noticed it when the teeth had had dried dirt on them but one of the upper right premolars was part of a bridge to the first molar, while the second premolar between them was made of porcelain.

About half of the missing Atlanta women had had crowns, but only a few had had bridge work. Of those few, not all were of African or mixed-race ancestry as she believed this skull to be. Jayne felt her pulse quicken as she pulled over a blank dental chart. The team would likely have a presumptive identification for this skull by the time she was done analyzing the cranium and mandible. She needed to get on with it.

6

At day's end, Jayne was relieved to not only climb up into the women's RV but also get there without seeing Scott. She'd been chewing on Gene's words, the name 'Callista' like a piece of celery, masticated but never broken down. She knew she'd eventually have to spit it out or swallow it whole. But she hadn't been able to figure out which while analyzing skulls and coding teeth – and she was exhausted.

She opened the door to the RV's sleeping compartment. Steelie was at her berth getting her toiletries bag together but she came over immediately, arms out for a hug.

'Jayne! Are you okay? We heard about the landslip.'

Jayne gave a quick hug in reply, trying to show that she was okay so that Steelie wouldn't examine her, lest she discern that something was wrong and it wasn't physical pain. 'Just need a shower. What happened at the truck stop?'

'No one told you?' Steelie rolled her eyes and went back to her toiletries bag. 'It was a freakin' circus. The Critters eventually got our material out but there was jurisdictional hot potato stuff because one of the fresh bodies was ID'd as a Canadian.'

Jayne was surprised that there was already an identification. 'They must have had fingerprints or something?'

'They did but that wasn't the only issue. She was both young and Indigenous so they're thinking trafficked.'

Jayne felt a sinking sensation. 'This is horrible.' She imagined Scott dealing with the overlap in the two investigations. He had so much invested in finding the missing women from Atlanta but a young trafficking victim warranted robust resource allocation. It could even take him from the mobile operation. 'Is the FBI taking the case or . . .?'

'That's where the dance came in,' Steelie said. 'San Antonio Homicide wanted Scott to take charge but he was like, "Dude, that's what the San Antonio Bureau office is for" and that went on for a while until Scott called the SAC in San Antonio and was basically the Homicide guy's gofer. Which, as you can imagine, is not a role Scott's used to playing.'

Steelie eyed Jayne, clearly waiting for the usual reaction to her joking that Scott's work style only spanned the distance between Alpha Male and maverick.

But Jayne could only eke out, 'Hmm.' Her feelings were jumbled. She was annoyed with herself for putting the successes of the day's work on the back burner so she could move on to thinking about when and how she'd be able to talk with Scott about Callista. She could see that Steelie had noticed her muted response so she went to retrieve her toiletries bag for the shower as well.

Steelie hovered. 'Did the police get your boot prints?'

'They did. What about the remains? What did you recover?'

'Ribs, one cranium – no mandible – but dental work on the maxillae. The guys are trying to get a hit on the dental now. Between that and what you gave them, they said they might be working through dinner.'

Jayne nodded but she was stuck on the word 'dinner'. Dinner meant facing the rest of the team, a bunch of people who probably knew Scott even better than she did. She went into one of the restrooms, sat on the toilet and wondered how in the hell she was going to muster up the chutzpah to walk into the trailer for dinner with everyone looking at her: Jayne Hall, Scott Houston's bit on the side.

When Jayne followed Steelie into the mess later, the high noise level that always seemed to accompany mealtimes suddenly stopped. Jayne was mortified and almost backed out of the room but then Scott stepped forward and he was smiling.

'Thirty-Two One, you missed it. We just heard from DC: five positive IDs from the two sites. Five families notified. Thanks to you.'

All the Bureau staff started applauding and whistling. There were yells of 'Yeah!' and 'That's how it's done!' People were shaking Jayne and Steelie's hands and slapping them on the back as they absorbed the news. Then Eric ushered them to the buffet and walked them through the options: enchiladas, tacos, beans, rice and all the fixings, plus empanadas both savory and sweet.

Jayne ended up at the opposite end of the table from Scott. Whenever she looked at him, he beamed at her. But she struggled to smile or even eat, wondering if she was looking at Callista Houston's husband and, even worse, why she still found this married man so devastatingly attractive. She resolved to stop looking at him and joined a conversation between Mark, Joe and Nate about the performance of the truck they were using to tow the mess trailer.

Toward the end of the meal, the door of the trailer opened and a tall, trim man with a military bearing entered. The noisy room fell silent. It took Jayne a moment to recognize Scott and Eric's boss in casual clothes. The noise of chairs being pushed back took over the room as everyone except Jayne and Steelie stood to attention.

Eric said, 'SSA Turner,' the surprise evident in his tone.

'Sir,' added Scott.

Turner acknowledged the room. 'Gentlemen, ladies.' Then he looked at Scott. 'Agent Houston – with me, please.' He located Jayne and Steelie and said, 'Ms. Hall, Ms. Lander, I will need you as well.'

Eric moved to join them, clearly assuming they were a package deal.

Turner gave him an understanding nod. 'At ease, SA.'

Eric stopped in his tracks. 'Sir.' He sounded distinctly ill at ease.

Scott, Steelie and Jayne walked to the door, watched by everyone in the trailer.

Outside, Craig Turner walked a few paces further on before turning to face them. 'I'm going to ask this once and once only. SA Houston, are you currently in a relationship with Ms. Hall?'

Jayne was totally taken aback. Turner's tone – his very presence here in Texas – suggested that there would be a problem if they were involved with each other. And then she put it together with Gene's words on the hillside: he was behind this. He was off in a jail cell somewhere but he was the puppet master. She looked to Scott, wanting to convey this to him telepathically, to warn him.

But Scott wasn't looking at her. He appeared to be formulating a response, then he squared his shoulders as though he'd made a decision about something. He said, loudly and clearly, 'Yes, sir.'

Turner's lips compressed. 'Thank you.' He looked at Jayne and she finally understood why Scott and Eric called Turner 'the Ice Man'; it felt like the temperature had dropped twenty degrees.

'Ms. Hall, Ms. Lander,' he said. 'As of now there is a hold on our MOU with your agency. You will be catching a flight back to Los Angeles. It may be tonight so please pack your things. I need you to surrender your badges at this time.'

As Jayne's fingers closed around the badge in her pocket, she was aware that Gene had just pulled off another kind of dismemberment. A bloodless one this time.

But Steelie wasn't going without a fight. 'SSA Turner.' Her tone said, *We're all friends here, right?* But her eyes were troubled. 'Why this sudden change?'

Turner breathed, looking at her with his unblinking stare before finally speaking in a measured way. 'It has come to my attention that there may be a conflict of interest that could jeopardize this operation.'

Neat, Jayne thought. Gene had called it 'playing house' when he'd intimidated her, but when he sent it up the chain, he'd called it 'a conflict of interest'. He definitely knew which knife to use for each cut.

Scott had been shifting impatiently. 'The only thing jeopardized by removing Thirty-Two One from the operation is the operation itself. We have five IDs from today, thanks only to them. Sir.'

Jayne had kept her hand on the badge while Steelie and Scott tried to change the outcome but she felt like Gene had set something in motion that was subject to the forces of gravity. There was only one way to go: down.

And then SSA Turner confirmed it: 'SA Houston, this is not up for discussion.'

Jayne handed over her badge, already resigned to the situation. Turner took the item with a nod, making brief, neutral eye contact with her. Steelie took a moment to unclip her personal lanyard, holding onto it as she handed over the badge.

Turner addressed Scott again. 'SA, escort Misses Hall and Lander to their accommodation unit to gather their things. Ensure they stay there until I summon you with transport.' He turned away before Scott could protest.

Jayne and Steelie walked in silence behind Scott to the women's RV, where he badged them in past the officer on the door.

Inside, Scott started pacing. 'This is hinky enough to have King behind it.'

Steelie said, 'But how could Gene be doing anything? He's in a cell most of the time.'

'He's capable,' Scott said bitterly.

Jayne looked at him, trying to find a way to tell him about what Gene said after the landslip but not wanting to – not feeling able to – conjure up the spectre of Callista with Steelie as an audience.

Scott misread her expression. 'Jayne, I know you're

embarrassed but that's just Turner. He's ice cold. And he's my boss, not yours. He's only got you going back to LA so this can be squeaky clean while he figures out – and he will figure out – that there's zero conflict of interest. And anyway, there's no conflict clause in the MOU.'

Steelie said 'I know. I remember that specifically.'

'So,' he said, 'something else is going on. Jayne, no phone calls or texts between us until we see each other back home, okay?'

Jayne nodded but she was thinking, *So, there really is a problem with our relationship. I wonder if its name begins with a C.* She sighed.

Steelie was her usual chipper self, rubbing her hands together as she gave Scott a wry smile. 'What about me?'

'Lander, you can do what you want. Blow up my phone. Blow up Eric's.'

'Alright.' Steelie put her arms out for a goodbye hug and she patted him on the back after they embraced. 'I'm going to get my "things" together,' she said, echoing Turner as she pretended to flip her pretend long hair.

The moment Steelie had closed the door behind her, Jayne said, 'Scott.'

But when he looked at her, she couldn't find the resolve to start with Callista. She slid into the booth. 'I think Gene knows about us, in here, last night.'

Scott's response came fast. 'He can't know that.'

She felt incredulous. 'Can't he?'

Scott absorbed her vehemence and then expanded on his previous response without altering his take. 'I know for a fact that he was in jail at the time. At the most, he might have found out that we were in here but he wouldn't have known what we were doing.'

He came to sit next to her. 'Trust me, even if Turner were to hear about it from someone on the team, he won't care about that part of it. It was downtime. R&R.' Putting his arm around her, he said, 'We're not the first.'

She hadn't even thought of this! Scott in the RV with another woman – an agent, or some cop on secondment?

'Oh, God,' she said, and covered her face with her hands.

Scott laughed. 'I didn't mean with *me*!' He rubbed her shoulder. 'Oh, come on!' he coaxed but she didn't want to show the emotion on her face.

He stopped laughing and pulled her closer. 'Do you remember what I said to you last night? When we gave each other . . . absolutely everything? I said that I love you. So, please, trust me.' He gently pulled her hands away from her face and kissed her cheek lightly.

Jayne shivered. Just the feel of his breath on her cheek was enough to give her goosebumps – and she knew why. Long ago, she'd decided that this man was perfect for her, from head to toe, inside and out, in word and deed. That meant that asking him about Callista would be like putting a coin in a slot machine in Vegas and pulling the handle: she'd have to be ready to lose him – to walk away. She knew she wasn't ready for that. She felt weak, almost childish, for this willful avoidance and looked down into her lap.

Scott apparently read her bent head as acquiescence and said, 'Okay, then.'

He kissed her on the cheek once more and stood up. 'Go get your "things" and I'll be right outside.'

DAY 3

Wednesday

7

Scott looked at his watch as he stood outside the laboratory RV. The door was closed and Eric had been inside with Supervisory Special Agent Turner for ten minutes. That was a record for Turner, who was a man of so few words, they'd never had a meeting with him that had exceeded seven minutes since they'd been assigned to him. So that could be good or it could be bad. Scott had no idea which because he'd been unable to get a fix on Turner's expression when his boss had stuck his head into the mess at breakfast to call him and Eric outside.

Scott looked at his watch again, this time with his mind on Jayne's schedule for the morning. According to the travel details he'd been able to get out of their administrator, Lance, she wouldn't even have left the hotel in San Antonio yet. That meant she was still breathing Texas air, just like him, but she might as well have been a world away.

The RV door opened and he jerked to attention but it was only Eric, who was closing the door behind him. Scott reached for the handle but Eric stopped him, shaking his head.

Scott frowned in mid-reach. 'He doesn't want to see me?'

Eric took on a placatory tone. 'It's not that. He's on a call.'

Scott considered this. So he'd have to wait a few more minutes before getting in there to untangle the mess and put King back in his box once and for all. He could live with that. 'Okay. So, what was your meeting about?'

There was the slightest hesitation before Eric said, 'He made me lead on the recovery.'

Scott had to avert his eyes. He didn't know why that stung so much; he should have expected it. If Turner was concerned enough about a conflict of interest with Agency 32/1 to put the MOU on hold, then of course Turner would take him off lead. It also meant that Turner probably wouldn't summon him about Jayne today; his boss had already made the one operational decision needed to keep the recovery of remains on track. It was a decision that made Scott feel like he'd been demoted. *And all because of King!* He impatiently batted away the thought that something or someone else could be responsible for this turn of events.

'Scott?'

Scott glanced at Eric and belatedly realized that his partner was concerned that this reassignment would cause friction between them. Scott didn't want that. Problems between them would be another triumph for King. He tried to push down his anger and self-preoccupation. 'Right. Good. That makes sense.'

Eric looked relieved.

Scott knew he should leave it there but he had to find out if Eric knew what Turner was planning about the conflict of interest investigation. 'Did he ask about me and Jayne?'

Eric's eyes flashed. 'No – and I'm glad he didn't. I told

you back in June that you shouldn't have been trying to fly that under his radar, man.'

'Alright already. I remember.' Scott wasn't in the mood for a lecture.

But Eric was still chuntering on, practically talking to himself. 'I'm amazed it took this long before he found out.'

Scott got a word in edgewise. 'What I'm interested in is how he found out.'

Eric glanced at the RV and then lowered his voice. 'The word around the office is that it came in on the tip line.'

Scott did a double-take. 'The word— The office? You called the office? Why didn't I think to do that?'

'Yeah.' Eric gave him a flat look, then continued in his hush-hush tone. 'Apparently, the tip referred to SF 86s and a quote-unquote lack of candor. It also linked Jayne's name with yours.'

Scott sorted through that quickly. 'Anyone calling the Standard Form "SF" is one of us.'

'*Was* one of us,' Eric corrected. 'He identified himself as an inmate, no name.'

Scott swore under his breath. 'So it was King. Had to be.'

Eric nodded. 'He'd have known the number would be traced back to whatever jail they had him in when he made the call. He probably wanted you to know.' He looked at Scott like he was wondering what he was thinking.

What Scott was thinking was that he wished he had X-ray vision to see his boss through the wall of the RV. He did not want to leave King's words ringing in Turner's ears any longer.

Eric moved into his line of sight. 'Patience, Grasshopper.'

Before Scott could vent his ire at being told to stay calm at this critical juncture, the door of the RV opened and SSA Turner alighted.

He was totally comfortable, as though they were meeting at their office in LA, not in a roadside rest area in Texas. 'Houston, thank you for waiting. I need you to accompany me to a meeting with my counterpart here in San Antonio. It will take the morning – bring your Bureau windbreaker.'

He switched his gaze to Eric, his tone still just standard Turner: businesslike, a little brusque perhaps, but not rude. 'Ramos, I will inform the team that this is a down day and the convoy will roll out to New Mexico when Houston is again available.'

'And the change of assignments?' Eric asked swiftly.

'That too.' Turner strode off toward the mess.

Scott watched Eric hustle to catch up with their boss. But as soon as the two of them disappeared into a trailer, he felt his self-righteous anger building up again. When he went to pick up his FBI-marked jacket for this meeting in San Antonio that was about who knew what, the silence inside the men's RV emphasized the fact that the entire team was elsewhere getting instructions from Eric. On top of not being able to clear his name yet, Scott felt he was being prevented from recovering the bodies of the very women he'd tried so hard to protect from King back in Atlanta. One or the other would have been bad enough, but not both. In fact, the removal bothered him more than he could have imagined. He would've slammed his fist into the wall if he hadn't been so aware that it was just particleboard with a fake wood grain printed onto it. Adding 'Damage to a Government Vehicle' to his list of transgressions was not going to help his case with Turner even if it would make him feel just a tiny bit better.

*

Steelie toyed with her phone as she ate her breakfast at the TexMex restaurant she'd found along the River Walk. Her waterside table was one of the perks of the Bureau putting her and Jayne up in a hotel in the tourist part of San Antonio rather than over at the airport. They would be on a flight to LA in a matter of hours but, before they took off, she wanted to call Matthew West to tell him they could go on their first date on Friday instead of Saturday. At least, this was the reason she would provide if she ever actually made the call.

The real reason was that, ever since Matt had asked her out, she'd found herself just wanting to hear his voice, which was kind of husky and deep. They hadn't seen or called each other since the invite and it felt far too long.

Steelie looked at the time on her phone. It was still very early in LA. Calling Matt now might denote an eagerness that she wasn't ready to reveal. She put her cell down again and signaled the waiter for another cup of coffee.

Taking in the river and the trees next to her, Steelie deconstructed why she felt a measure of calm, despite what had happened with Turner the night before. She decided it was because she trusted her own reading of their agency's MOU with the FBI that there was no conflict language in it. She also trusted Scott when he'd said he would sort things out. It would be important that it did in fact get sorted out because the MOU represented a measure of financial stability for Agency 32/1.

She turned her mind to the recovery operation itself. The antemortem database she and Jayne had put together after meeting the missing women's families was robust and the identifications that had been made so far would be enough to get at least half the families to provide DNA. DNA samples would, in turn, take the pressure off the Critters to use anthropology in an effort to make presumptive identifications on skeletal remains in New Mexico and Arizona. The main challenge the Critters might have without her and Jayne would be in locating even smaller bony elements. But, having done that side by side for a few sites now, Steelie thought the team of guys had their eye in.

This left the only lingering worry: Scott's belief that Gene King was able to get anyone to listen to him after he'd been convicted of crimes for which he'd admitted his guilt. If this all came down to Gene, then his personal knowledge of Scott, Jayne and herself was a big part of the problem. He could mix enough truth in with a lie to make the lie believable. Actionable. Like the action Turner took by removing her and Jayne from the recovery operation. *Ugh*. Steelie chased her coffee with some water, settled the bill and left. She knew what she would rather do than think about Gene any longer.

Stopping on a picturesque stone bridge, she halted at the apex and dialed as she leaned against the balustrade.

Matt answered on the first ring. 'Steelie?' He sounded both surprised and concerned.

That made Steelie concerned. 'Yeah. Why are you saying my name like that?'

'Like what?'

'Like you're shocked I'm calling. You gave me your number.'

'Yeah, but I thought you were on an operation. Out of state. I figured something was wrong.'

Steelie relaxed. It was kind of cute, actually. Him worrying about her. And something was wrong but she wasn't going to talk about that now. She'd called so she could think about nicer things. 'I am out of state but we're coming back early.'

'Oh. Okay.'

Steelie discovered that she was doing a weird, girly thing with her fingers on the balustrade, tracing out imaginary curlicues. She stopped and gripped the stone surface manfully. 'So, how about moving our date up to Friday night?'

'Uh . . .' Matt's voice fell away.

Steelie pulled the phone away from her ear and looked at it, but that didn't help to explain why he didn't seem to know what she was talking about. She brought the phone back to her ear. 'We're going out on Saturday?'

'I know all that; I was just thinking. And I can't do Friday.'

'Got a date with someone else?' She couldn't help but tease him.

'No! Jesus! Why would you say that?' He sounded alarmed.

'I was kidding!' Steelie wondered why she'd brought up the one thing she *didn't* want to picture in the first place.

'Well, I'm not like that. And no, the reason is, we have reservations for Saturday and they can't be changed because . . . well, never mind why. They can't be changed.'

'So the chance to see me a day early isn't a draw?' As Steelie anticipated Matt's reply, she had to work hard to not do the curlicues again.

After a beat, he said, 'I think you're the one who wants to see *me* a day early.'

Steelie had to cover the mouthpiece of her cell phone so he wouldn't hear her laughing.

He chuckled. 'I thought so. See you *Saturday*,' he said and hung up.

DAY 4

Thursday

8

Jayne looked around the small Agency 32/1 parking lot as Steelie turned her Jeep Wrangler into one of the two spots marked 'Reserved'. Even though they'd been summarily removed from the recovery work with the FBI, it was good to be back in LA and good to see their brick building's low-slung 1950s frontage with its metal-framed windows.

Steelie was unzipping the back window out of the Wrangler's soft top. 'Not that I mind driving you around but when do you think you'll get a new car?'

Jayne began unzipping the window on her side. 'My dad's offered to come with me so probably this weekend.'

'Elliott's willing to get off a flight from Caracas and go car shopping?'

'It's not like we'd go straight from LAX.'

'Any thoughts yet on which car?'

'No. Just not—'

'Another pick-up. I know.' Steelie took the window from Jayne and rolled it with the other to stow it in the Wrangler's small tailgate area.

A white-haired woman wearing a blouse with embroidered flowers at the neckline and blue Capri pants walked into the parking area. She was carrying a cloth bag over her shoulder and held a paper bag in her hand.

'Carol!' Steelie exclaimed. 'Donuts?'

Carol smiled and the skin around her eyes puckered. 'Of course.'

Jayne greeted their volunteer receptionist with a hug. 'Somehow you knew we'd be in need of baked goods today?'

'Well, neither of you said why you were back a day early but I rather assumed it wasn't by choice,' she said drily.

'You could say that again,' Steelie said.

While Jayne unlocked the front door, Carol asked, 'How was the flight yesterday?'

'Easy. We had a quick stop in Phoenix.'

The bells on the door tinkled as Jayne opened it wide. 'You re-arranged!'

'A little,' Carol said as she crossed to disable the alarm. 'I thought it would be good if prospective clients had the option to pick up their own pamphlets from the front counter instead of waiting for me to hand them out. And then I moved Fitzgerald to get a little more light.'

'I like it,' Jayne said.

She joined Steelie in opening the Venetian blinds covering their front windows. Jayne never tired of looking across to the hills that undulated toward Dodger Stadium. Their existence made a valley out of the flatland below, where the Los Angeles River flowed between the Golden State Freeway on one side and the rail yards on the other. The agency sat on San Fernando Road, a four-laner flanking the train tracks and home to small businesses, a FedEx depot, a second-hand car dealership and a few factory buildings left over from the 1940s and 1950s. It was a great location for Jayne and Steelie, who lived in Silver Lake and Atwater Village respectively – each less than twenty minutes away on surface streets. And while San Fernando Road provided a bus line to help clients who needed public transport, the light industrial neighborhood kept their rent low.

Carol busied herself with making coffee at the refreshment table in reception, saying, 'I'll bring it to the kitchen.'

'See ya there,' Steelie said, taking the donut bag with her as she went down the hall to the laboratory, her domain at the back of the building.

Jayne went through the frosted-glass double doors that led into her office from reception and sat at her desk, the wall of filing cabinets behind her. She booted up the computer; there were a few emails Carol had left for her to attend to, but when she heard the others in the kitchen, she walked down the hall to join them.

Over coffee, Carol asked for details on the mobile recovery operation and listened to both of them with interest. 'Six identifications – seven, if you include the ID in the summer. I'm blanking on her name.'

'Mrs. Patterson,' Steelie supplied.

'Mrs. Patterson,' she repeated as though committing it to memory. 'Seven IDs sounds like astounding progress to me.'

Carol's assessment made Jayne realize that she'd left Texas focused more on the seven women they hadn't yet found, instead of the ones they had. And then there was that other woman. The living one: Callista. Who probably didn't eat donuts. Jayne put her own down uneaten.

Steelie waggled her hand side to side as she responded to Carol. 'I wouldn't go so far as astounding because it's a closed system. We already knew that any remains we found had to be from one of only fourteen people, all of whom were known to us.'

Carol said, 'Decomposed remains still provide quite a challenge. On more levels than one. Wouldn't you agree, Jayne?'

Jayne nodded. She'd just been thinking about how Scott had shut down temporarily when they'd identified Ellen Collins. Carol's previous career as a law enforcement grief counselor was on show.

Carol looked back at Steelie. 'How will the team be handling IDs in your absence?'

Steelie spoke with pride. 'Oh, those guys can do a fair bit.'

'These are the Critters?' Carol spoke the nickname hesitantly, like she was trying out a word in a new language.

Steelie said, indulgently, 'You *can* call them the Critical Stabilization and Recovery team, Carol.'

Carol laughed. 'I would prefer that! Critters sounds . . . I don't know. Like a pest control service.'

Steelie guffawed but Jayne only smiled. She broke off a small piece of donut and deposited it on her tongue. It was delicious.

After giving Jayne and her uneaten donut a curious look, Steelie said to Carol, 'The Critters have our database – or, I should say, their database – with everything we gleaned from the families but they're probably going to need DNA for a lot of the remains.'

Carol looked concerned. 'But what are their chances of getting that at this point? My sense from what you told me when you were in Atlanta was that the families only trusted the two of you.'

Steelie looked pointedly at Jayne.

Jayne galvanized herself. This was her area, after all. 'I tilled the ground for a future ask on DNA. I'd say there are a handful of families who'd be willing to provide samples if the Bureau came back to them in the right way.'

Steelie added, 'And some can lead to more.'

'A domino effect one actually wants to see.' Carol used her napkin to pull together the crumbs of her old-fashioned glazed. 'Now, what about the Memorandum of Understanding? Any updates?'

Steelie said, 'Turner hasn't reached out yet.'

Carol rummaged in the donut bag. 'My guess is that, if it turns out Gene King is indeed behind all of this upheaval, he's just stirring the pot, as he's done before. Jayne, you may not need to be as concerned as you clearly are.' She handed her the wax paper her donut had come in.

Jayne took the wrapper and shrugged. 'Maybe.' She wasn't planning to share that it was more than just Gene and his stirring that was worrying her. It was also Scott and his wife – or whatever Callista was. The bells on the front door rang out in a loud, musical jangle. It was a different sound than the mail carrier made and the wrong time for that, too. Carol went up front to see who it was.

Steelie said, 'Saved by the bell, Jayne. Because I can tell you're avoiding something.'

Jayne tried acting clueless. 'I'm just not that hungry.'

Steelie gave her a flat look. 'I'm not talking about donuts. Those only work as a litmus test for people like me, the true donut hounds. But you're avoiding eye contact. You're avoiding *talking*.'

A loud, accented voice traveled down the hall. 'This is the place that does profiles of missing persons, right?'

Even as Jayne caught Carol's calming tones, she placed the man's pronunciation of 'Right'. *Roight*. Australian.

Steelie got up. 'Sounds like it's for you.'

Wearing her hat as the agency's main interviewer, Jayne walked into reception. She saw an agitated man of about forty holding a piece of paper that looked like it had spent time folded into quarters and sat on in a pocket. A scuffed leather bag bulged at his side, straining the strap over his shoulder. Wraparound sunglasses with yellow fluorescent frames were pushed up into his short dark hair above suntanned skin. He turned bloodshot brown eyes onto Jayne.

'Jayne! Thank God I'm in the right place.' He crossed to her. 'You gotta help me. My sister's missing.'

Jayne glanced at Carol but she, too, looked mystified at the man's use of Jayne's first name as though they knew each other. Was this a client she'd emailed? The Agency had fewer than 120 clients and she thought she'd remember an Australian. 'I'm sorry; have we met before?'

'No – look, my name's Graham and I know you from your photo.' He unfurled the square of paper. It was a print-out of the *Contact Us* page of the Agency

32/1 website, showing Jayne and Steelie's portraits and biographies.

Jayne took in the redness around the man's eyes and the slight scent of alcohol that seemed to emanate from the open neck of his dark blue shirt on which was emblazoned the word *Holden*. His anxiousness made her think his sister's disappearance was recent. If so, she had to make sure of one thing before they got started on any forensic profile.

'And your sister. Has she already been reported as missing to the police?'

He looked indignant. 'Too right she was! Sixteen years ago!'

*

Special Agent Scott Houston stood in the shade of the laboratory RV drinking from a water bottle while watching dust swirl around the tires of the Corrections sedan. When the Corrections officers helped the handcuffed King out of the back seat, Scott knew the inmate had seen him because the man deliberately flashed him a smile. Scott reflexively crumpled the water bottle in his hand. The bottle wasn't empty and water splashed to the ground. Scott looked down in annoyance. He noticed that the dust at his feet was so light and copious, the water was beading up before being absorbed. He looked back to King. Eric and the Critters were following him on foot to the dump site along this New Mexico segment of Interstate 10. Scott wasn't invited. He scowled. The fact that King had orchestrated this demotion was intolerable.

But the best way he could get through this day was to stop looking at it like he'd been demoted. In fact, he told himself, the job required both the hunters and the gatherers. So, today, he would gather.

He glanced around the rest area. New Mexico State Police had a small patrol on its perimeter and officers were stationed near the door of each Bureau vehicle. The logistics team was clearing up from breakfast and moving on to refresh the accommodation units after yesterday's drive from San Antonio to Lordsburg. Scott could see that their logs people were moving fast and efficiently, stopping to talk only when absolutely necessary. Minutes spent talking cut into the time they would have to sleep during the day in readiness for the overnight drive to Phoenix. This was assuming New Mexico didn't offer up any surprise fresh bodies like San Antonio had.

King and the entourage were out of sight now. That helped. Scott turned to climb up into the lab RV. Angie was sitting at her workstation in the cool interior.

She looked up from her laptop. 'Hey, Houston.'

They fist-bumped and then pulled out to their usual fingertip clasp as he said, 'Reporting for duty, Agent Nicks.'

'It's not like that, Scott,' she said with a genial chuckle.

'Uh, it is exactly like that.' He took off his sunglasses and sat down in the chair next to her. 'You heard Turner.'

'What I heard was him making reassignments for coverage. Eric taking lead, you liaising with Atlanta Missings once you were done helping the San Antonio Bureau Office.'

'And since you were already liaising with APD

Missings – and doing a beautiful job – that would make me your caddie.'

'I've always wanted a caddie.' She smirked but when Scott didn't even smile, she became serious. 'Aren't you good with Eric taking lead?'

'Of course.' Scott felt surprised; he hadn't been thinking of Eric at all. 'It's not that. It's King.'

'King?' She frowned and swiveled her chair to face him. 'Are you telling me something went down? He's the reason you were taken off lead?'

'I'm pretty sure he's the reason Turner's acting like he has a stick up his ass,' he said grimly.

'I heard he's always like that.'

'Well, he's not. He's good – but he's by the book.' Scott paused as he debated about telling Angie what he thought was going on. He'd trust her with his life, let alone with this information, but wasn't sure if it was fair to burden her with an injustice she couldn't do anything about. Then again, it *was* Angie. They'd been through thick and thin together in Atlanta.

He sighed. 'Turner got a heads-up that Jayne and I are involved. It came in on the tip line – anonymous – but the tipster said he was a federal inmate. And there's only one federal inmate in the whole country who fits the bill: Eugene King.'

Angie's mouth made an O, then she reconsidered. 'But surely Turner read the King interrogation transcripts from when we did the arrest? I remember King calling you Jayne's "lover boy" more than once.'

Scott rolled his eyes. 'You would remember that. Added it to the collection of my nicknames, didn't you?'

'Well,' she winked, 'it's been looking pretty accurate. I can tell you and Jayne are tight.'

She'd made him grin. He said, 'I took that advice you gave me.' He waited to see if she remembered telling him, 'Don't let that one get away' about Jayne earlier that summer. She did: she was holding her fist out for another bump.

Scott resumed. 'The thing is, Ange, back when we arrested him, King was only guessing that Jayne and I were involved. Okay, it was a good guess 'cause he figured it after tapping Jayne's phone. But she and I weren't, y'know, together-together then. Turner wouldn't have found it actionable.'

'Together-together?' Angie teased.

Scott waved this off. He knew he didn't have any experience of labeling the kind of relationship he had with Jayne. 'The point I'm trying to make is, King didn't enlighten Turner about me and Jayne from three months ago. He was talking about now.'

'But he could still only guess at that.'

'He didn't have to guess. He found out.'

Angie was immediately incredulous. 'From who? Not one of our guys!'

Scott shook his head. 'Someone who wasn't at our briefing when I said, "Don't engage King under any circumstances": local police in Texas. A rookie no less.'

'Ah shiiiiiit,' Angie said with feeling.

'Yeah. It took me a while to find him last night but I did.'

She lifted an eyebrow. 'Does he still have a job?'

Scott grinned. 'I tried not to scare him too much. King

was clever: this greenhorn was guarding the car while Corrections took a leak before getting on the road to the jail. Back window was open. King dropped a crumb about how lucky we Bureau people were to have these men's and women's RVs and how there's probably been some fraternizing going on—'

Angie finished the sentence. 'And the rookie knew about you and Jayne.'

Scott nodded. 'The kid didn't know our names but had enjoyed relaying how he'd heard from the cops over in Orange that the team leader – that would've been me at the time – did some trailer swapping when we stopped to gas up.'

'Stupid idiot,' Angie muttered.

'Me?'

She gave him a benevolent look. 'Him. For talking.'

'Yeah, well, King wouldn't need too many details to get something juicy in front of Turner.'

'Oh. Yeah. Hm.' Angie brooded on this for a moment. 'Turner thinks there's a conflict?'

'His exact words? "There *may* be a conflict." Gotta love his eternal correctness,' Scott said ruefully.

Angie turned from brooding to indignant. 'I don't think Turner should have reassigned you, Scott. It's not like we're building a case here; I mean, King's already pleaded out. This is a recovery operation. For the families.'

'Yes and no, Ange. You know that someone like King will use any tiny thing to undermine the safety of a conviction or shorten a sentence, even when they've confessed. Remember, he used to be one of us. He knows how to work the system. In fact, he just did – and got me reassigned.'

'To be my lackey.'

'Caddie.'

'I'm changing it to lackey.'

They shared a smile but then the radio on Angie's desk crackled to life. Eric's voice came through. 'Kilo Alpha to Base, Kilo Alpha to Base.'

Angie activated her radio. 'This is Base. Go ahead.'

'Location confirmed. Site active. Live package is en route to Base. Kilo Alpha out.'

'Roger. Base out.' She looked to Scott. 'Well, King's still playing. Corrections is bringing him back already.'

Scott was matter of fact. 'Of course he's still playing. Showing us his dump sites is what's getting him out of his cell for a whole week.' But his statement prompted an uncomfortable thought: *King's out of his cell but I may as well be in one.*

9

Now that Graham Ayers was settled on the couch in Jayne's office with a cup of coffee and a plate of buttered toast, his bloodshot eyes and duffel bag were explained: he'd arrived that morning on a Qantas flight that had left Melbourne, Australia the previous day. He'd only slept for an hour or so of the fourteen-hour journey, finding the jet too small for someone habituated to the wide-open skies of rural Australia. He had spent much of the flight walking up and down the aisles, asking for and getting drinks from the obliging and friendly flight attendants. Jayne suggested Graham might want to get some sleep at his hotel and then come back later for the full interview.

He pushed half-chewed toast into the corner of his mouth. 'Can't. Got a flight up to Seattle tonight. Hotel's booked up there.'

'Seattle?'

He washed the mouthful down with a swig of coffee. 'I'm going to sound like I'm starting at the end but, look, my sister went missing in Seattle and I've got myself an appointment with the coroner up there next week because me and my mum reckon they've got her body but I don't know how to explain it all to them and we want you to do that.'

'Okay . . .' Jayne tried to sort through all of that.

'Sorry, I didn't mean you'd have to go up there off your own bat!'

He re-started. 'My mum sold a paddock so I'd have the dosh to buy two tickets for you and your workmate to fly to Seattle and go to the coroner up there – it's called King County? And while you're doing that – if you do – I was going to meet my sister's bloke. I've left him an answering machine message for the first time today, told him I was in Los Angeles to get your help and I'd be glad if he'd sink a tinnie with me because I'm going to have a go at finding out what happened to Alex.'

Jayne was scribbling notes and could see that she'd have to get Graham to untangle what were clearly long-held hopes and ideas. 'Okay, if we can hold the part about going to Seattle? I'd like to understand why you believe your sister's been found but not identified.'

''Cause she's a girl but she has a . . .' He faltered. 'Well, you're a doctor so I guess it's alright for me to say it. She's got a penis,' he whispered.

Jayne looked at him. She wasn't a doctor but she was a forensic anthropologist and the word 'penis' was simply one level of detail beyond 'external genitalia'. It wasn't a word that required a hushed tone.

But she only asked, 'Was Alex born intersex?'

This question was key because someone born with both male *and* female sex characteristics could have a very different skeleton to that of someone born with solely male or female sex characteristics who transitioned genders.

Graham swallowed his coffee and pointed at her. 'That's the word. Intersex. We couldn't remember the word Alex used when she got older because it wasn't what the doctor told my parents when she was a baby. The way Mum explained it to me, Alex didn't have a uterus and she had a penis of sorts so the doc recommended that her birth certificate say she was male.'

Jayne nodded. She knew that parents the world over felt forced into making abstract decisions when their baby was born intersex; most people weren't aware of the totality of human variation and most cultures did nothing to increase that awareness. Indeed, some cultures actively suppressed it.

She made a note. 'And did she have other documents with her identifying her as male, that you know of?'

'Yep, she went through school as a boy, so that's what's on her driver's license, her passport. But that never stopped her. M'sister knew she was a girl from an early age. Scared my parents to bits – they thought it meant she was gay but she wasn't. She was a girl who was into boys, that's how she explained it to them. She loved Mum and Dad to pieces but it got hard for her to deal with the fact that some doctor made a choice for her when she was a tot but then she had to actually live with it. She at least made it up with Dad before he popped his clogs . . .' He exhaled.

Jayne pushed the box of tissues on the coffee table closer to him.

He shook his head. 'I've just realized you're taking notes 'cause you're actually going to look for m'sister. In all these years, people I've talked to could only speculate no better than I could.' He pressed his eyelids closed with his palms.

She let him compose himself. 'It's going to be a group effort, Graham, and you're the most important part of it because you can tell us about your sister. Are you okay to go on?'

He opened his eyes and nodded.

'So Alex did develop a female identity?' Jayne said.

'Oh yeah. I mean, at home we all knew. But she'd asked us not to say anything to anyone else till she was ready. When she was younger, she was a tomboy – always in her tracky daks, never wore a dress – but when she started getting breasts, there was a lot of teasing, and it got worse and more upsetting for her the older she got, even though she was a battler.'

He appealed to Jayne. 'You gotta understand: we live in a country town. People don't get it if a young bloke doesn't drink VB and watch the footy, hoonin' it around on the streets after dark, tryin' to get a sheila into the back of the kombi . . .' He reddened. 'Not that I was a larrikin myself but at least my voice changed, hair grew on my chest and all that. That didn't happen for Alex.'

'And when did she decide to live as a girl, or as a woman?'

'Well, after Dad died, she moved down to Melbourne. Joined a theatre troupe, acted, danced, sang. All the stuff she loved and was good at. No one knew her as Alexander in the city, just Alex, so life was less tricky. Then her troupe got selected to go on a tour to four cities here in America. She went but she wasn't on the plane back to

Oz from the last stop in Seattle – but she wasn't missing at that point.'

'She told you she'd overstayed her visa or . . .?' Jayne was adding notes to what documentary material they might be able to access to build Alex's profile.

'She did. She got a little cash job, moved in with another girl. She wrote to us a lot. She was happy and she'd even met a bloke, had a huge pash on 'im. The last letter we got from her was about him. She thought things were going great, getting serious, maybe they might even tie the knot but she hadn't told him yet that she had the little penis bit. And it was little. It wouldn't be a big deal if a bloke loved her. That's what I thought but she wasn't sure. She liked him heaps and she was trying to find the moment when she'd take the chance. That's how she put it.' Graham teared up again.

Jayne waited.

This time, Graham took a tissue and wiped his eyes. Then he blew his breath out. 'That was the last time we heard from her. When we wrote back, we didn't get a reply for a month or two, and when it did come, it was from her roommate. She was the one who told us that Alex had gone missing. She'd done the missing person report and everything. The police had talked to her and Riley – he's the boyfriend – and the cops said Alex had probably decided to leave to do something else, somewhere else.'

Jayne annotated the presence of a missing person report in Seattle.

Graham was looking at her notebook. 'At first, me and my mum tried to accept what the cops said but it didn't sit right. I wrote to the police and they sent me back some kind of form to report someone missing. That didn't make sense to me but I filled it out and returned that. Didn't hear anything. Wrote back to the roommate; didn't hear anything. Got an international phone card, called the number at their flat and didn't get a reply. I didn't have a number or an addy for Riley, I just knew where he worked. We didn't know what else to do and didn't have the money—' His face contorted in distress.

When he'd composed himself, he started again. 'We didn't have the money to fly to the States. We just hoped the phone would ring one day and it would be Alex. A few years passed and then one day, I was at the doctor's and they had a magazine in there and I was skimming this article about the Green River mongrel.'

Jolted, Jayne looked up from her notebook. 'The serial killer from Washington State?'

'Yeah!' He pointed at her notes like he was expecting her to write that down.

But Jayne probed a bit more. 'Information is still coming to light about how the Green River Serial Killer targeted his victims in and around Seattle, but I recall a focus on sex workers. Do you think Alex could have been involved with that?'

'Not bloody likely! But the thing is, the article had a list of names of women he'd killed all around Seattle, they said, and, strewth, there was Alex's roommate's name!' He raised his eyebrows at her, waiting for her reaction.

Jayne got goosebumps. Almost speechless with shock, she managed, 'My goodness.'

Graham gestured at her. 'That's about what I said but I was a bit more flowery. So me and Mum got to thinking: maybe that feral bastard got Alex first – before he went back for her roommate – and maybe the cops found Alex's body but they thought she was a boy because of her penis!'

He sat back and threw up his hands, like he'd put all his cards on the table.

As Graham had been speaking, Jayne's mind had been moving fast along multiple avenues, none of which were connected to the Green River Serial Killer. They were about the fact that while an intersex person like Alex could assert her sex and gender identity in life, in death she could very well fall through the cracks. American postmortem identification systems were designed to categorize sex as male *or* female, a binary standard that could literally leave Alex behind in a coroner's freezer – forever.

Alex's case was all the more critical because her missing person report was put in by a roommate who knew her as female but her identity documents labeled her as male. In underlining those two facts in her notebook, Jayne realized she was literally holding Alex's identification in her hands. Her workaday notebook suddenly seemed as precious as an illuminated manuscript: fragile but luminous. She needed to convey it to the Seattle ME's office as soon as practicable. What she neglected to consider was that when she brought the light, there would be another person whose only goal would be to snuff it out.

*

FBI Special Agent Eric Ramos was following Tony, Duane, Xavier and Steve as they walked on the highway shoulder to their base camp just inside the city limits of Lordsburg, New Mexico. The Critters were carrying two stretchers laden with multiple body bags holding long bones, ribs and vertebrae, most held together by mummified tissue as far as Eric could tell. He felt responsible for those bones, for getting IDs on them. He always felt a strong sense of responsibility about his job but this time it was different, with SSA Turner making him lead.

The feeling of responsibility had ratcheted up that morning when King, who had behaved like his usual playful-yet-contrite, shitty self, had been removed from the site. Duane had come up to Eric and voiced concern that he and the other Critters were only recovering remains that were 'postcranial'. Duane had been doubtful that they'd be able to make identifications from that kind of material without Jayne and Steelie's involvement. But Eric had decided to be positive – maybe there'd be some healed injuries, some surgical pins. It seemed like Jayne and Steelie always found some; so could the Critters.

The local police guarding their base camp came to attention as the team walked into the graveled area. All eyes were on the body bags. Finally, after a long day of standing around, some action. Eric followed the Critters to step up into the mobile lab.

Scott and Angie both turned to watch the men spread the body bags out across tables and make photoboards while pulling equipment from cabinets.

Eric called out, 'Lunch break, guys?'

'We thought we'd do some quick prelims,' Duane replied.

'Okay. I'll be back,' Eric said.

He went to the men's RV, where he used the restroom, showered, detoured for a bite to eat then went back to the lab. He was desperate for a result already; it would be unbelievably fast but he still wanted it. When he entered the lab, however, the mood was subdued, deflated. Numerous bones were out and images were up on the screen but the Critters were standing back.

'What's happening?' Eric asked, looking at the tables.

Tony broke the news. 'We won't even get presumptive IDs off this stuff, Eric. No marks, nothing obvious to check against the antemortem database.'

Scott and Angie had swiveled their chairs around and were listening in.

Steve asked, 'Can we get Thirty-Two One's eyes on this?'

'No,' Eric said.

Steve blinked at him. 'Just . . . no?'

'Just no,' Scott confirmed on Eric's behalf, coming to join him. 'Why can't you guys figure it out?'

'Because we're not anthropologists,' Xavier said in an exasperated tone.

Angie glanced at Eric in consternation.

Eric asked, 'What else would help?' Then added, '*Besides* Thirty-Two One.'

'DNA, man.' Duane opened his hands, palms out.

'Okay.' Eric turned to Scott. 'Get in touch with the parents of Ellie and Jessica.'

Scott shook his head, lips pursed.

Eric took that in. Was he seriously trying to opt out? He addressed Angie. 'Set up a call with Atlanta Missings. Explain that we need a video conference call with Mr. Collins and Mrs. Belport and we need it by tonight. Scott'll work his magic.'

Scott grimaced. 'I'm not feeling too magical right now, Eric.'

Eric gazed at him. So he was serious. 'Let's take five. Outside.'

As he went to the door with Scott trailing behind him, Eric called back to Angie. 'Start making the call, please.'

She nodded. 'Ten-four.'

The excitement of the cops milling around the base camp was still palpable to Eric. He walked out of their earshot and then he turned to Scott.

'Do you have a problem with me telling you what to do?'

Scott smiled slightly. 'Hell, no. You're always telling me what to do.'

'Seriously, Houston? You just rejected my strategy in there.'

Eric watched Scott look back at the lab like he was mentally replaying what had gone on in there. Then his face creased and he wiped a hand over it. 'Shit. Sorry, I didn't mean for it to come out like that. My head was somewhere else.'

'Okay,' Eric said, folding his arms across his chest. 'Tell me where your head is, and when you're done, get your head back here.'

Scott exhaled but that's all he did.

Eric prompted, 'Is it King or is it Turner?'

Scott shook his head. 'No, none of that stuff. It's talking to Ellie and Jessica's parents.'

'They've already been notified. You're not doing the notification call.'

'I know.'

'So?'

'Eric, you know how much time I spent with the parents after Ellie and Jessica went missing.'

'That's why I want you to be the one to ask them to help us get DNA from the rest of the families.'

'And I'm saying I don't know that I can handle talking to them now that they know their daughters are, y'know, dead.'

Now Eric knew what the problem was. 'You're worried they're going to remind you of Kate Alston's parents.'

Scott met his eyes. Then he nodded, lips pursed.

Eric thought back to how Scott had said he'd felt after meeting the Alstons: impotent. No wonder he wasn't eager. But this was the job. So Eric said, 'Look, we accept that sometimes the crimes, the vics, even the survivors affect us. That's why they debrief us.'

Scott burst out, 'I had a goddamned breakdown after I met with the Alstons, Eric, and the debrief didn't do shit for me. Not that time.'

Eric patted the air in a calming gesture. 'I know. But if you hadn't been affected by it, that would have been worse. It would be wrong to find a kid dead in a freezer and then meet her parents and not feel upset. In fact, we know some agents like that. Don't be like them.'

Eric waited for the smile he was trying to coax out

of Scott. He detected a hint of one, so he said, 'And you should stay in touch with those feelings when you talk to the families, Scott. I'll clear the room.'

Scott glanced at him sharply. 'You'll stay, though, right?'

'Of course, partner.' Eric had managed to sound reassuring but his mind was on the fact that they didn't have anyone on this mobile operation who could debrief Scott if he needed it after this call. But this call had to happen; Eric needed results.

10

Jayne had to put her hands against the dashboard of the Mercedes as Marie brought her 450SL to an abrupt halt in the Agency 32/1 parking lot.

'Mom. Honestly.' She gave Marie an exasperated look. Every drive ended with her getting closely reacquainted with the dash, no matter how many times she asked her mom to remember that she wasn't alone in the car and it wasn't the Grand Prix.

'Yes, darling?' Total sweetness and light.

'You have a lead foot.'

'I drive as I live. With verve. With *panache*.' Marie flung a hand through the air with a flourish, only to catch a glimpse of herself in the rearview mirror and lean forward to inspect her lipstick.

Jayne was amazed that her mother could find anything amiss with her make-up. Marie was done up to perfection as always, her style falling somewhere between Sophia Loren and Catherine Deneuve. Her hair was blow-dried and sprayed into an upswept brown and auburn style that made her appear perennially in front of a photographer's fan. The whole arrangement was topped by a colorful Hermès scarf Marie wore when driving her Mercedes with the top down, as it was today. Jayne actually found the consistency of her mother's flamboyance oddly comforting, even though it came with baggage.

Watching her mother, Jayne said, 'I thought you were maybe extra excited about getting over to LAX to pick up Dad.'

Marie finished applying the touch-up to her lips before answering. 'I'm not driving this car to pick him up. He told me last night that he was bringing many, many suitcases. "Trunks", he said. I don't know where he expects to put everything.'

'It *is* his house as well,' Jayne said for the fiftieth time. 'Just because he's back and forth between Caracas and Altadena doesn't make it any less his house.'

'But I've arranged it just so, darling. And now I've had to concede space so he can paint in his retirement.'

Jayne got out of the car and started to lift shopping bags out of the back seat. 'Listen to you: "concede", like it's some kind of negotiation.'

'It *has* been a negotiation. Ever since he said he was ready to retire, I've been negotiating my space and my schedule. Oh, and I want you and Scott to come over for dinner tomorrow night. Scott's first chance to meet your father.'

Jayne just said, 'Um.'

Marie dropped her sunglasses down to the tip of her nose and looked up at Jayne. 'Why "um"? You told me Scott would be back tomorrow, no?'

Jayne tried to picture having a conversation with Scott about Callista right before dinner with her parents, possibly by herself because she and Scott had broken up. She prevaricated. 'I'll keep you posted.'

Marie started the engine and revved it as she pushed her sunglasses back into place. 'I have something special planned so I'll expect to hear from you!' She blew Jayne a kiss, reversed with 'panache' and rejoined the lunchtime traffic on San Fernando Road.

Jayne picked up her grocery bags and then realized she hadn't specifically thanked her mother for taking her shopping. She would call her later. She went inside the Agency and greeted Carol.

'Was that both of your parents?' Carol was looking out over the top of the counter in reception.

'Just my mom. My dad doesn't arrive until tonight.'

Carol stood up as she cleared away her lunch. 'How long did you say he's been teaching in Venezuela?'

'Pretty much since I was in high school. But he's always traveled home regularly.'

'Still, it's going to be quite a change.'

Jayne raised an eyebrow. 'You forgot to say, "for Marie".'

'I thought that was implied,' Carol said playfully. 'Steelie said for you to come to the lab when you got in.'

Smiling, Jayne stopped in her office to pick up the Alex Ayers file before heading to the lab. She found Steelie peering through her tortoiseshell glasses at Alex's medical X-rays, now illuminated on the wall-mounted lightboxes.

Without looking over, Steelie said, 'Did you eat?'

'If you consider kale and pine nuts to be food. Well, I suppose you'd have to, being vegetarian.' Jayne giggled.

'Ha,' Steelie said humorlessly. She used her glasses to push her bangs off of her forehead and pulled a stool over to the U-shaped counter that ran around three walls of the room. 'These X-rays were shot when Alex was fourteen?'

'Yes, after a horseriding accident.'

Steelie tapped the radiograph of the upper leg, ignoring the ones of right wrist, elbow and shoulder. 'So at this stage, her bones were still fusing. The angle's just decent enough to make out the sciatic notch.'

Jayne looked to where Steelie was pointing. Behind the hip joint, the ilium flared and curved above an arch-like opening. Steelie made a fist with her thumb jutting upwards and then put her hand against the X-ray film so her thumb was inside the arch. She tilted her thumb to the left and then the right. Each time, her thumb quickly passed the extremities of the arch and overlapped bone.

Jayne said, 'Pretty narrow.'

Steelie translated: 'Pretty male.' She dropped her hand. 'And she'd gone through puberty.'

'Well, she was going *through* puberty. We don't know exactly what stage she was at. How can we know if this is the final width of the sciatic notch?'

'We don't know if it's the final width but it might be the final relative width. Like, it was narrow from birth and it's always going to be narrow.' Steelie looked across the lightboards. 'And it might be all we have to go on. We can't really use the long bones because younger age, rather than sexual dimorphism, has everything looking gracile.'

Jayne picked up the dental X-rays and mounted the small films into a frame, which she clipped to the light box. There was one large dental X-ray on the counter. She held this up next to the frame.

She said, 'At least we've got a panogram. Alex was eighteen when it was taken. It's the most recent of the dentals Graham had. He didn't know if she underwent any dental work while she was in the US and before she went missing. But thanks to how they shot this panogram, we can see Alex's whole jaw and . . . look: it's gracile.'

'Not just gracile,' Steelie said with interest. 'That's a textbook female gonial angle and a nice pointy chin to seal the deal.'

'And some fillings to help speed us on our way.'

Steelie looked back to the medical X-rays. 'If you weren't telling me these were from the same person, I'd have said those postcranial bones are likely from a young male and this . . .' she tapped the panogram, 'is a female jaw – and not an Angelina Jolie type but über gracile, like, Elizabeth Taylor or Halle Berry. Do we have any photos?'

Jayne spread the photographs from the folder across the counter. 'I had Graham write her approximate age on the back of each one.'

'Okay. I'll label them accordingly when I scan them.'

They perused the photos. There was a batch of a very young Alex in the gray shorts of a boy's school uniform, short hair parted on the side and a huge smile exposing gaps between growing teeth. And some of Alex just before departing for the States, wearing a long, full skirt cinched at the waist by a wide belt, allowing a peasant top to flounce above it, its frilled edges catching the same breeze that lifted her shoulder-length hair. Graham stood next to her, wearing a blue T-shirt with bleach stains that might have been an eighties fashion statement and board shorts that left great quantities of reddish-blond lower leg hair on display. He was holding his fingers behind Alex's head in a V-symbol and was mid-laugh.

Steelie murmured, 'You can tell they're family by their features. And, next to her brother and on first glance, Alex looks feminine. Looked at more closely, she's actually pretty androgynous.'

Jayne shrugged. 'Examine anyone closely, especially with an anthropologist's eye, and a lot of people will come out looking androgynous.'

'Some people.' Steelie sat back. 'Did Graham happen to say why their parents raised her as a boy?'

'He understood it to have been a doctor's idea. Because of the penis, the doctor advised her parents that if female secondary sex characteristics developed in puberty, surgery could take care of any issues. Like breasts.'

Steelie shook her head in disbelief. 'Charming. I mean, what's a little mastectomy when you're studying for finals?'

'I know. She did develop breasts during puberty but she also grew some light facial hair. And by that time, she identified as female. Had done so for years but only privately.'

'Well, we have enough to do a good profile here.' Steelie scooped up the photos and used her stool to roll across the room, catching hold of the edge of the counter in front of the scanner. 'I'll get started on digitizing these.'

Jayne headed back to the hall. 'And I'll see if anyone's still in the office up in Seattle.'

*

From his position at the top of the step stool, Joseph reached past the veinous cluster of wires that held the closet ceiling light in place. His fingers landed unerringly on the freezer bag. After he replaced the ceiling light and ensured the bulb was still working, Joseph folded away the step stool, closed the closet door from the inside and turned off the light. He was in total darkness but he closed his eyes anyway because that was part of what brought it all back. Ever so slowly, he pressed his fingers into the join of the bag's zip lock, giving it a little more pressure, then more, and a bit more until it yielded with a soft *pop*. Joseph almost sighed. Oh, the thrill of it, the openness. Inserting his fingers into the bag, he fluttered them against the hank of hair within. It was still silken after all these years, thanks to his ministrations. He'd washed it, conditioned it, dried it. Joseph unfurled it to its full length as he removed it from the bag, then he smelled it, inhaled it. He dragged it across his lips, let it sweep across his eyelids, and then, finally and for the last time, he wound it tightly around one hand – under and over, under and over, tighter and tighter until he was ready. Then he jerked his fist up. The hair snapped taut between his hands. *Yes*. It felt the same. The long hair of one Alexander Ayers, wound tight around his hand while Joseph used his other to choke out the man's life. Alexander's long hair, like a maiden. Joseph sneered; he'd made it his handmaiden to murder. One life ended and another begun. Rebirth – followed by a reburial. But now the reliving was going to have to end. Joseph released his grip on the hair and felt blood pump back into his fingertips in an achy, rhythmic tingle. He would dispose of the hair where no one would find it. He needed to be nimble and free, to plan and to kill again.

*

Eric felt subdued eating lunch in the mess trailer with Scott and the Critters as he waited for the word from Angie that the call had been set up with the Atlanta Police Department's Missing Persons Squad. When Angie finally summoned him, Eric gestured for Scott to follow them back to the lab.

Angie explained, 'You've got Mr. Collins and Mrs. Belport in the conference room at APD Missings but no detectives present; it's just them.'

John, their IT coordinator, was leaning over a monitor, blocking the screen as he made an adjustment to a cord. 'Just doing some fine-tuning,' he said.

He moved aside and Eric glanced at the screen. The two people visible on it, both in their early sixties, were sitting at a table as though they didn't know where to look while waiting for the screen on their end to go live. The woman was fiddling with a shawl whose colors picked up on her burgundy hair dye, the overhead lighting in the room exposing both her white roots and the freckles spread across her pale cheeks. She looked nervous, whereas the man next to her looked ready for anything.

He was wearing a dark blue button-down shirt with all the buttons done barring the topmost one, and no tie. His salt-and-pepper hair was close-cropped and his brown skin clean-shaven. He took up one of the bottles of water on the table, looked at the label and put it back next to the box of tissues that had clearly been provided for them. He looked at the screen and then away.

John said, 'A/V is all tee'd up, Eric. Here's a couple of lavalier mics and then I'll hit the button when you're ready to start.'

Eric took the microphones. 'Actually, we're going to need the room.'

Unperturbed, John nodded, but Angie's eyebrows went up a fraction before she, too, nodded and turned to leave.

While John instructed Eric on what buttons to press for transmission and muting, Scott called out to Angie's retreating figure. 'Thanks, Ange.'

'Anytime, Houston,' she replied without turning around.

Once John was gone, Eric attached the lavalier microphone to Scott's shirtfront but ignored the second one; he wasn't planning to be on the call. 'You good?'

Scott nodded, and Eric activated the camera and microphone. The moment the feed went live with Scott's head and shoulders, the woman gave a start of recognition and burst into tears. The man next to her pulled the tissues closer, patted her hand and then folded his arms across his chest again. He resumed looking at Scott but not speaking.

Scott cleared his throat. 'Mrs. Belport. Mr. Collins. It's good to see you again. You have my deepest sympathy for the loss of your daughters, Jessica . . .' He paused as Mrs. Belport tried to compose herself behind the tissues she was holding to her face. Then he looked at Mr. Collins. 'And Ellie.'

Mr. Collins gave a single nod of acknowledgment.

Mrs. Belport sniffed behind her tissue, the first flow of tears tapering off. 'Thank you, Mr. Houston.'

Scott continued. 'Thank you so much for providing the DNA samples that allowed us to positively identify your daughters. Has Atlanta Police Department's Missing Persons Squad communicated with you about funeral arrangements staying on hold a little while longer as we still hope to recover more . . . remains?'

From his position outside the camera's view, Eric glanced at Scott. Why did he sound so hesitant? He saw that Scott's hands were tightly clenched together on the desk.

'Yes,' Mr. Collins answered. 'They've been very helpful.'

'Good. Now, you may have heard that we've identified four other women besides Jessica and Ellie, but our team is still searching for Rizza, Alana, Lisa, Tal, Ruth, Ting and Journey.'

'Yes, we know.'

'Well, Mr. Collins,' Scott said carefully, 'Ellie was friends with Alana and Journey. They looked out for each other. And Mrs. Belport, Rizza was your daughter's go-to for babysitting little Des and she considered Ting to be her best friend.'

Watching their faces, Eric could tell that at least some of this was news to these parents.

'How is little Des?' Scott's voice had softened.

Mrs. Belport gave a teary smile. 'He's doing well, despite everything. He remembers you, Mr. Houston. He told us you said he's going to do great things.'

'I remember him, too. Give him a hug from me and tell him I know he's already doing great things.'

Mrs. Belport's smile was overtaken by a sob when she tried to reply. She finally said, 'I will.'

Scott said, 'You both know I spent a lot of time with Jessica and with Ellie, so I'm aware that your daughters spent a lot of time with some of the women who worked around them. I know they all cared about each other and were also trying to take care of themselves, their kids, their families.' He took a deep breath. 'No one on the team here thinks it's enough simply to convict the man who took their lives. We want to get all the women home.'

Eric saw Mr. Collins' eyes begin to well up with tears.

'But to do that . . .' Scott's voice thickened. He cleared his throat. 'To do that, we need DNA from all the other families the same way you provided it. We can't make identifications at this point without it. I am speaking with you today to ask if you would talk to the families of the rest of the women. Can you help us by doing this?'

A tear coursed down Mr. Collins' cheek but he didn't reach for the tissues. He spoke slowly with his arms tight across his chest. 'Agent Houston, I'm not going to thank you for trying to help my daughter when she was alive because you didn't protect her from that monster.'

Eric noticed Scott's clenched fingers unfurl, as though the thing he'd been tensed up for had finally happened, but his knuckles were white.

Mr. Collins wasn't done. 'But I recognize that you're not the reason Ellie's dead and I will thank you for your help in getting her body back to us. The ladies – Steelie and

Jayne, that is – they explained what you've done to make this happen and how big a job it is. And they explained about DNA. So. Yes, I will help you, so I can help the other families get to where we are, which is planning a fune—' His mouth twisted as another tear dropped and he fought to gain control of his voice. 'A funeral instead of just wondering . . . wondering all the time where Ellie is or what condition she's . . . in.'

He finally took a fistful of tissues and wiped his face, taking his time with it, and then he looked at Mrs. Belport. He put his hand over hers and shook it gently. 'We'll talk to them, won't we, Missy?'

She nodded at him and then looked back to Scott. 'Des will be glad you remember him.'

Scott nodded gravely. 'Thank you, both of you, for your assistance with this. Again, you have my deepest condolences. I will sign off now.' He looked at Eric, who read the mute appeal in Scott's eyes and cut off the transmission.

Eric drew breath to speak but Scott shook his head as he pushed back from the desk. Eric watched Scott almost collide with Angie as he left the trailer. She looked back at him as she stepped inside. Eric got her up to speed with the status of things after the call, asking that she kept an open line to Atlanta Missings in case any families responded to the call for help and started providing DNA as of that night. Then Eric left the lab and scanned the base camp for Scott. He eventually spotted him sitting on the split rail fencing that ringed the site, about as far away as one could get from their vehicles.

As Eric approached, he smelled cigarette smoke. His shoes were silent on the dusty earth-packed surface so he called out Scott's name. A plume of smoke went into the air.

Eric leaned his elbows on the fence and looked at the cigarette Scott was dragging on again. 'Where'd you get *that*?'

Holding his breath, Scott said, 'Nate.'

Eric tracked the next plume of smoke into the air above them. 'You okay, man?'

'Not really.'

'You want to talk?'

'No-ot really.' Scott took another drag but then he did start talking, his tone combative as smoke streamed out of his mouth and nostrils. 'You know what I want, Eric? I want to forget.' He impatiently blew the last of the smoke out. 'I want to forget all the shit with King – how he almost cost me my job in Atlanta, how he held Jayne and Steelie's lives in his hands, how he . . . Eric, King killed those people's daughters just because he had a beef with me.'

He pointed back at the lab trailer. 'People are dead because of *me*.'

Eric shook his head vehemently. 'Scott, you're buying into King's excuses. He's a homicidal maniac, remember?'

Scott made a strangled noise and stubbed out the cigarette on the fence post while pulling the packet from his shirt pocket. He dug around for another cigarette but apparently there wasn't one because he jammed the spent butt inside and crumpled the packet in his hands.

Eric eyed the debris. 'How many were in there when you got started?'

'Not enough.'

Eric was silent. It was bad if Scott was parroting King's bullshit. It was King who bore full and sole responsibility for his actions.

Eric looked around. 'Look, it's going to be a while before we convoy out. So you and me are going to catch a ride from the locals and go to a bar that ideally also serves food. They can bring us back here before our drivers roll out.' He gestured with his head toward the patrol cars. 'Let's go do some forgetting.'

11

Officer Vicente from their New Mexico State Police detail had told Eric he knew just the place to take the two FBI agents: a bar called The Ocotillo on the other side of Lordsburg. He said it did 'mean' burritos and margaritas and was lively but not the kind of lively that produced disturbance calls to the police.

So, with Officer Vicente waiting outside, Scott and Eric were sitting in a booth in The Ocotillo, their badges and weapons obscured under their clothes. The bar was everything the cop had described: pleasantly noisy from a mixture of music, talk and people playing darts, plus two televisions mounted above the bar tuned to different sports events. Meanwhile, the low lighting was punctuated by shafts of colored spotlights made visible by the cigarette smoke wafting around.

Scott had been watching one of the televisions, mostly drinking, while Eric had been looking at Scott and around the room and mostly eating. Scott eventually ordered some sliders and ate them while taking a call from Matthew West. Based on what Eric could hear of Scott's side of the conversation, the LAPD homicide detective was asking Scott something about Steelie because Scott confirmed that 'Steelie' was a nickname and then spelled out her full name. Whatever else they talked about, as soon as he hung up,

Scott went to the bar. When he returned, he was lighting a cigarette while tucking the pack into his shirt pocket. Eric looked at that. Scott saw him looking and indicated that he was going to go over to the darts board.

Eric went on to his next beer. He was getting buzzed now but he knew Scott was well past that as he watched him making his way through the crowd. Drunk would be about right based on the number of shots Scott had downed. Eric sipped his beer and felt annoyed, irrationally, with Detective West. Matt was one of those trying-to-quit smokers who always seemed to have a 'spare' cigarette if someone asked for one. And since Scott had started hanging out with Matt, Scott was the someone asking. Eric told himself that he didn't care if Scott smoked; he just didn't want it to turn into that unhealthy, every-time-I-have-a-drink-I-need-a-cigarette-in-my-hand thing that Scott used to do in Atlanta, usually whenever work was bothering him – or when Callista was. The tobacco industry could have paid that woman for how much she'd prompted Scott to smoke. Moving to LA hadn't just ended it with Callista, it had broken the nicotine habit.

Eric got up and moved through the crowd to get a look at the darts game. A lot of people were clustered around Scott because, as Eric had already known, Scott was as good a shot with darts as he was with his gun despite inebriation and the smoke from his cigarette making his eyes squint. The crowd was enjoying his success and now other players were backing out so they could take bets on Scott's prowess instead.

And then there were the women. Two in particular,

both wearing jean shorts, one in a white vest and the other in a black T-shirt trimmed to expose her midriff. They were wearing cowboy boots and hats and were definitely gravitating toward Scott. One of them managed to get behind him, her hand on his shoulder as she bounced up and down on her toes after each throw. Eric noticed that each downward bounce was revealing a lot of her attributes. He scanned the crowd, looking for which people the women might have been with, but no one was paying particular attention to them. It was like everyone knew each other, like they were regulars.

Eric looked back to Scott. His expression had become tense and focused. Eric knew that Scott was no longer seeing the darts board; he was seeing King – thinking about King. Every single dart was slamming home to the bull's eye now, coming so fast no one could get to the board to remove them. They were starting to land on each other and fall to the floor in a pile and the crowd was loving it. No one seemed to notice that Scott was acting like an automaton. *Enough is enough*. Eric made his way over and put his hand on Scott's arm to pull it down. Scott didn't resist.

Over the general noise, Jean Shorts #1 said something like, 'Hey!' And maybe, 'You're spoiling our fun!'

Eric could barely hear her so he shouted, 'What?'

Then he felt a tap on his shoulder. It was Jean Shorts #2, reaching up to cup his ear with a hand so he could hear without her resorting to shouting. 'How come you don't wanna play? You look like you have strong arms.' She squeezed his bicep, more than once.

He looked at her fingers on his arm, unprepared for this level of flirtation from someone he hadn't been talking to or even making eye contact with that night. When he looked at her face, he estimated that she was in her late twenties and she was smiling at him in a way that possibly no woman ever had. He smiled back but was tongue-tied, distracted by her touch. It was a long couple of seconds before he remembered Scott. He turned back but Scott was gone.

Eric went up on his toes and located his partner past the booths near the restrooms. Jean Shorts #1 had her cowboy hat off and it was dangling behind her from the cord around her neck. As Eric watched, she took Scott's cigarette out of his mouth and put it in hers. Eric could see that Scott was coming out of his darts-killing haze to finally notice her.

Eric immediately shouldered his way through the darts crowd, which had moved on to some kind of championship round. When he reached the pair, Scott's fingers were playing through the frayed edges of the woman's shorts. Eric thought it unlikely that it would stop there so he interrupted, pulling Scott's hand away. Scott stumbled drunkenly into him so Eric put a hand to Scott's chest to prop him up while he tried to apologize to the woman.

Smiling friskily, she shouted, 'A threesome, huh? I'm open to that!'

Eric was beginning to wonder if everyone's hearing in this bar had been ruined by the noise. He needed to shut this down. Raising his voice, he said, 'He's with me.'

He instantly realized she'd misunderstood because of the way her expression changed. He was about to say, *I didn't mean like that* when Scott leaned over and kissed him, full on the lips.

Eric immediately pulled back in shock but Jean Shorts had taken it all in stride. 'I'm so sorry. My gosh! You guys don't look . . .'

Eric couldn't deal with her as well as Scott. He gave his partner a look. *What the— Was that for her benefit?*

Scott was looking right back at him but his eyes were glassy.

'Anyway!' Jean Shorts summed up cheerfully. 'This was fun! You guys are way cute, I should've realized.'

Eric dragged his eyes over to her. She was using two fingers to hold the cigarette out from her body while she adjusted her cleavage, kind of pumping it up like they weren't there.

Then she fluffed her hair. 'How do I look?'

Her voice suddenly sounded deeper, as though she pitched it higher when she'd thought she was talking to straight guys. She didn't wait for Eric's reply, which he couldn't formulate anyway, and headed off like she was going back into the ring, re-seating her cowboy hat on her head.

Scott had leaned his head back against the wall and closed his eyes. He mumbled, 'I think I'm a little drunk.'

Eric found his voice. 'A *little*? Jesus Christ, Houston!'

But then he had to vault forward to prevent his partner's knees from buckling under him as Scott fell asleep standing up. Half-carrying him, Eric managed to get outside into the blessedly quiet parking lot. He looked up at the night sky, almost surprised to find that the stars were still where they were supposed to be.

Officer Vicente saw Eric and came over to lend a hand. He chuckled as they bundled Scott into the back seat of the unmarked car, and said, 'That place can get pretty rowdy. But not in a bad way.'

Eric got in next to Scott and spent a moment trying to push him up into a seated position so he could put on the seatbelt. It was impossible.

Vicente started the car and Eric looked back at The Ocotillo's neon sign, which featured an outline of the eponymous desert plant in full bloom, pinky-red dots on each green stem. The place looked so benign from the outside but inside it had felt like some kind of Twilight Zone.

He called up to Vicente as they pulled away. 'I'm not sure if rowdy is even the word. The women in there were . . .' He whistled to show his surprise.

'Yeah,' Vicente said knowingly. 'Small town, so they love seeing anyone new. And they *love* guys in uniform.'

Due to his buzz, Eric had to look down at himself to double check what he was wearing. 'But we're not *in* uniform.'

The officer glanced at him in the rearview mirror. 'Two clean-cut guys like you who're over thirty but can still wear a belt? Around here, you don't need to *wear* a uniform. The girls know.'

Eric raised an eyebrow and joked, 'I should see if I could get transferred out here.'

As the car sped up, Scott slumped into his lap, snoring lightly. Eric remembered he hadn't succeeded with the seatbelt so he put his arm around Scott's chest to simulate one and then shook his head, annoyed with himself. It was only alcohol that had him thinking his arm could save anyone in an accident.

He called up to the front seat. 'Just FYI, my partner's not buckled up.'

'Roger,' Vicente confirmed. 'Not much traffic at this time.' But he slowed the pace anyway.

As they traveled under the streetlights, the car's interior was alternately illuminated and plunged back into darkness. Eric looked down at Scott, whose chest was rising and falling, causing the pack of cigarettes in the shirt pocket to crinkle softly. Eric removed the pack and lighter. Then he thought back to what had just happened in the bar.

He decided that the glassy look in Scott's eyes that he hadn't been able to read at the time was gratitude: primarily for stopping Scott from doing something with another woman that would have hurt Jayne but also for getting him away from the job for a few hours. It hadn't even been a kiss, Eric told himself, although he briefly backtracked to how Scott had held him firmly in with a hand on the back of his head. Then he rejected even that as evidence of a kiss. It had just been all of Scott's gratitude manifested in an action, the kind of action that someone who was in extremis and without words might take. Oh, and someone who was drunk. Very drunk. That made Eric smile: there was no way Scott would remember what had happened. After all, it had been a night for forgetting.

DAY 5

Friday

12

Scott opened the door of the Bureau RV and instantly knew he was in Arizona. The desert didn't look the same as it had in New Mexico. And it was hotter. Not as hot as it had been in Phoenix earlier that summer when he and Eric were on the Alston case but hot enough for it to feel like he'd bumped into a wall when he opened the door. He put on his sunglasses and looked around the rest area.

Like all their other base camps along I-10, this one had been transformed by the presence of Bureau vehicles and attendant local police cars. It was a graveled court ringed by a low adobe wall against which a variety of cacti and succulents were growing. On the other side of the wall, the desert expanded ever-outward but it wasn't completely flat: in the distance to both east and west, mountains rose, their slopes covered in gray-green shrubs up to rocky summits not quite tall enough to produce the drop in temperature that would result in a change in vegetation at this time of year. According to the map, Phoenix was to the north and Tucson to the south, but neither city was visible from their location.

Scott brought his focus down to the mess trailer. He had purposefully emerged from the RV only after Eric and the Critters had headed out for breakfast. He didn't want to engage with anyone while he dealt with the alcohol-fuelled headache from a night he could barely remember but which had resulted in him waking up fully clothed on top of his berth. The only problem with this approach was that, at this point, he did actually need food. As he stepped down from the RV, the door of the mess opened and Eric came out, followed by the Critters, who were moving to the lab trailer to get suited up in protective gear. Eric spotted Scott and raised his hand in greeting before walking off toward the road. King would be arriving soon.

When he got to the mess, Scott saw that he'd missed the huevos rancheros and sausages but there was still plenty of fruit and pancakes. He was helping himself to coffee when Agent Mark Wilson stepped up into the trailer.

'Hey, Scott. I saved you a plate,' Mark said, going behind one of the buffets. He brought out a foil-wrapped paper plate. 'Eric said you'd need it.'

Scott lifted the foil. The plate had everything on it and smelled delicious. 'Thanks. This is perfect.' He took hot sauce and maple syrup over to the end of the table and sat down to eat.

Mark had stopped to look out the window. 'King's here.'

Scott looked up but didn't stop eating or rise from his seat.

Mark glanced back at him. 'Had enough of him, huh?' He went back to looking out the window.

'Haven't you?'

'I don't have the history with him that you have. Or, I should say, the history he has with you. When I think back to how we apprehended him, to how he'd buried body parts, kept trophies, he came across like any other serial killer. You know, just self-absorbed and in his own world. Then – hup, there he goes again. Laughing like something's really funny.'

'He's probably jerking Eric's chain about where I am.'

'Probably. They're getting him underway now. Ankle cuffs are off.'

Mark went to pour himself an orange juice and sat down across from Scott. 'It was during the interrogations that I saw how truly creepy he was, how he'd taken his Bureau training and twisted it. But once he was booked, I could move on from all of it like it was a case, whereas you had to deal with the part of it that was directed at you. All the surveillance crap, the meddling.'

Scott grimaced as he pushed his chair back to get some more fruit. He hardly wanted a reminder of this stuff.

The door opened and Nate, Sara and Joe came in carrying trash bags and cleaning supplies.

'Killer eggs, huh?' Nate said, sounding punchy.

Scott nodded. 'Thanks, guys. You did us proud – again. Glad this was the last breakfast?'

Sara laughed as she started clearing one of the buffet tables. 'We've had a great time.'

'And we have a surprise for dinner,' Joe added. 'You haven't said anything, have you, Mark?'

Mark mimicked zipping his mouth shut as he got up from the table. Scott poured himself another coffee and turned to leave.

'Hang on a second,' Sara said as she poured out a second cup and put together a small bag with creamer and sugar packets. 'Take this to Angie, would you? She wanted some in the lab.'

Scott tucked the bag into one of his cargo pants pockets and took the second cup. Mark held the door for him as he left. Even for the few seconds it took to walk to the mobile lab, he worked to hold both cups in one hand so he could pull his sunglasses down and reduce the sun's glare.

Inside the lab, it was cool and quiet since the fume hoods were off. Angie was cleaning her workstation.

'Ah, my coffee!'

Scott went to put everything on the desk but then hesitated. 'Okay to put this down here?'

'Absolutely. I was just doing a little clean-up while it's quiet this morning. I'm presuming we're on target to finish up today and give these trailers back tomorrow?'

'As far as I know.' He indicated the radio on the desk. 'Any word from Eric yet?'

'Yeah. They've already located the first of the three sites. Eric's left Tony and Xavier on that one and they're on foot again, looking for the second one.'

Scott was suddenly aware that, although he missed being actively involved in the recovery, he was glad he wasn't out there baking in the sun because his deep fatigue would undoubtedly mix unfavorably with his antipathy toward King. He held King responsible for him having to speak to Collins and Belport, and therefore for him drinking too much last night, and smoking – which made King responsible for the hangover he had right now. Adding Arizona's supercharged heat to all that would lead him to do or say something that would either jeopardize his job or play into King's hands. He put his arms on the table and laid his forehead on them.

Angie's chair squeaked as she leaned back to look at him. 'Why don't you go lay down?'

He looked at her from under his eyebrows. 'On the job? At, like, nine in the morning?'

'Yeah, that does sound wrong. What is wrong anyway?'

'I'm just wiped out.' He closed his eyes again.

'From talking with the parents yesterday and then "missing" dinner?'

He opened one eye to look at her. 'You always could read me, Ange.'

'Like a book, Houston. Like a book.'

13

Eschewing the telephone's intercom in the Agency 32/1 reception area, Carol called out through the French doors. 'Jayne, it's Olivia Caldwell from the King County Medical Examiner's office on line one.'

Jayne exclaimed happily. She and Steelie had become fast friends with Olivia when they had all studied at UCLA. Olivia had been a medical student from Orange County while Jayne and Steelie had just declared for anthropology. Jayne had hoped to reach Olivia when she'd called her Seattle office the day before but had been routed to another staff member.

Jayne picked up her desk phone. 'OC! I didn't expect it to be you.'

'Are you kidding, Jayne? As soon as I saw that you'd talked with Umar last night, I scooped it up.'

'It's so good to hear your voice. How are you?'

'Busy, busy, busy. But it keeps me out of trouble. How are you – how's Steelie?'

'We're both fine.'

'It's been too long. Please tell me you have kids. I know Steelie won't have.'

Jayne laughed. 'Steelie is actually going on a serious date this weekend – with a very unlikely match.'

'Don't tell me. A prosecutor.'

'A cop.'

Olivia let out a whistle. 'Was he previously in the Peace Corps or something? And how'd they even meet now that she's done with defense lawyering?'

Jayne smiled; OC had always liked the details. 'They met last month on one of our cases. I've seen them together and he's smitten. But why'd you ask me about kids? Are you and Keith . . .?'

'Ah . . . no, I'm not sporting a breast pump under my autopsy gown, though my office did change a closet into a lactation room. Currently being used as a panic room by our college intern every time we get a floater, poor sucker. Anyway, about your call yesterday: you're looking for a body in our freezer?'

Jayne rolled with the total shift in subject from lactation to morgue freezers. It was a relief to be talking with someone who was just like her and Steelie when it came to that.

She said, 'King County is just the first place we want to rule out for this one. Umar said he would do some checking last night?'

'He did,' Olivia confirmed. 'But just with the dental, figuring that teeth were the most likely to get us a hit given that you're looking for someone with a mixed male and female skeletal profile. And . . . let's see . . . there was no match with our in-house records using just dental data. However, since you'd so helpfully coded the teeth for NCIC already, Umar uploaded the charts into NCIC. But you struck out there too, at least among coroners who've uploaded dental on their Jane Does.'

Furiously taking notes, Jayne could barely wait to tell

Steelie that Alex's dental records had been added to her missing person record in the National Crime Information Center database. That was a coup, as they had no access to NCIC themselves. 'I would love to run the dental against John Does too but that's—'

Olivia cut her off. 'Impossible since the missing person's coded female. NCIC won't go for it.'

'That's what I was about to say. But thank Umar for uploading it to NCIC, will you?' Jayne was about to thank Olivia for doing her best but Olivia was making noises akin to a heraldic trumpet.

'All is not lost, my friend! My county has a backlog of unidentifieds, a percentage of which we've examined but haven't yet databased. They're not in our local systems, let alone NCIC.'

Jayne felt a frisson of excitement. There was still hope for finding Alex in Seattle. 'Our misper could be in that batch, OC. Any chance you could check it for us?'

'Believe me, I would love to because it would mean I wasn't on an autopsy roster from sunup to sundown. But I've talked to my boss about it and he's good with you and Steelie reviewing the twenty files.'

Jayne couldn't believe her ears. 'That would be fantastic. Do the twenty files represent twenty people or what? What's the breakdown?'

'It could be more than twenty people because we've got commingled remains plus partials in there.'

'How complete are the files?' Jayne looked up from her notepad to see Steelie walking into her office from reception, sunglasses in her hair, her expression curious. Jayne gave her a huge smile.

The sound of rustling paper came down the line to Jayne, and then Olivia said, 'Not bad actually. We've got field notes from the anthropologist . . . quick and dirty anthropological analyses. You can use those. There are photos and criminalists' notes but these are all either sub judice homicides or cause of death undetermined so you won't get a look-see, sorry.'

'Of course,' Jayne said. 'We wouldn't expect that.'

'The offer on the table is, if you want to look at the files and give our office a short – my boss said "very short" – shortlist, we will compare any radiographs of your misper to those remains. He hasn't said which day the comparisons would happen, or which year, but I can run interference there.'

Jayne gave Steelie a thumbs-up while saying to Olivia, 'Thank you so much!'

'Then we have a deal,' Olivia said. 'Umar has a note here that you were coming in this Monday for a meeting on behalf of your client? Let's convert that meeting to this file dive and then see if we still need a meeting.'

'That works.'

'And if you get here before I start my first post, we can have coffee in the cafeteria. Say, seven-thirty? Catch up properly.'

As Jayne hung up, Steelie settled herself on the edge of the desk, trying to read Jayne's notes upside down. 'OC came through for us?'

Jayne nodded. 'She's been fantastic. They have a small backlog of unidentified material—'

'No surprise there.'

'Yes, but not all of it has been databased, so when Umar checked the dental we sent up for Alex yesterday and didn't get any matches, it turns out that wasn't the end of the road. Oh, and he added the dental to Alex's NCIC record.'

'That was nice of him!'

Jayne told her about Olivia's plan. Finally, she said, 'We can't examine the remains or see any photos, but if we can make the pile smaller, they'll do comparisons for us by hand.'

'Sounds like OC pulled some strings.'

'Indeed. I got the sense that if we didn't know her personally, we might not have got a pathologist to answer our call. So I now need to call Graham and confirm that you and I are on to fly up to Seattle on Sunday.'

Steelie put her hand on the phone to stop Jayne picking up the handset. 'First: critical business.'

Jayne had an idea of what was coming because Steelie's stern expression looked a lot like one of Marie's stern expressions, minus the arched eyebrow, the lipstick and the blowout.

Steelie recited something she'd clearly prepared earlier. 'If whatever is bothering you is about the MOU, then make it about the whole MOU, not just the U.'

Jayne just raised her eyebrows, waiting for Steelie to decode this.

'U as in y-o-u.' Steelie grinned and pointed at herself with both thumbs. 'That was pretty good, right?' She raised her voice to be heard in the next room. 'I could give Carol a run for her money in the therapy department!'

'Nice try,' Carol calmly retorted from reception.

Steelie started straightening the office supplies on Jayne's desk. 'Seriously, Jayne, if your bleak mood is about the MOU, that's between Scott and his supervisor. Sure, it's also about money for the Agency, but that's just money.'

Jayne gave her a wry smile. 'Just money, huh?'

'Yeah. And if it ends up that we have to return the Bureau BlackBerry, I'm okay with that because it's been stretching out the back pocket of my 501s.'

Jayne toyed with blurting out the Callista story but stopped again. She didn't want Scott to be lowered in Steelie's estimation, nor did she want recriminations for not talking to him about it yet. She sighed. 'This isn't about the MOU. Okay?'

'Well, what then?' Steelie leaned in and lowered her voice. 'Did you and Scott break up or something?'

Jayne shook her head.

'Something you saw during the mobile operation, then, or something someone said?'

Jayne accidentally looked at her on the word 'said' and then quickly turned to busy herself at the computer, waking up the screensaver.

Steelie said, 'Hmph. But whatever it is, you're saying it isn't to do with Scott?'

Jayne didn't want to lie. 'It is and it isn't. And I can't talk about it – yet.'

'Okay. You should call him.'

Jayne's response was more explosive than was warranted.

'What, while he's out on an interstate highway looking for body parts, I just call on a personal matter? We agreed we wouldn't talk until he's back.'

'But you're not acting like that's what's happening!' Steelie countered. 'You've had a face as long as Ventura Boulevard since we left Texas, like he's not in your life anymore. You need to call him.'

Since Steelie's hand was no longer on the phone, Jayne reached for it. 'The only person I need to call right now is Graham. Our client.'

*

Eric looked back at the highway, gauging how much Arizona desert he'd just traversed. It was probably only a hundred feet but it felt farther because (a) it was as hot as Hades with the sun glaring straight down on him, and (b) he didn't feel too sparkly after drinking as much alcohol as he had last night. When he looked forward again, he felt sure King was taking them on a wild goose chase. It was the last day of the recovery operation – *unless* King could string it out to another day by pretending he couldn't remember where he'd left the body parts. Again. Eric swung out to the side to pass Duane and Steve and walk up alongside King and the Corrections officers.

'Lost your bearings, King?'

'Like you've lost your partner, you mean?' King looked around. 'Where *is* Special Adversary Houston this morning? Had to chain him up so he wouldn't do any more damage?'

'The only person in chains is you. Where are the remains?'

King smiled. 'You're adorable when you try to talk like him, Agent Ramos. But even in these shackles,' he held up his wrists, the metal chain between them tinkling, 'I can dance circles around him. Always have; always will.'

Eric rolled his eyes behind his sunglasses. King didn't make him angry like he made Scott; he was just a royal pain in the ass. 'Where, King?'

They were approaching another one of those spots in the desert where people who've parked their cars on the side of the highway walk into the sand and brush and make piles of stone they've found by scouring the area. They'd already passed a cluster of such shrines closer to the highway.

King stopped without warning. 'You're looking at them.'

Lifting his sunglasses, Eric shaded his eyes and looked at the area, but he could only discern piles of stone.

King sounded pleased. 'You still can't see them, can you?'

Steve had come up alongside Eric and he pointed out one of the piles. Eric stared, and then he finally saw it. King had piled up linear bones, shorter lengths atop longer ones, to make a pyramid. Eric nodded that he'd seen it and the two Critters moved forward to begin documentation and recovery.

As King observed this, he said, 'You might be wondering how I got the bones to stay put.'

Eric dropped his sunglasses back down. 'I'm not.'

'Well, you're going to want this for your report, Agent Ramos. I drilled holes so I could insert a fishing wire frame. If I hadn't done that, all the non-human animals around here would've scattered them too quick. Though it looks to me like . . . yes, they've had a good chew on the ends. For the animals without opposable thumbs, my frame would've been a godsend, holding the bone steady so they could insert their little tongues in and lick out the marrow.' King's grayish tongue suddenly snaked out of his mouth and retracted on an audibly wet inhalation.

Eric hadn't looked away fast enough and he felt the bile rise from his stomach.

King laughed softly.

The Corrections officers looked like Eric felt. He addressed them. 'You can take him back to base.'

They nodded and moved King toward the highway.

Eric walked over to the Critters, who were taking digital photographs of the site. He said, 'King claims he wired these together.'

'Found the wire,' Steve said. 'But the bones are from more than one person. He wired a couple of people together.'

Eric bit back an expletive. 'Anything looking good for IDs?'

Duane said, 'Not yet. But we're barely into it.'

Eric pulled out his radio. 'Kilo Alpha to Kilo Delta.'

It was a moment before Tony answered. 'This is Kilo Delta, go ahead.'

'What's your ETA for completion? Over.'

'Sixty minutes for completion and transport, over.'

Eric glanced at his watch. 'Ten-four. Do you require assistance? Over.'

'Negative.'

'Roger. Kilo Alpha out.' When Eric heard Tony sign off, he clipped the radio back onto his belt and went back to observing Duane and Steve figure out how they were going to lift and transport the bones: still connected by the wires, or cut the wires first. Steve was in favor of cutting the wires but Duane felt that the lab would provide better lighting to re-photograph the bones before the wire was cut. They tried to get the pyramid into a body bag, and then two bags. Nothing was working and, for some reason that Eric didn't understand, the two agents were starting to raise their voices. Eric realized he was going to have to adjudicate even though he felt out of his depth when it came to the minutiae of body recovery.

He stepped forward. 'Steve. Sparky. Take me through it and take it down a thousand. It's hot enough out here without you two adding to it.'

*

Angie's phone rang. Looking at the readout, she said to Scott, 'It's Atlanta Missings.' She reached for her notebook as she listened to the caller.

Scott could tell it was good news. He felt a stirring of excitement but knew he'd have to wait to get the details until she'd hung up from the call.

When Angie rang off, she grabbed him by the shoulders. 'Scott! All of the mispers' families back in Atlanta are providing DNA samples. Every single one. Everyone's going to go home.'

The jubilation Scott felt astounded him. He hugged Angie, their knees bumping as their chairs met. In the midst of their embrace, he realized that what he was really feeling was relief.

Angie straightened up, eyes misty. 'Let's radio Eric.'

When they got Eric, he sounded harassed. 'This is Kilo Alpha, go ahead Base.'

'Message received from home base,' Angie said, her voice trembling with emotion. 'We are go for all items. I repeat, we are go. Over.' She gave Scott an irrepressible smile.

There was a moment of silence before the radio crackled back to life.

'Copy. Over and out.'

Angie settled the radio on its charging stand and looked at it. 'That was . . . restrained. For Ramos.'

Scott had noticed and felt a stab of worry. What was Eric having to deal with out there? He said, 'King said he got creative by the time he got to Phoenix.'

'What the hell did that mean?'

Scott grimaced. 'God knows. I'm going to notify Turner.'

When he got through to his boss, Scott couldn't help but point out Thirty-Two One's work in Atlanta had led to this success.

Turner cleared his throat. It was a dry, efficient sound unrelated to a cold – or emotion. 'Message received loud and clear, SA Houston, however, I'm also aware that you did a Hail Mary pass yesterday.'

Scott realized that someone had told Turner about his video call with Collins and Belport. Probably Eric.

Turner had continued. 'While I've got you on the horn: the testimony you and SA Ramos were due to give in Anchorage on Friday?'

Scott was hoping his boss was going to say that their presence was no longer required and he waited for the good news.

Turner said, 'They've moved you up to Monday.'

Scott frowned. 'This Monday? But we haven't been prepped for that.'

'The Assistant United States Attorney up there has everything and will prep you.'

Scott didn't want this. He wanted to get on a flight to LA tonight – in the morning at the latest. He wanted to be with Jayne, badly. 'But how can this AUSA prep us for Monday? It's Friday already.'

'I have command of the days of the week, Agent Houston. You and Ramos are not coming back to Los Angeles. You'll fly out from Phoenix tomorrow and the AUSA will prep you both on Sunday. Lance will be in touch with you before close of business with the details.'

Scott slumped back in his chair, wondering which incredibly helpful AUSA this was.

Turner sounded impatient. 'Houston, do you copy?'

'Yes, sir.' He heard the line go dead in typical Turner style.

Scott threw the phone onto the desk.

'What's up?' Angie said.

'Eric and I are on our way to Anchorage tomorrow.'

'Transferred?' She grinned.

He gave her a quelling look.

'C'mon, Scott,' she said. 'You should be happy right now.'

He knew she was right, but the boost he'd received from

the DNA news had been knocked down by this schedule change.

It didn't help that when the Critters returned at lunchtime with the body parts they had recovered, it was clear that DNA would be the only avenue to identifications in the absence of Jayne and Steelie's forensic anthropological skills. There wouldn't be any quick presumptive IDs for him and Angie to transmit to the missing persons unit in Atlanta. Instead, there would be a slow, opaque process that only required his supreme patience.

And sure enough, in the afternoon, while Eric went back out with Tony, Xavier and King in search of the third site, Scott and Angie could only watch as Duane and Steve set up stations divided by plastic barriers, then used Stryker saws to cut out samples from bones. They repeated the process on all the unattributed bones recovered on the prior days of the operation, now that there would be comparative DNA available for all the missing women.

It was hours of listening to the whine of the saws alternating with the scratchy, grinding noise that the small, circular blades made against bone. Scott watched as each cut released a cloud of fine bone dust that would rise but then remain bounded by the plastic barriers that prevented cross-contamination. The only break in the monotony was when the Critters switched to locating and retrieving samples from teeth and hair.

Scott felt drained from watching them and not doing anything. There was no reason for him and Angie to contact Atlanta Missing Persons until this process was done. Angie didn't even need him to be there to complete that step, so he was superfluous as well as tired.

Knowing that Anchorage would now come between him and an in-person reunion with Jayne had made him even more aware of the feeling of being trapped. It was settled. King was shackled and he'd made Scott his new cellmate.

14

The moment Eric was satisfied that King had indeed led them to his third and final body dump site outside Phoenix, he informed the Federal Corrections officers that King's hall pass was now expired. Eric walked back with them to the Corrections vehicle, which was parked on the shoulder of the highway. He watched, arms crossed over his chest, as the officers made the adjustments to restrain King in the backseat. When Officer Harrison finished, King and Eric looked at each other. King's expression wasn't the defeated look Eric had seen on the faces of arrestees nor was it the resigned, watchful look of federal inmates being transported from one lock-up to another. King looked exultant and he had the tone of voice to match.

'Until we meet again, Ramos.'

Eric gave him what he hoped was a piercing look and closed the door in his face. Feeling sure King was laughing his goading chuckle from inside the sedan, Eric took a moment to thank the officers for their patience and cooperation. The three of them shook hands and he could tell that they were happy the assignment was over; it was the first time he'd seen either of them smile.

As the sedan made the U-turn to take King back to Georgia, Eric registered the lifting of some tension in his shoulders. This was a milestone in the recovery operation:

if the inmate was leaving, then they had located all the sites. Now it was down to other processes to make the IDs and finally get these women's remains to their families.

He turned back to monitor Tony's progress in photographing the remains, which were two skulls King had placed, when fully fleshed and frozen, at the base of a rock less than a hundred feet from the shoulder of Interstate 10. People had been driving past two decapitated heads for the months it had taken them to decompose to their current bony state and no one had ever noticed them.

When Tony and Xavier had completed documentation, bagging the skulls was straightforward, but then the Critters went onto their hands and knees.

'What's up?' Eric asked.

'We're trying to locate some head hair,' Xavier said. 'We expected to see it once we lifted the skulls but there are only a few strands here. This could take a while.'

Eric came forward and took the clear plastic evidence bag Tony was holding out. With effort, he discerned some long white or gray hairs. 'Okay. What can I do?'

Tony said, 'We need to move out from the rock in a systematic fashion and look for hairs that aren't just a strand here or there. We're expecting clumps. Xavier's doing the base of the rock toward the highway. I'm taking this side, if you can take that one? Starting at the base of the rock. And you'll need to suit up.'

'You got it,' Eric said and dug around in the backpack the Critters had placed on a plastic sheet. He pulled the Tyvek suit on over his clothes, booties over his shoes, and put on a single pair of surgical gloves. Taking off his sunglasses and stowing them in the bag, he called out, 'Xavier, do I need the mask?'

Xavier looked back at him. 'I would, but even more important is the hood on your suit. That should be up so we don't mix our hair in with the recovered hair when we're bending over it. Save us having to exclude it later.'

Eric nodded and retrieved a mask as well as knee protectors from the backpack. Once he had those two items on, he pulled up his hood and walked to the south side of the rock. The minute he got down on his knees, the coverall felt hot. The elastic was also pulling at his forehead. He adjusted his suit so that the lower half wasn't pulling so much on the hood. Then he got to work.

As his eyes adjusted to the task, he found himself surprised that he'd been able to find something as thin as hair, but he'd done it. He called Xavier over.

After the Critter looked at the find, he said, 'Non-human – see the banding of color – but that's okay. Let me give you some flags. That way, you can mark whatever you're finding and we'll check it when we're done with our sections.'

'Right.' Eric felt like a fraud wearing all the Tyvek.

Somehow Xavier picked up on it. 'It's a big area, so what you're doing helps. It'll save us being out here after dark with floodlights and scorpions.'

Eric nodded and went back down to his knees, moving in a southerly direction. He used two flags after spending too much time trying to figure out if the items he'd found were human hair. He didn't have those skills. When he reached a clump of gnarly shrubs, he finally found such a copious amount of long gray hair that he was sure it was human. He got to his feet and looked for the Critters. He couldn't see either of them, which meant they had to be on the north side of the rock.

'Guys,' he called out, knowing they would hear him, and returned to his crouch to look at the area around the hair. He couldn't see anything else caught by the shrubs other than a piece of desiccated cactus that had tiny holes where the thorns had once been.

Tony and Xavier arrived. Eric stood and pointed out the hair.

'That's more like it,' Tony said, sounding energized.

Xavier went into a crouch. 'I think it's the mother lode too because there's some scalp tissue right here.'

Eric was shocked he'd missed that. 'Where?'

He saw Xavier pointing to what Eric had thought was the piece of cactus.

Xavier explained, 'It was probably dislodged by an animal at the right moment in decomposition when the hair was still attached. Then the scalp lay here, and over time the hair fell away. The holes are where the roots were. You can't see them all, but under a 'scope, you—'

Eric didn't hear the rest of Xavier's comment because he had to walk away, quickly. He felt like his lunch was about to come up. He needed out of the Tyvek suit, the mask, the hood – all of it.

He became aware that Tony had caught up to him.

'Eric!'

'Yeah.'

'I think maybe you're dehydrated. These suits can be hell out here.'

'No shit. I don't know how you guys do it.'

'Not to put too fine a point on it, but you and Scott reeked of booze when you came in last night.'

Eric glanced at him and then away. 'Point taken.'

'I'm not judging you, man. Just saying that you were probably already dehydrated last night, then you've been standing around in the heat all day. You need to take a pew. Here, this one's clean.'

Tony gestured at the stretcher they would be using to take the body parts back to base. Eric looked at the stretcher and then at Tony with an expression that he hoped said, *Seriously?*

Tony stared right back. 'I'm not saying you have to lay down on it, Eric. Sit down, put your sunglasses on and I'll get you an electrolyte drink. And a hat.' Tony was taking off his gloves as he started bustling around.

Eric decided not to fight it. He peeled off the protective gear, sat on the stretcher and accepted Tony's ministrations for a minute. Then he insisted that he didn't need a minder. Tony hesitated but picked up the camera and some evidence bags and went back to the scalp.

Eric took his time to drink the full bottle of electrolytes. The turquoise liquid looked alarmingly human-made in this natural landscape of dirt, insects, the occasional hawk and endless sky. Gradually, he felt better. He could even feel a slight breeze. The hat Tony had given him didn't fit but it was helping and he wondered why he hadn't been wearing one anyway. It was probably another sign of last night's hangover.

Once Tony and Xavier had completed their search,

which had turned up another clump of hair but no more scalp tissue, they loaded the body bags onto the stretcher. Then they walked in single file on the shoulder of the lane Highway Patrol had cordoned off for their safety. The occasional vehicle passed; some slowed in acknowledgment of the caution tape strung between the cones while others sped past. One of the types that didn't slow down was approaching now, a sky-blue International Scout in convertible mode. Its music was loud and the occupants were conversing at a shout.

Eric squinted at the vehicle as it came closer, hoping it might slow down out of respect for the fact that they were walking just a few feet away. And then it did, as though the driver had finally taken in the caution tape. Eric looked over as the Scout came alongside and saw a woman in the passenger seat before the truck was past him.

Eric spun around to confirm what he thought he'd seen: Jean Shorts #2 from The Ocotillo bar who'd put her hand on his arm. He could almost feel her hand there still. Now she was turning in her seat to look at him too, giving him a wave of recognition as the truck sped on. Eric started to wave in reply but then he froze. *What am I doing?* If the woman came back to say hi, he would have to stop her, to tell her she couldn't be there, that they were transporting forensic evidence in a criminal case, that he wasn't available for a quick hi. But the Scout didn't stop and Eric turned to follow on behind Xavier and Tony, who were now quite a way ahead of him. It was like he was out there alone. A lone man walking on a highway. It was depressing.

His mood improved at their base camp between the air

conditioning and the scene inside the lab. The room was abuzz, literally, with multiple Stryker saws running as the Critters worked on producing samples for DNA testing. While Eric surveyed the productivity, he drank a Coke, which settled his stomach and made him realize how hungry he was.

He walked over to Scott and gestured through the plastic barrier at the Critters. 'Scott, all this is happening because of your call with Collins and Belport. I know it cost you, but shit, look at the result.'

Scott nodded but all he said was, 'Corrections has taken King back?'

Eric made a motion with his hands like a bird flapping its wings. 'He's gone.'

Then he listened as Scott updated him on the situation with Anchorage. Scott's monotone told him that his partner was less than pleased about their testimony being brought forward, but Eric didn't mind. Then again, he didn't have a situation going on with his girlfriend. He didn't even have a girlfriend.

He dropped his voice to a more confidential tone. 'Are you worried about Jayne? We'll only be delayed by, like, two days.'

Scott said, 'I'm not worried, I think I need to get some sleep. I don't know how you're awake.'

Eric jerked a thumb outside. 'They're going to bring two food trucks out for us. You don't want to wait for that?'

'Not even for that.'

They fist-bumped and Scott left.

*

Joseph slammed the lid of the laptop shut but the footsteps – his wife's careful tread – carried on past the bedroom door. He listened for a moment and then opened the laptop again. He examined the few photographs he'd been able to find online of the women he'd learned about today, this Lander and Hall. Assuming they hadn't gone through any great changes in weight, he would be able to neutralize them. Lander looked to be about five-foot-five-and-change, and slim with it. Hall could be as much as five-foot-six and she was shapely, but not as curvy as his wife, whose form was altered completely after carrying first one child and then another. He clenched his fists. The children. He had to protect them from this at all costs. He'd disposed of Alexander Ayers' hair but now that wasn't going to be enough. Not if Ayers' body had been found. Not with scientists like Lander and Hall in the mix.

He checked his watch, wiped his search and shut down the laptop. He needed to check the location tonight to see if the bag was gone. If the bag was still there, he would need time to come up with another plan. He clenched his jaw. Time. He could feel it running out.

He tried to re-set his facial expression from one of tension to one of tranquility and opened the door to the hall, stopping to pick up his outdoor coat. He could hear that everyone was now in the kitchen because it was almost dinnertime on Family Friday. His wife would be upset but he had no choice.

Walking into the den, he could see his wife with the kids at the kitchen counter, peeling and dicing potatoes.

The kids were using those child-safe plastic knives they'd bought to let them practice chopping but which mostly resulted in a mess.

His wife looked up at him and her smile faded. 'Honey! You're going out?'

'Just need to pick up a couple of things, hon.' He'd have to remember that he'd said that and figure out what to bring home.

'But it's Friday.'

Acting as though he hadn't heard her, he walked over to her purse on the sideboard and took her car keys from the side pocket. He switched to addressing the kids. 'Helping Mommy make dinner, guys?'

'Yes, Daddy!' They spoke in unison.

He went over and ruffled their hair as he kissed their mother on the cheek. 'I'll be back soon. I've got my phone if you need to reach me.'

Despite the look of distrust on her face, she knew him well enough to know that he wouldn't be going to a strip club or meeting another woman – she didn't realize it was much worse. As he put his hand on the doorknob, Joseph paused, reviewing in his mind whether or not he'd removed all traces of his search on the computer. There was a chance she'd check it. But then he distinctly remembered doing it before he'd put the laptop back on the dresser. He stepped out the door.

15

Steelie navigated the driveway up toward the KDIG radio station where the massive transmission dish on the roof cast a shadow over the xeriscapic landscaping to the east of the building.

'There's your dad,' Steelie said. 'Look at him. The consummate artist. Does he think he's still on a university campus or what?'

Jayne looked up from her phone, which was decidedly not ringing with a call from Scott, and saw her mom's convertible parked in front of the building. Elliott was reclined across the two front seats. His ankles were crossed over the passenger door frame, putting on show his canvas shoes, which were splashed with paint in every color. The navy-blue beret he frequently wore was right now over his face and they could hear music.

Steelie grinned. 'Should I honk my horn really loud?'

Jayne shook her head. 'He told me last night that he felt jet lagged for the first time ever.'

'That's not jet lag. It's entering retirement and putting your old house in Caracas up for sale.' Steelie parked the Jeep.

Jayne went over and gently shook Elliott's shoulder. 'Dad.'

He lifted a corner of the beret and squinted up. 'Sweetheart.'

'So you weren't asleep.'

As he got out and hugged her, he said, 'I was just taking in Harry James' "Malaguena Salerosa" courtesy of KJazz.'

'As one does,' Steelie said, clearly tickled.

'As one does.' Elliott smiled at her. 'Hello, Steelie.'

They hugged as Steelie returned his greeting and then she started dancing to the music. Elliott joined her.

Jayne watched with a smile.

When the playlist on KKJZ moved on, Elliott leaned into the car to turn off the radio. 'So, Steelie, how are your parents?'

She said, 'Did Jayne tell you my dad got them into a condo?'

Elliott nodded. 'Ruben's master plan coming to fruition at last. How is Nixie liking having to use an outside studio space? Is it in Downtown?'

'It is. And she likes it enough to send you, through me, an open invitation to the studio. That's on top of the usual lunch invite. But don't worry, she promises she won't cook.'

Steelie headed for her Jeep, tooting her horn lightly as she pulled away.

'Steelie's looking well,' Elliott said as he and Jayne turned toward the building, arms around each other. 'Maybe a little thin?'

Jayne rolled her eyes. 'It comes from running everywhere – unnecessarily. Like when she gets gas. She runs inside to pay, runs back to pump, then runs back in for her change. It's silly.'

'To be fair, she's done that since she was a teenager.' Elliott hugged Jayne closer. 'I was expecting Scott to bring you. Or maybe even coming along to the house?'

Jayne leaned her head on his shoulder. 'Oh, Dad.'

He stopped and looked at her. 'Why the heavy tone?'

She shook her head. 'No, nothing. He's not back yet, that's all.' Saying that aloud reinforced her commitment to Scott's request to hold off talking until they were both in LA. She'd hear from him whenever he was back.

Elliott raised an eyebrow at her but didn't say more as they walked into the station. The receptionist escorted them to a control booth for one of the smaller studios where they heard Marie finishing up her promo for the next day's episode of *Weekends with Prentis*, her popular call-in program about cooking and gardening. Her producer, Art, acknowledged Elliott and Jayne with a smile. Marie was on the other side of the glass but they could hear her voice through a speaker. The interplay of her Spanish accent with the British one she'd retained from years in a British boarding school in Caracas made her voice instantly identifiable on the Southern California public radio dial.

'This is Marie Prentis on KDIG. Tune in tomorrow to join me and my regular guests, landscaper Jess Heywood and chef Andrew Chen, for our semi-annual garden food episode – that's food for the garden and from the garden, my friends. If you've been wondering when to give and when to take, from lettuce to leeks, listen in and call in. Ask Jess how to stop those slimy snails and then Andrew will tell you how to cook 'em. Sneak peek, listeners: it's all

about the garlic. Weekends with Prentis *Saturday edition right here on KDIG – can you dig it?'*

Art pressed a button and a red light went out. He spoke into a microphone. 'A perfect promo, Marie. You nailed it.'

Marie snapped her elegant fingers. 'Third time was the charm, Art. And I see my chariot has arrived.'

As Marie cleared up in the studio, Art came over and shook hands with Elliott. 'So good to see you again, Elliott. You look great!'

Jayne looked appraisingly at her dad. He'd taken to wearing his wavy hair on the long side, brushed back from his tanned forehead. He did appear relaxed, like he'd been living in a place with sun and good food.

Art smiled at Jayne. 'It must be nice to have your dad back here full-time.'

'Definitely.' Jayne slipped her arm through her father's. 'We're going car shopping this weekend.'

'Aha! Are you replacing your truck or is this for you, Elliott?'

Elliott patted Jayne's hand. 'For Jayne. I'm used to public transport from living in Caracas. It'll be a while before I want to drive much again.'

'I hear you,' Art said with feeling. He had a well-documented commute between Sunland and Pasadena.

Marie came through then, her full white skirt flowing around her as she settled her cardigan over her shoulders, taking care to not let it catch on the row of sequins decorating the large white leather purse she held in the crook of her arm. She kissed Elliott, flashed a dazzling smile at Jayne, had a bit more chat with Art and then they left.

When the trio reached Marie's car, Jayne took the back seat so her parents could sit together up front. Marie started chiding Elliott for 'always' wearing the paint-splattered shoes and Elliott was countering that the many colors meant they 'matched everything'. Listening to their banter, Jayne felt like a child again. Then she thought that that was probably about right for her maturity level when it came to talking with Scott about Callista – or the future of her own relationship with him.

She was painfully aware that she was thirty-five but hadn't formed relationships that had warranted conversations about the future. Since coming home from working in post-conflict zones and particularly since Benni's death, her forays into dating had been hampered by Herculean efforts to appear 'normal' rather than someone controlled by her trauma. She'd go out on dates to restaurants or concerts, but once there, she would surreptitiously maneuver herself to sit with her back to a wall or stay near an exit, in case of a sudden threat.

It turned out that she hadn't been good at hiding anything. The men she'd dated had noticed her behavior. They'd asked. So she'd explained: how she still sometimes worried about driving over land mines in LA or that fireworks sounded like gunfire or that she couldn't buy a whole, raw chicken because it reminded her of a dead baby. Unless she tried *really* hard to see it as a chicken, and even then, it still looked decapitated. She'd weathered the looks of confusion and disgust. Ending dating ended the explaining.

But Scott got this part of her! And in him getting her –

and letting her know he did – she'd relaxed the hold she'd been keeping on herself. In fact, she felt free with him, none more so than when they made love. Their chemistry pulled her brain and her body into the present; not one part of her was available for reviewing the past or fearing the future. It was revelatory, almost addictive, and it was into this world that Gene had dropped the Callista bomb. If the dust cleared to reveal it had all been a fantasy . . . Jayne couldn't bear the thought. She pressed her left hand hard onto the seat of the Mercedes, fingers outspread. The warm leather pushed back into her palm like a responding hand. Looking down, Jayne saw her own unadorned, and she imagined the other wearing a ring.

She realized her mother was speaking to her. Jayne looked around. They were stopped at a red light.

'Jayne?' Marie was looking at her in the rearview mirror. 'Scott is meeting us at the house? I left both slow cookers on so we would have plenty of food.'

Jayne let her exasperation take an easy exit. 'Mom! You talk about him like he's a growing boy! It's ridiculous.'

Marie retorted, 'Well, to me he is a growing boy!'

Jayne now felt sullen and somewhat apologetic. She mumbled, 'He's thirty-seven. He's in a state of bony degeneration, as we all are after the age of thirty.'

Elliott chuckled but Marie made a short, impatient noise. 'Speak for yourself, darling.' She accelerated off the green light. 'And . . .? Scott?'

Elliott put his hand on her shoulder. 'He's not back yet, cariña.'

Marie examined Jayne in the rearview again and drew

breath to speak but Elliott squeezed her shoulder and she relented.

*

When Joseph drove into the village, which had expanded since he'd last been there but remained quaint, if gentrified, he found a place to park in the lot for those visiting the local shops and boutiques on the one main street. He retrieved his bicycle from the rear of the car and started cycling back the way he'd come.

Although the sky was still just light, it was darker at ground level in this thickly forested area and he turned on the bicycle's headlamp as he coasted down the two-lane road. Only a few cars passed and most of them were heading the other way, toward the village and its welcoming shop windows. He was looking for the tilted tree, the one that had grown leaning against another, and then he saw it. Braking gently, he pulled onto the shoulder and dismounted. Looking around, he saw that he was alone so he turned off the bike's light, stowed the machine in the bushes and walked into the forest.

Vegetation abounded around him: old trees, saplings, vinca and other low-growing ground covers whose names he didn't know. There was no path but he had a good sense of direction and his feeling was that the location would be slightly uphill from where he was. He turned to his right. The hill eventually became a little steeper and he knew he was getting closer. It was dark under the heavy canopy of leaves but he didn't dare turn on the flashlight he'd brought, just in case someone else was out here. It could only be someone with a true-crime interest but there were plenty of them around. As he approached the area, he stopped and stood still for another whole minute. He couldn't hear or see anyone.

He got down on his hands and knees and moved slowly and carefully around the place where he'd left the bag. There was a chance it had moved a few feet one way or the other over the years so he would have to be thorough.

And he was. By the time the cold dampness had seeped all the way through the knees of his corduroys, he was sure: the bag was gone. He had no way of knowing when it had been taken or by who, but he would have to assume it had been the police. He couldn't take a chance that it was someone else. He stood up and accidentally trod on a stick, which snapped. The noise was loud in this quiet place but he was no longer concerned if anyone saw him. The bag wasn't here so there was no real danger in being here. The danger was now bound up in Lander and Hall.

*

Steelie took a break from digging the trench that now demarcated three sides of her backyard in Atwater Village. She'd been enjoying these early-evening dig sessions after work, making steady progress on what would become the undulating border of a garden bed filled with drought-tolerant trees and shrubs.

Sitting on her old bench, she reviewed the pencil-drawn plan that she'd enhanced with watercolors. It included artificial grass spanning the space between the borders, a larger patio, outdoor furniture and a pergola off the back of the house. She knew some of this would eventually require a professional – a landscaper or maybe a contractor – which was what Jayne had been advocating after she'd helped Steelie do the weeding a few times. Steelie found it interesting that Jayne could see so clearly what Steelie needed but couldn't do the same for herself. Steelie was about to call her, to needle her about Scott, but then a thought occurred her. She popped the lid off a bottle of Blue Moon and dialed Eric's number.

'Steelie!' Eric sounded genuinely pleased that she'd called.

'Hi, Eric. I'm not going to ask you any details but are you guys still in the field?'

'We are but we'll be back soon. You doing okay?'

'Yeah. But I'm pretty sure something's going on with Jayne. Is anything going on with Scott?'

'No. Not in relation to Jayne at least. Aren't they holding off talking on the phone because of the whole MOU thing? What's up?'

'I can't tell.' She took a sip of beer. 'You know in Texas when we split into two teams? Did anything happen? With Gene, I mean, at the other site.'

'Not that I saw. We were trying to ensure he didn't get up close and personal but during the landslip situation he was kind of close to her for, like, thirty seconds.'

Steelie registered this new fact almost physically. Jayne hadn't mentioned that on the day. 'Could he have said something to her without anyone else hearing him?'

'Maybe. Hm, okay. You're thinking King . . . well, what are you thinking?'

What Steelie was thinking was that thirty seconds was a long time to be alone with someone who felt like a threat. But she didn't want Eric to start blaming himself for letting it happen. 'I don't know.'

'Well, that guy loves him some games. I'll check in with Corrections. See if they heard or saw anything. They were closer to him.'

Steelie felt grateful for Eric's logical mind. While she'd started going down a rabbit hole of all the things Gene might have said or could have done, Eric was going to look for evidence. 'Thanks.' Her relief was evident in her tone.

'No problem. So. Heard you're going on a date this weekend with Detective West.'

Steelie had just started to take another swig of beer and had to swallow it quickly. 'Please don't tell me you heard that from one of the Critters, 'cause that would just be weird if they knew details of my personal life when I know nothing about theirs.'

'No, I heard it from Scott. He's become buddies with Matt. We've hung out now and then.'

It had been obvious to Steelie during the UCLA case that Scott and Matt had become friendly but she hadn't realized that Eric and Scott had seen Matt since then. *She* hadn't even seen him since then. 'Oh? What do you all talk about?'

'What do you think two Bureau agents and a homicide detective talk about? War stories.'

Steelie snorted. 'Male bonding, in other words.'

'Like you don't do the same thing – with lawyers *and* forensic folks,' Eric scoffed.

He was right. 'Okay, that's true. So, where've you been

hanging out? The gym? A shooting range?' She smiled at her own joke.

Eric chuckled. 'I don't think Matt's the type to have a gym membership, do you? Actually, don't answer that. Don't want to test your loyalty at this early stage.'

'It's so early, it's not even a stage, Eric.'

'So you keep saying. Anyway, Matt works in Downtown and Scott lives there, so drink has been taken, y'know, after hours. A few times. At least, that's where I've seen him.'

Steelie looked at her beer and wondered what Matt's drink of choice was.

Eric had taken on an intimate, conspiratorial tone. 'And will you be taking off your law enforcement boxing gloves tomorrow?'

Steelie liked that her background as a criminal defense lawyer had been distilled down to this. 'I won't be wearing them but I always have them nearby.'

'Just remember, you can't hold hands while you're wearing boxing gloves.'

'Since when do I want to hold hands with the guy?'

'Oh, that won't fly, Steelie. We all know he's the only person with a badge you have time for.'

'You mean, besides you and Scott?'

'Well,' Eric said complacently, 'our badges *are* special.'

She laughed. 'Over and out, *Dad*.'

When Steelie heard Eric's bark of laughter, she cut the call, enjoying having the last word, and then she picked up her shovel. Back to work before it was too dark to see anything. She felt good, like she didn't have to worry about

Jayne for the minute. Eric was on the job. That meant she could go back to her new favorite pastime, which was guessing where Matthew West had made reservations for them to have dinner in exactly twenty-four hours.

*

Back by the road, Joseph retrieved his bike and put on both headlamp and taillamp to illuminate the increasing darkness. He cycled steadily uphill, keeping on the shoulder whenever a car came up behind, thinking back over his carefully constructed life. He'd done everything right after dodging that bullet at the beginning, when he'd been naïve and gullible. Now Lander and Hall were aiming at him like a double-barreled shotgun holding two slugs with his name on them. But he could see them coming just as clearly as he could see the SUV picking up speed on the straightaway out of the village and heading toward him.

Once he was safely in the parking lot, he stowed the bike in the car and then sat inside to change pants. In the fresh set of corduroys he'd brought along, he walked over to the general store, thanking the couple that held the door for him as they were leaving in a bubble of their own chat. Inside, the atmosphere was cozy as the few short grocery aisles gave way to a small café doing brisk business in hot chocolate and homemade apple cider, if the posted sign was accurate. The people at the tables were mostly seniors plus a few women who had parked strollers around their tables as they talked above the gurgling and mewling of their babies.

Joseph turned to browse the aisles, looking for what he

could take home with him – some legitimately desired item that would save him coming up with answers to his wife's questions. Just as his hand went to the chrome-plated, single-serve French coffee press, he noticed the plug-in egg cooker. His wife had mentioned this appliance more than once; had talked about how it would save her time when she was getting ready for work in the morning if she could put on the breakfast eggs for him and the kids at the same time as she made his lunch. That decided it. He bought that with cash and then ordered a pepper beef sandwich and a hot cider, which he consumed at a table near the counter while looking at the local paper he'd found on the bench. The paper was good cover. He wasn't reading it. He was only picturing himself this time next week – rid of Lander and Hall.

Back in the car, with the egg cooker in a brown paper bag on the seat next to him, he drove home, willing his mind to stop going over the plan. It was solid. There was no reason to re-think it or make tweaks here and there. Indeed, it was probably the only plan that he could implement; the other ones were too risky.

The journey was fast and he got a parking space just across from their townhouse on their residential street. Taking the parcel inside, he found that the house was quiet. The kitchen was dark but when he looked in the refrigerator, he saw that his wife had left him a serving of food in a labeled Tupperware. He wouldn't eat it now – the sandwich from the café had taken care of his hunger – but it was good to see that she'd done as she should. He put the parcel on the kitchen counter and then washed up in the bathroom, noting that both kids' toothbrushes were wet; his wife had had things under control.

The light was still on in their bedroom but his wife didn't stir when Joseph entered the room. This annoyed him even though she did have a longer workday on Fridays and he'd left her the full load by going out tonight. He was aware that some in their circle of friends would say that it was unfair, given that he didn't work and only had to walk the kids to and from school on weekdays. But he knew the truth: he'd been making everything right by going out tonight. Thanks to his plan, his wife's comfortable routine of home-work-home could continue and the kids would be safe. That was his role as a man, wasn't it? To provide that security for them.

The squeak of the mattress springs under his weight didn't fully wake his wife. He tried to breathe through his annoyance but it didn't work. It had been a long evening, during which he'd taken risks for her – for *her* happiness – and he intended to have this part of Family Friday even though he'd missed dinner and the movie. He pulled her into position. That woke her up. He was digging his fingers into her flesh when he remembered the wet corduroys he'd left in her car. He would have to get rid of those before morning.

DAY 6

Saturday

16

The first thing Steelie noticed about Matthew West when she opened her door to him was that he seemed nervous. He was running a hand over his light brown hair and his brown eyes were on the move. Then she noticed his clothes. His shirt was an exceedingly crisp white button-down that was open at the neck and his gray slacks sported a faint stripe that made them look nicer than something he'd wear to work.

But she didn't get a chance to do more than greet him before he rushed off to open the passenger door of a double-cab Ford pick-up – white with a blue metallic band running from front to tail, she noticed – parked at the curb in front of her garden. He muttered something about the truck doors being stiff.

While Matt drove, Steelie took in the horse-blanket-style seat cover on the front bench and, in the back, the wide-brimmed straw hat sitting on top of a young but sorry-looking ficus tree with its root ball wrapped in a burlap sack. The tree was riding high on the backseat, a seatbelt strapped across the burlap, and just visible under a fall of leaves was the edge of what was unmistakably a soft pack of Marlboro Reds.

Steelie swiveled back and flicked down the sun visor on her side. 'I feel like I just hopped into a John Wayne flick. Left your gun rack at home, didja?'

'Guns, I keep in the glove box.'

'And your throw-down?'

He smiled. 'Wouldn't you like to know?'

Steelie enjoyed that. 'So what's with the plant? Scared it to death?'

'What's with all the questions?' Matt countered.

'Just curious.'

He raised an amused eyebrow. 'You're curious about the plant but not about where we're having dinner?'

Steelie bounced up and down on the bench seat. It had plenty of bounce. Fun.

He looked over at her. 'Everything okay over there?'

'Just noticing how much this truck is like Jayne's old one.'

'Hers was a 150. This is a 250.'

Steelie was surprised that Matt had total recall of Jayne's truck. He was steering onto the north side of the Golden State Freeway where Griffith Park was still catching late-afternoon sunlight along its uppermost ridgelines.

She finally settled down, having become aware that she was nervous too, she just showed it differently than he did. 'Okay, so, where are we going?'

Matt was checking the traffic as he merged across two lanes. 'It's a place where there won't be any cops who'll know me nor any lawyers who'll know you.'

'A senior home, then?'

He frowned. 'Come again?'

She gestured at the sunset. 'Who else eats this early?'

'Oh.' He shook his head. 'No. You'll see.'

'You remembered I'm vegetarian, right? Because most cops I know dine at places where all I can eat is the lettuce from inside their burger.'

'I'm just a cop to you?'

'Until I have evidence to the contrary,' she teased.

He smiled. 'Got your ID on you?'

She gave him a withering look. 'What self-respecting forensic anthropologist leaves the house without her ID? Sheesh.'

Matt laughed.

'What's so funny?' she said. 'There's nothing funny about being caught dead unidentified. You know that as well as I do.'

'Don't get me wrong,' he chuckled. 'I totally agree. It's just that your whole lawyer-meets-bone-doctor thing is . . . You don't talk like anyone else I know.'

He exited the freeway and within a few turns they were entering the grounds of Burbank Airport.

Steelie was floored. They were going on a plane? 'Uh . . . Maaaatt?'

He had pulled into a short-term parking space by the time she finished dragging his name out.

He killed the engine. 'What?'

'What are we doing at the airport?'

'Relax, we're just getting appetizers here.'

She stared at him as he hopped down and retrieved something out of a dry-cleaner bag hanging from the rear window. She swiveled to the front and switched to staring at the airport terminal in disbelief.

Matt opened her door but Steelie still couldn't make

a move to get out. He extended his hand. She took it and felt the warm, slightly dry, rough places of his palm, like he was no stranger to a shovel. She felt the first stirrings of excitement and alighted.

'This is nice,' Matt said. 'Finally, some peace and quiet from your non-stop questions.'

Steelie couldn't parry because an American Airlines flight took off nearby, sailing deftly into the westering sun, its engine noise preventing easy conversation on the ground. Walking toward the terminal, Steelie realized she was still holding Matt's hand and expressively dropped it.

He shouted over the airplane noise, 'Suit yourself but I walk fast.'

'So do I,' she yelled, wondering why she was trying to compete. She was out of her depth with Matt and she knew it.

And Matt did walk fast. Steelie was left hurrying behind him as he entered the terminal. She watched with interest as he badged the security staff and declared his weapon, which she noticed was in fact in the standard throw-down location, strapped to his lower leg. She went through the metal detector as Matt watched, talking and laughing with a male airport police officer. They finished up as she rejoined Matt. The officer touched his cap as he gave Steelie a friendly smile.

Matt headed for the departures area and Steelie followed, glancing back at the cop, who had already moved on to making some kind of circuit of the security area.

She said, 'Know him, do you?'

'My cousin.'

'You didn't wanna introduce me?'

'You could meet him when we come back.'

'About that. Where will we be coming back from again?'

Matt tilted his head. 'I think I heard another question there. It's weird. Is it your lawyer background?' He veered off toward a gate where the flight was already boarding.

Steelie immediately looked above the desk at the departures board.

She tried to pull Matt to the side. '*Vegas?*'

But he was already proffering two tickets to the gate agent, who was asking for Steelie's ID in such a polite tone that Steelie automatically dug out her wallet and flipped it open for approval. Matt looked on and then led the way through the door to cross the tarmac to the plane.

The mix of engine noise and airline fuel fumes got Steelie over her last mental hurdle. She was going to Las Vegas, Nevada, for dinner. *Dinner.* She grinned and mounted the air stairs. A warm breeze suddenly billowed out her shirt and sunlight glinted off the cockpit window, through which she could see the left-seat pilot. She saluted him happily and got a wave in response.

Matt called up from behind her. 'By the way, I don't do window seats.'

'Nor do I,' she called back. 'And I don't do center seats.'

'Make an exception so we can sit together?'

'I sit on the aisle so I can get out in an emergency, so no, I won't be making an exception.'

'Me too, so—'

Steelie realized why Matt broke off. On entering the Southwest Airlines cabin, they could see that the aisle seats faced each other in the first two rows. Neither she nor Matt would have to compromise.

Steelie took the aisle seat facing the front of the plane and watched Matt as he asked the flight attendant to hang his jacket in the closet. Then Matt talked to the second flight attendant, gesturing at his and Steelie's seats.

When Matt sat down, he shot his cuffs and smoothed down his shirtfront. The flight attendant emerged from behind the bulwark and gave Matt six packets of Southwest's signature salted peanuts. Matt promptly counted off three packets and held them out for Steelie.

She rolled her eyes. 'Let me guess. These are the appetizers?'

He smiled. 'Enjoy.'

She shook her head. It was cute. He was cute.

'What?' He pretended to examine the packet. 'They're vegetarian, aren't they?' He emptied most of it into his mouth and grinned at her with bulging cheeks.

'Absurd,' she said, trying not to laugh.

The flight attendant was closing the door now and a PA announcement came from the overhead speakers: 'Ladies and gentlemen, this is your captain speaking . . .'

Steelie buckled up her seatbelt and shot a few nuts into her mouth. This was, hands-down, the most fun she'd had in years and they hadn't even taken off yet.

*

'Saturday night.' Ari, the salesman from the Toyota dealership, pointed out the front window of the Corolla. 'Everyone's out.'

Oh right, Jayne thought, having lost track of the fact

that Saturday night was when most people were cruising Brand Boulevard in Glendale, taking it from the top, down through the shopping and restaurant district, all the way to the Boulevard of Cars.

Elliott did his part from the back seat. 'Nice night for it,' he said amiably.

As Jayne pulled out of the dealership and turned right, Ari looked over his shoulder at Elliott. 'You guys from out of town?'

Elliott said, 'No, we're local. Ish.'

Jayne caught his eye in the rearview mirror and tried not to laugh.

Ari turned back to Jayne. 'Allow me to put on the radio so you can hear how nice it is. What stations do you like?'

That was easy. '98.7 or 106.7 – or how about 102.7 since it's a Saturday night?'

He looked happy that she had answered with such detail. 'I'll put all three on the pre-sets for you!' He executed the task in a flash and then picked the station that wasn't on a commercial break.

Jayne heard a snippet of Everclear and rejoiced that they would help get her past a few minutes of superficial chat with yet another salesperson.

Jayne smiled.

Ari smiled.

But Ari couldn't not talk. He said, 'So, how do you like the car so far?'

'It's nice!'

She could tell he was disappointed by this generic

response so she added, 'I'm used to a pick-up truck so I'm not sure if I can ride this low. I feel like I keep having to get taller in my seat.' She mimicked this as she turned right onto San Fernando Road.

Ari enthused, 'The seat's adjustable. Everything's adjustable. And I'd be happy to give you a trade-in price on your truck.'

Why did she mention the truck? This was why she shouldn't make chat. She gave her father a pleading look in the mirror.

Elliott tried to sit forward to talk but the three-point seatbelt stopped him short. He looked down at it in surprise and started again. 'Actually, the truck was totaled.'

Ari gave Jayne a sympathetic look. 'I'm so sorry! What happened? If you don't mind me asking.'

Jayne chose her words. 'A guy drove me off the road.'

This wasn't strictly true and she saw her dad looking at her. He wasn't one to side-step like she was doing right now. *Or like Scott apparently did all the time*.

She turned up the volume on the radio. Ari was just a young guy trying to make his shift pass faster. He didn't need to know that a murder suspect had burst into her pick-up while she was driving and forced her, truck and all, into the Silver Lake Reservoir. Nor did he need to hear about how she'd been powerless to stop him and had almost drowned. *Ugh, that powerlessness* . . . like when Benni was lying there bleeding into the ground and her eyes had gone dry with the effort to see other trip wires. Jayne gripped the Corolla's steering wheel as she remembered staring into the grass around her and Benni, looking for more mines wearing camouflage . . . She should be looking now. And then, suddenly, there was a plastic bag! She was about to drive over it! Jayne swerved wildly, slewed the car to the curb and stood on the brakes.

'Whoa!' Ari shouted.

Jayne looked over and didn't recognize him for a second because he wasn't a UN colleague. He also looked highly alarmed. She forced out a viable explanation. 'Testing. A hard stop.'

'Really?' he squeaked.

The plastic bag floated up next to the car. It was completely empty. It hadn't been hiding a landmine, the way bags sometimes did in post-conflict zones where she'd worked for the UN war crimes investigations. She'd been trained to never drive over a plastic bag as a matter of life or death, and then Benni's death had trained her for life.

Elliott's voice came from the backseat. Calm. Reasonable. 'Ari, would you mind driving us back?'

The young man got out with alacrity. Jayne cracked open the driver's door and checked for the plastic bag's whereabouts. It had drifted away. Still just a bag.

Embarrassed, she avoided eye contact with Ari, but as she switched sides, she kept a hand on the hood of the car for a tangible reminder that it was a Corolla, not a Humvee or a tank.

The three of them rode in silence back to the Boulevard of Cars, where the Saturday-night slow dance was still in full swing, people window-shopping on the car lots while others pulled out from dealerships on their own test drives, moon roofs and windows open in the balmy night air.

No doubt for the first time in his career, Ari did not try to sell them the Corolla or, in fact, any other car on the lot, and they were able to leave within moments of getting back.

As Elliott started the engine of the Mercedes, he said, 'So, the bag. Does that still happen often?'

Jayne did up her seatbelt. 'Not as much as it used to.'

He pulled out of the lot. 'Well, since we're on the topic of explosives, how about we take a dinner break?'

She looked at him. 'What's explosive about that?'

'I wasn't done. Over dinner, you tell me what's happening with Scott so I can be a buffer between you and your mother. Like a missile defense system.'

Jayne felt apologetic. 'Was she that bad after you dropped me off last night?'

'You know your mother. She made the topic last for the entire journey home.'

'Sorry.'

'Don't be.' Elliott took a left onto San Fernando but moved into the right lane immediately.

'Algemac's?' Jayne said hopefully.

'Yes. That way we can run right back over to Brand if you want to try another car.'

He pulled in at the coffee shop, its roofline a 1960s diagonal line under the massive ficus tree on the sidewalk. Their parking space faced the large window that did as much to display the people sitting at the counter as it did the pies revolving in the adjacent glass cases. The patrons had the usual median age of about sixty and the waitresses were on the move with a coffee pot in each hand – black spout for regular, orange for decaf. Jayne had been there often enough to know that the waitresses would be asking if anyone wanted a 'top-up'. It was like an Edward Hopper painting, only cozier and busier.

Elliott turned off the engine but faced Jayne. 'Leaving aside Marie, I'm curious about what's going on, Jayne. You told me on the phone – many times! – that you were excited to introduce Scott to me. Then I get home, he's nowhere to be seen and you're running for cover from your mother's questions.' He paused. 'Is Scott like the other ones? Not really made for the long haul?'

She widened her eyes. 'You make me sound like a broken-down freighter that needs a tug boat to get to shore.'

'You know what I mean,' Elliott said. 'Maybe it's turned out that he's not someone with vision, with gravitas? Someone you can walk with. Someone you can sit with.'

In an Algemac's booth, eating a Tom Turkey Dinner and getting a 'top-up', Jayne finished in her mind. She didn't know how to explain that it wasn't about Scott's qualities. It was about his availability. She said, 'It's not that.'

'Okay, so can you tell me what it is while we eat?'

'I can't, Dad. Or . . . I could, but I need to talk with him about it first.'

'Then we'll just eat.' Elliott gave her an encouraging smile and opened his door.

*

Steelie clocked the flight to Vegas at a smooth forty-five minutes when they began the final descent featuring the bumps and lifts that were evidence of the valley's hot day, now cooling as the afternoon gave way to dusk. Steelie leaned forward slightly so she could see the lights of some of the iconic hotels twinkling against a sky layered with blue, pink and gold, but then she pressed her back firmly into the seat as the airplane touched down. She saw Matt raise an eyebrow at her, mouthing the word *Okay?* She nodded in reply and they were soon unbuckling seatbelts to leave.

The flight attendant said, 'See you on the way back, Detective,' as she handed Matt his jacket.

Before Steelie could ask her question, Matt explained, 'They know me.'

Steelie began to wonder if Matt was some kind of serious gambler for whom Vegas was a second home. Then she wondered what difference that would make.

In the arrivals hall of McCarran, they were surrounded by travelers who were loud with excitement, pulling overstuffed carry-on bags as they looked for baggage claim carousels or rental car desks amidst ringing slot machines.

Outside, Steelie enjoyed the heat after being in the ultra-cooled airport terminal and they took the first taxi on the rank. On Las Vegas Boulevard, Steelie felt herself picking up on the anticipation of others who've been whisked down that broad, smooth advertisement for spectacle and entertainment. But when the taxi turned into the sweeping driveway of the Bellagio Hotel, she turned to Matt with concern.

'I'm not wearing the right clothes for a place like this!'

'Steelie, when I picked you up, I looked at what you were wearing. You're fine.'

Feeling unsure, she got out and looked around. It felt as if half of the airport had come with them and she saw that she was indeed dressed appropriately. Her white linen shirt was one that she'd ironed for an occasion she'd never gone to and her deep navy linen trousers were sailor-style: wide-legged below the golden buttons decorating the flap front. The cut produced enough drape to both play it semi-formal as well as hide her shoes, which were her standard white sneakers. Her only jewelry was, well, literally her only jewelry: her grandfather's Omega Seamaster, which she'd long ago discovered dressed up anything she was wearing in a pinch. She was finger-combing her short, tousled hairstyle as Matt joined her after paying the taxi driver.

'You look really great.' He smiled at her as he put on his jacket. Then he held his elbow out in invitation. 'Shall we?'

She took his arm. 'Let's do this.'

A few minutes later, they were at the entrance of something doing a great imitation of a cave or maybe a grotto. When Matt identified his reservation, the host standing at the podium said, 'Ah, Mr. West!' and glanced over his glasses at Steelie before he called over a waiter and murmured something.

They were shown to a table situated on the edge of a room that appeared candle-lit, with a curved ceiling and illuminated Italianate oil paintings along the stone walls. There was a hushed hum from tables where couples talked and ate amidst soft background music. As Steelie took her seat, she spotted a dessert cart making the rounds and she commented on it.

'You're hungry then?' Matt said.

'I just haven't seen a dessert cart in years.'

He looked at the waiter advancing toward them with

leather-bound menus and then turned toward Steelie. 'So this restaurant is doing this thing tonight. It's a fixed menu and it's all vegetarian. I hope you're okay with that?'

The second the waiter departed, Steelie said, 'A fixed *vegetarian* menu? Let me see that?'

He handed it over.

She ran her eyes over the menu and then she laughed. The dessert section was covered by a temporary paper insert that read *Choice of Fresh Donuts*. She faced it toward Matt and pointed at it. 'Is that for me?'

He nodded but looked anxious.

She sat back in disbelief. 'Jeez, Matt. I just can't figure out how you planned this. And who told you I like donuts? Was it Scott?'

He looked even more uncomfortable. 'Bud Reese, actually. But Scott was the one who told me that you're vegetarian. Because most places I eat do tend to have something, like, roasting on a spit in the front window. When I saw that the Bellagio was doing this whole . . . climate-change-save-the-world theme night or whatever, I decided on it. I come here a lot so I asked them to add the donuts for you; told 'em it was your birthday.'

Steelie was shaking her head slowly. 'What I'm also hearing you say is that there's not much on this menu that you'd want.'

He blinked. 'To be perfectly frank, what I want isn't on this menu.'

Steelie's grin was, she knew, both stupid and impossible to wipe off her face, so all she could do was look away, desperately scanning the room for the dessert cart, wondering if the donut selection included Krispy Kremes while also thinking that this was the third time Matthew West had left her at a loss for words. Still, no matter how hard she tried, she couldn't think of a damn thing to say.

17

Standing at the Alaska Airlines departure gate at Sky Harbor Airport in Phoenix, Eric looked at the readout on his cell phone, which had just begun to vibrate. The caller ID read, *Harrison, Latasha*. Eric was gratified that the higher-ups in Corrections had reached her this quickly. He stepped away from Scott and took the call.

'Agent Ramos, this is Latasha Harrison from Corrections. My sup got me a message that you needed to speak to me?'

'Yes. Sorry to bother you on your downtime.'

'Is there a problem?'

'Not at all. I wanted to see if I could pick up any intel from you about the day we worked the site out in San Antonio.'

'The truck stop or the landslide?'

Eric stopped himself from correcting that to 'landslip'. 'The landslide,' he confirmed.

'Huh. I'm not going to forget that place anytime soon,' she said with feeling.

'Oh?' *This is going to be easier than I expected. Corrections saw King do something.* He readied himself.

'Had to order a new uniform,' she said. 'Turned out that all the dirt stains wouldn't come out.'

Eric tried to absorb his disappointment while also responding to Scott, who'd given him an interrogative look: it was time to board the flight to Anchorage. Eric commiserated with Officer Harrison about her uniform while waving at Scott to go ahead and board.

Then he said, 'I was thinking of after the landslip, when you were making your way back up the slope toward the inmate. Did you hear him say anything?'

'Like what?' She sounded like she'd suddenly realized Eric was on a fishing trip and she didn't want to end up on the hook.

Eric wanted to assuage her concerns but he didn't want to lead her. He went for a friendly tone. 'Anything at all.'

'No, I sure didn't.' She sounded like she'd reviewed the event in her mind. Now he could ask more direct questions.

'How about seeing him move around to another position, try to slip his cuffs—'

'Ain't nobody slips their cuffs around me and Mercier.' She laughed but it seemed to Eric that it was to someone next to her.

'Right. So, nothing odd at all about the inmate when you got back to him?' Eric watched the line of people moving through the gate, showing boarding passes and making small talk with the gate agents.

'Hmm.' She sounded thoughtful. 'Maybe it was odd that he was smiling when we got there. But that guy was always smiling, right, Mercy?'

Eric pressed his phone harder against his ear. 'Officer Mercier's with you now?'

'Yeah. Our kids are in the same soccer league. We're sittin' here on the sidelines watchin' 'em.'

'Any chance I could have a quick word with him? I have to catch a flight in a minute.'

'Sure,' she said easily, like she'd accepted that this was just a chat. 'Hold on.'

Eric saw that the second boarding group was moving toward the jet bridge now. He moved closer to the gate, his boarding pass sitting proud of his blazer pocket so the staff would know he was also on this flight.

A male voice came on the phone. 'Agent Ramos? Charles Mercier here. Harrison says you want to know if we saw anything that day we all went down the slope?'

'Yes, that's correct.'

'Well, if there'd been anything untoward, anything not within Corrections protocol, we would've informed you at the time.' He'd clearly listened to his partner's side of the call and wanted to end any suggestion that they had been remiss in any way.

'Of course,' Eric reassured. 'There's no suggestion of that. This is informal, just us talking, in case there was something you noticed.'

Mercier was apparently mollified by the explanation and became more conversational. 'In that case, I'd just confirm what Tasha said. The inmate was smiling when we got to him. Couldn't tell why. Probably just enjoyed seeing us slide around on our asses.'

'And when you got to him, he was, what, about five, six feet from our scientist?'

'Yeah, I'd say that's about right. But you saw that yourself.'

I did, Eric thought, *but what did I miss?* He noticed

the gate agent inviting him to step forward. He looked around. The airline staff had been efficient; he was the last one in the gate area. He pulled out his boarding pass as he thanked Officer Mercier and apologized for interrupting their evening.

As Eric walked alone up the jet bridge, he found his mind was back on that hillside in Texas, hunting again, but not for dismembered heads. He decided he would use the flight to Alaska to run over the whole thing, starting from when they had first arrived at the site and Jayne was inside the mobile lab. He'd take it all the way up to the point when he'd found her a stone's throw from Eugene Frederick King.

*

Joseph set the timer and practiced putting the parts of the weapon and silencer together again, going through the steps he now had memorized. The instant he was done, he whipped up the stopwatch but he still hadn't been quick enough. He also noticed that the faster he went, the louder his assembly became – and it wasn't just the sound of the metal racking into place. It was him, breathing noisily through the process. This wasn't going to work, especially now that he would have to deal with not just Lander and Hall but the man he'd seen tonight too. And what about Riley? It might be the end of the road for that guy as well. Joseph grunted. He shouldn't get distracted by the thought of ending Riley's run just now. He could end him any time. He refocused. Why not just leave the weapon *assembled* in the kayaking bag and bring the ammunition separately? He would need to find a suitable hiding place for the bag but he had confidence in himself to do that.

As usual, his confidence wasn't misplaced: after a short hunt, he found an ideal spot. He wedged the bag between some large rocks where it wouldn't slip down, no matter the weather. He practiced pulling it down from the hiding place and opening it several times. Then he set the stopwatch and went through the motions, loading the ammo and aiming the rifle, picturing Lander and Hall taking it in the chest, the stomach, the back, anywhere – everywhere. He was good; he was doing it fast enough.

He sealed the bag, stowed it in the hiding place and then stood back to look at the area with a critical eye. A casual glance returned the usual cluster of boulders and evergreen saplings. Only a closer look from a dedicated hiker would reveal the bag. He realized then that he had another weapon. Opening his pants, he urinated on the bag and everything around it. Now, anyone coming across his stash wouldn't even want to touch it.

*

Steelie and Matt had made their way through the entire menu of Bella Terra at the Bellagio, from the appetizers of Temperature Drops accompanied by thin slices of Reversal Roulade, to the main of NoCow Gnocchi with a Go Green Salad. From the dessert cart, they'd sampled Carbon Offset Cannoli and two different Krispy Kremes. Between the names of the dishes and several bottles of bubbly, they'd stayed in the moment, making up alternative dishes and generally being the loudest pair in the room, earning mildly disapproving glances from other diners. This had only made them find everything funnier.

'What's *in* this champagne?' Steelie said, as Matt poured close to the last of it into her glass and then the very last of it into his.

'Right?' Matt held his glass up to the light to examine it.

He was still tilting his glass back as the waiter reappeared, holding a discreet bill jacket.

'Will this be on the room, sir?'

Matt almost choked as he looked up at him. 'There's no room!' Then he spluttered to Steelie, 'I didn't book a room. I wouldn't want you to think there was a room. There is *no* room.' He cut his hand through the air.

Steelie couldn't stop laughing. 'This is like watching an episode of *Seinfeld*!'

Matt put his hand out for the bill only to find that the waiter was also struggling to rein in his amusement.

'Not you too,' Matt said, but he was smiling an embarrassed smile.

'Apologies, sir. A pleasure to have you with us this evening.'

When Steelie and Matt eventually walked out of the hotel's front entrance, the temperature was just right to enjoy the night. The Bellagio fountains were finishing a performance set to Michael Jackson's 'Billie Jean' and the surface of the massive pool was rippling from a finale perfectly timed to the moment the music ceased booming out over The Strip.

Matt said, 'Want to catch the next show?'

'We have time?'

'Yeah. We go back on the last flight.'

They strolled down the driveway and managed to snag a balcony which appeared to be suspended over the water.

Steelie leaned her elbows on the parapet and took in the scene for a while. 'This is really nice.' She turned around to observe the wave of humanity walking past. 'Even all these tourists are nice.'

Matt looked over at her. 'Yeah.'

Steelie mimicked him from earlier. 'There isn't a room. I'm telling you: there's *no* room!' But as she guffawed, she took in his expression. 'Sorry. I'm embarrassing you; I'll stop. Eventually.'

He looked into her eyes. 'You're not embarrassing me.'

'Good. Because joking is my thing.'

'I like that about you.' He held her gaze.

Steelie felt sure Matt was going to kiss her, but he didn't. She looked at his lips. They had been the first feature of his that she'd noticed when they'd met at UCLA a month ago. They had looked kissable then and they looked kissable now. But two things happened at that moment: the opening notes of Frank Sinatra's 'My Way' blasted the area and a clutch of tourists pressed into their balcony, trying to get the best view of the fountains.

Matt looked displeased but he moved behind Steelie to give others space at the balustrade. But more people continued to push in behind them, loudly singing along with Frank in American and international accents. Matt put his hands on the balustrade, an arm on either side of Steelie. She felt his chest against her back.

She spoke over her shoulder. 'I don't need a protector, Detective.'

His voice came close to her ear. 'You're really misreading this, Ms. Lander.'

She turned around then. Matt didn't move an inch, causing her body to brush against his for the full 180 degrees. The grin on his face was about as stupid as hers had been earlier, she was glad to see, but still he didn't kiss her. She could smell donuts and champagne on his breath: a heady mix. So she went on her toes, put her arms around his neck and kissed him. He had a delayed reaction before he put his arms around her and kissed her back. It was so good, Steelie almost whimpered.

She only pulled away when there was an outburst of clapping from the crowd watching the fountains. She turned to look and was rewarded by seeing the towering water jets swooning in time to Sinatra's first chorus.

Matt put his cheek to hers and said, 'So I'm sensing that, maybe, possibly, there *could've* been a room?'

As Steelie burst out laughing, Matt hugged her from behind and she felt rather than heard his pleased chuckle.

18

Eric settled back into the second-row captain's seat of the Cadillac Escalade sent from the livery service to collect him and Scott from Anchorage Airport. The young driver had the radio on low up front, tuned to a rock station. Eric yawned and pulled out his BlackBerry. It was close to midnight Alaska Daylight Time.

Scott caught his yawn; he didn't even try to stifle it. 'What's the itinerary for tomorrow?'

Eric tried to focus his eyes on the screen. 'Uh, they've helpfully given us a pick-up time of 1000 hours, which will give us a chance to catch up on sleep. The AUSA will kick us loose at 1600 hours. Monday, we have to be at court at 0800. Pick-up time: six-thirty. Although . . .' He brightened the screen. 'Judging from the fact that we're booked on a flight to LA at 1300 hours, we must be the first witnesses of the day.'

Scott had been looking out the window during this recital. 'I didn't hear any mention of meals.'

'When has anyone remembered agents need to eat?' Eric grumbled. 'Like right now, in fact.' He looked out the windows. 'Everything looks closed. And what do you want to bet the hotel isn't serving food at this time of night?'

The driver looked at him in the rearview mirror. 'Yeah, they won't be. Sorry.'

Scott smirked. 'Be glad we ate the "snacks" on the flight.' He looked at Eric's BlackBerry. 'Is the flight to LA direct?'

'No. Travel has us going through . . .' Eric scanned again. 'Seattle. And not a quick connection.'

'Great.' Scott's voice was heavy with sarcasm.

'Hey, at least it gives us time to get something to eat. On Monday afternoon. A day and a half from now.'

'There is that,' Scott said, leaning his head back against the headrest and closing his eyes.

Eric fiddled with his BlackBerry. He'd been working and reworking the angles on why Gene King would've been smiling just after the landslip. The likelihood that it was generalized amusement from sliding down a hill while handcuffed seemed nil to him. Seeing Corrections officers out of control might merit some mirth but, in Eric's experience, what got King going was something more complicated. Something psychological and related to either Jayne or Scott. But before he devoted any more time to divining what King had done, Eric wanted to rule out the possibility that Jayne had already told Scott what happened.

He pitched it casually. 'Any word from Jayne?'

'No, but I didn't expect any. Why?'

Still keeping it casual, Eric said, 'Steelie was saying—'

'When'd you speak to Steelie? Is everything okay?' Scott had opened his eyes.

'Yesterday. She only said Jayne's a little off and she was asking, well, she has an idea that maybe something went down with . . .' Eric glanced at the driver and decided not to say King's name. 'Our perp this week.'

Now Scott lifted his head from the headrest. 'When exactly?'

'Remember when you split the sites on Tuesday?'

Scott squinted, clearly picturing it. 'I knew I should have gone with her.'

'You couldn't. You were already on point at the truck stop.'

'Did he do something?' Scott turned in his seat to look squarely at Eric. 'Were you really on his six after the landslip?'

Eric took a steadying breath. This was the crux of it; he hadn't been there. And yet he couldn't have gotten there faster; it's not like he knew there was going to be a landslip. But to say that to Scott right now would come out like a weak defense. 'He couldn't have done anything; he was cuffed. And I checked with the others: nothing. At the most, he could have said something.'

Scott swiveled back, his body rigid.

Eric read his partner's body language. 'Houston, don't go there.' But it was too late.

'*Fuck!*' Scott slammed his hand against the back of the passenger seat, which reverberated on its base.

The driver jumped, turned to look at Scott and then quickly turned back to the face the road, his eyes darting to and from the rearview mirror.

Eric leaned forward to catch the driver's eye. 'Sorry, he's just . . . Everything's fine.'

'Uh. Okay,' the young man said but he jerked the vehicle into a cutaway.

They had, in fact, arrived at the semi-circular driveway of their hotel. Scott was out the door before the vehicle came to a full stop.

Eric retrieved their bags and dismissed the driver. After the SUV moved out of the way, he saw that Scott was back down the driveway a short distance, pacing.

Eric went down to him. 'How about you get it out now before we go inside and you start breaking furniture?'

Scott pulled his hands backwards and forwards through his hair as he paced. 'You know what, Eric? I haven't spoken to Jayne since Tuesday night because we agreed: low profile 'cuz Turner's on the rampage. The thing is—'

He broke off and shook his head, a humorless smile passing across his lips. 'On Tuesday night, I could tell – I could just *sense* that something was wrong. But I put it down to her embarrassment in front of Turner.' He stopped pacing. 'If it turns out King's come between me and Jayne, I'll kill him, Eric. I'll fuckin' kill him with my bare hands.'

Eric had listened patiently to all of this. 'So. Before you kill him, go to jail *and* tank your career, how about you ask Jayne about it? You're standing here talking about killing a guy who about a dozen families of the victims need to see facing something other than just your fists . . .'

Scott grimaced and looked at the sky.

'Yeah, remember them?' Eric continued, his tone light. 'So selfish, just killing him for yourself. At least kill him for their sakes if you're gonna do it.'

Scott held up his hands in surrender.

'So, to get back to my point,' Eric said. 'Jayne's a smart woman who's capable of drawing her own conclusions about anything King said.'

Scott focused on him for the first time. 'King's manipulated her before.'

'Replaying the past isn't—'

Scott sounded exasperated. 'I'm not, Eric.'

Eric wasn't going to be fobbed off with that, not when Scott literally just referred to what King had done *in the past*. 'You are and it isn't helping. Just talk to her. It's not like she unplugged her phone.'

Scott's eyes flashed angrily. 'And when exactly do I explain to Turner that I wasn't calling Jayne about our potential-conflict-of-interest-related MOU? That I was, in fact, calling her about our potential-conflict-of-interest-related personal relationship? No way. Turner won't even give me a chance to explain.'

Eric took this in. 'You think it's that bad with Turner that you can't call Jayne? He didn't seem that frosty when he was with you in Texas.'

'Not that frosty? Ramos, he fuckin' demoted me.'

Eric raised his eyebrows. So him being made lead had made Scott feel demoted.

Scott immediately looked apologetic. 'I don't mean demoted.'

'I think you do.' Eric shrugged.

Scott put his hands up, palms out. 'Eric, I don't. But it did feel like I got . . . knocked back.'

That made sense. Eric exhaled. 'You got reassigned by our boss – who's a rule-follower – because he perceived that you might have broken some rules.' He pointed at Scott's BlackBerry. 'If you don't want a record on a Bureau device, call Jayne from the hotel's landline.'

Scott looked like he was considering that. Then he said, 'If that piece of shit King has been playing games, I'll need to talk to her face to face so I can read her. I know how he gets into her head.'

Eric didn't totally get this but he accepted it. Maybe he'd been out of a relationship so long, he'd forgotten how to do it. Or maybe Jayne needed special handling. He said, 'Fine. But go see her as soon as we get back to LA on Monday. Because at the office first thing Tuesday is more Turner, more King, the SitRep on the MOU, and God knows what case or six we've been assigned to on the roster.'

Scott gave him a tight but grateful smile.

Eric looked over to where their bags were still sitting in front of the hotel's glassed-in entryway. 'Let's go find out if our shiny badges will get us some food in an Alaskan hotel at midnight.'

*

Steelie woke up as the Southwest jet taxied into Burbank. 'I can't believe I slept.'

Matt covered a yawn. 'I can't believe I took a middle seat.'

Steelie looked around. 'Why is it so crowded? It's so late.'

'Last flight out of Vegas,' Matt mumbled.

They walked back to Matt's truck. The airport was quiet and the temperature had fallen. He opened the passenger door for Steelie.

She said, 'Hang on. I almost forgot.' She pulled out her slim wallet, extracted two $20 bills and slapped them onto Matt's blazer front. 'You won this one.'

His face lit up. 'I did, didn't I? Our first date did not end in tears.' He took the bills. 'A pleasure doing business with you, ma'am.'

'Throwing my words back at me? Touché.' She stepped up into the cab and Matt closed the door behind her.

Steelie regretted how little traffic there was on the roads because she wasn't ready for the night to end. Her neighborhood was as good as silent when Matt walked her up to her front door. He stopped with one foot on the porch and the other down a step, equalizing their height when she turned to him.

She said quietly, 'I had a good time. A really good time, actually.'

'Me too. But don't sound so surprised. Maybe. If possible.' He leaned toward her. 'Do we have to whisper?'

She whispered back. 'What I meant was, I didn't realize how much I needed a break.'

'You spend your time matching missing persons to dead bodies but you didn't realize you needed a break? Fascinating.'

'Very funny. I'm trying to say thank you.'

'I know.' He smiled. 'I'm just teasing you.'

That made Steelie happy. He could give as good as he got. She lingered, gazing at his lips. 'So, I wouldn't be against going on another date with you.'

He cocked his head to the side. 'Interesting sentence construction. But fine. When? Tomorrow?'

She loved that he said this. 'Tomorrow I have to go to Seattle—'

'For the FBI?'

'No, a Thirty-Two One case. Missing sister.'

He raised an intrigued eyebrow but didn't ask questions. 'So, not tomorrow.'

'No. But, um . . . soon.' Steelie realized that the grin on her face had made her voice sound like she was teasing him, even though she really did mean 'soon'.

He'd taken it like a tease. 'In that case, see you soon Steelie Lander.' He took his foot off the porch and started walking to his truck.

He was going without a last kiss? She hissed, 'Wait! Matt!'

He sauntered back with a look of feigned puzzlement.

Once he was close enough, she pulled him in by the lapels and kissed him. Then she kissed him again. Finally, she pushed him away. 'Argh!'

He walked backwards down the driveway, watching her watching him, a pleased grin on his face until he tripped over a solar path light.

'Shit!' he said as he stumbled.

She whisper-shouted, 'Are you okay?'

But he just brushed down his slacks, righted the light and waved a farewell.

Steelie went inside and stood with her back against the door, heart beating fast as she listened to his truck leave. Then she pulled out her phone and dialed Jayne.

Jayne's voice was muffled. 'Hi, Steelie.'

'Did I wake you? Is Scott there?'

'No and no. My pillow was just halfway on the phone. I was hoping you'd call. Oh, I just saw the time. How was your date?'

Steelie was pulling her overnight bag toward the front door in readiness for their departure for Seattle the next day. 'Guess where we had dinner?'

'I have to guess? Okay, the Polo Lounge.'

That surprised Steelie. 'The Polo Lounge? Why the Polo Lounge?'

'I don't know. Matt just seems kinda old-school.'

Steelie grinned. 'Yeah, he is. He's even got an old truck like yours.' She cringed inwardly. 'Like your old one, that is.' Now she felt like she was dragging Jayne through the reservoir crash all over again. 'Sorry to bring that up.'

'It's okay. I want to tell you something about cars too, but first tell me where you ate.'

'The Bellagio.' Steelie perched on the couch and waited for Jayne's reaction.

After more pillow noise, Jayne exclaimed, 'Wait, as in *Vegas*?'

'As in.'

'You flew? You must have.'

'Uh-huh,' Steelie said smugly.

Jayne sounded like she didn't know where to start. 'I'm amazed you let him take you out of state.'

Steelie flopped back on the couch, ready to gush. 'I know! But I decided to go with it.' She gleefully told Jayne about the vegetarian menu and the modified dessert cart. 'I was like a kid in a candy store.'

'I bet.' Jayne sounded wistful. 'I can't believe he made those kinds of plans and then surprised you with them. He must be . . . he must have thought about it – about you – a lot.' She paused. 'You weren't weirded out by that?'

'No. I like him, Jayne.' It felt good to say that out loud. 'He's down to earth, he's funny, he likes my jokes *and* he's a good kisser.'

Jayne whistled. 'Well, well, well. Very nice. And when are you planning to see him again?'

'On the level that I currently consider him more attractive than a Krispy Kreme, I can't wait to see him again. But I told him how we're going to Seattle tomorrow so we didn't make immediate plans.'

'And the cop part?' Jayne said gently. 'Are you over that?'

'I think I am. I mean, he doesn't seem like a cop to me anymore. He's Matt.'

Jayne laughed. 'He always was.'

Steelie knew that this was Jayne's way of calling out the danger of Steelie's enduring biases. 'Yada yada. So. What did you want to tell me about cars?'

'I have a new one.'

'Hey, that's great! You shouldn't have let me go on about Matt.'

'No! I wanted to know.'

'So, what'dja get?'

'Jeep Cherokee.'

Steelie knew the car so wouldn't pronounce approval until she had more information. 'Before or after the redesign?'

'Before. It's a '96 and it's in my driveway as we speak.'

Steelie nodded happily. 'That's a vehicle made to take

us places! Wanna drive to Seattle instead of fly? Road trip!'

'It would take us more than a day to drive there! Dating Matt is making you even more ridiculous, which I didn't think was possible.' Jayne paused. 'And it's lovely.'

DAY 7

Sunday

19

Scott sat next to Eric, both agents waiting for the Assistant United States Attorney who had greeted them in a brisk manner in the lobby of Anchorage's Federal Building that morning. Victoria Johnson was in her thirties and had been dressed in casual clothes but she'd been all business, not stopping for small talk. Instead, she'd ushered them into a conference room to review two binders of evidence the agents would be testifying to in the cross-border kidnapping case she was prosecuting. Scott and Eric had played a minor role in the case nine months earlier when stationed in Atlanta, so the review was necessary.

The two hours they'd spent going over the evidence that morning had been useful, and then they'd broken for lunch, which AUSA Johnson had had delivered for all of them. She'd left the agents to eat together while she'd had a working lunch in her office. When she returned, she had a highlighter in one hand and a cup holder with three coffees and fixings in the other.

'Help yourselves,' she said as she placed the coffees on the table and adjusted the hair band holding her bobbed hair behind her ears. 'Okay, we've reached the roleplay part of my prep. Agent Houston, let's start with you. I'm going to move this chair over here . . .'

She began to drag one of the armchairs to the corner of the room. It looked heavy so Scott quickly got up to help but she said, 'I can handle it, thanks.'

He returned to doctoring his coffee. When he looked back, the chair was sitting like an island of its own over by the wall, as distant as it could be from the conference room table.

AUSA Johnson saw him looking. 'This is to replicate as much as possible what it will be like for you on the witness stand.'

'I have given evidence before,' Scott said defensively.

'Not on one of my cases.'

Scott shrugged and took a sip of coffee as he walked over to the chair.

She said, 'Will you have a cup of coffee in your hand on the witness stand?'

Scott looked at her sharply. She smiled. He backtracked to the table and put the cup down.

She added one more instruction. 'And put your blazer back on, please, Agent Houston. I need to see how you handle yourself in what you'll be wearing tomorrow. You will be wearing that blazer or something similar?'

While Scott put his blazer on, he shot Eric a meaningful glance, but Eric was leaning back in his chair as he blew on his coffee, grinning like he was settling in for a show. Scott sat in the 'witness box' and looked at the attorney.

AUSA Johnson moved around in front of him, sometimes blocking his view of the room and of Eric. She asked the first question without preamble, her back to him.

'Please state your name and title for the record.'

'Scott Houston, Special Agent, Federal Bureau of Investigation.'

She turned around to face him. 'I thought you said you'd testified before.'

He frowned. 'I have.'

'Then why didn't you pause?'

'Why would I pause before saying my own name?'

She shook her head. 'You pause after everything so that when the defense gets you on cross and you start pausing to formulate your responses, it won't stand out.'

Scott tried to think back to whether he'd tended to do that when he'd testified in the past.

Johnson supplemented, 'If the jury sees you answering some of the defense attorney's questions fast and some slow, it'll look like you're parsing the truth.'

Her words cut through Scott's train of thought. 'Parsing the truth,' he repeated slowly, trying not to sound like he was in total disbelief. 'Is that the same as lying?'

Johnson took on a level tone. 'It's not the same but I don't want to have to take bets on jurors knowing the difference, so I'm getting you to suppress your natural inclination to jump the gun and be a hothead.' She looked at him like she was waiting for his quick comeback.

Scott didn't know what to say.

She relented. 'Your reputation precedes you.'

Scott leaned around her to look at Eric, but his partner wasn't leaping to his defense. In fact, he looked amused. Scott realized sheepishly that Johnson could easily have had this précis of his character from AUSA Edwards down in Los Angeles or even AUSA Trent in Atlanta.

But he wondered if one or both of the attorneys had also conveyed to Johnson that, overall, he was a good witness on the stand.

Taking up her back-and-forth pacing again, Johnson relaunched. 'Please state your name and title for the record.'

He paused, counted 'one, two' in his head and then said, 'Scott Houston, Special Agent, Federal Bureau of Investigation.'

He was able to continue putting in a beat before he answered each question, and then it was Eric's turn in the hot seat. Eric had had the advantage of seeing Scott get schooled so he was pause-perfect during his roleplay session and kept his hands clasped loosely in front of him no matter what inflammatory statement the attorney threw at him.

When Eric was done, AUSA Johnson sat down and declared herself happy with their preparation. She was even happy with how they wore their clothes: 'Nice. Both of you. No fidgeting, no cuff-shooting, no running a finger around a collar. And don't start those habits tomorrow either, gentlemen.'

She leaned back in her chair and exhaled as she pulled off her hair band. Shaking out her hair, she finger-combed her bangs down onto her forehead; they reached the tops of her eyebrows. Her bangs had coppery-bronze highlights just lighter than the brown of her skin color. Scott was surprised at how she no longer looked like a defense lawyer badgering them with questions.

She caught him looking at her. 'Forgot I was on your side, didn't you?'

He gave her an embarrassed smile. 'Yes, actually.'

She beamed. 'That's good. It means the roleplay was working. And it's part of why I know you'll *both* be stellar for me tomorrow.' She gave Eric a friendly smile.

Eric cocked an eyebrow. 'You make it sound like it's all about you, AUSA Johnson.'

'Oh, but it is, Agent Ramos,' she said as she gathered her papers. 'I've got my eye on a judgeship and I don't intend to have any mishaps in a courtroom stand in my way.' She crossed the room to pull the chair that had stood in for the witness box back over to the table.

Scott, having learned his lesson, did not go over to offer assistance, but when Johnson returned to the table, she indicated the two binders of evidence. 'I'll take you up on your earlier attempt at gallantry and let you carry those binders back to my office while I bring the rest.'

Eric gathered up the coffees and spoke *sotto voce* to Scott as they followed her out. 'Gold star for you, Houston.'

*

As soon as the waitress for the hotel restaurant left with their order, Steelie moved to the other side of the booth to join Jayne.

She reviewed the progress in Jayne's notebook. 'So this is the cheat sheet for tomorrow?'

Jayne nodded. 'I'm almost done.'

The waitress returned with their drinks. 'One Arnold Palmer and one Earl Grey.'

Jayne looked up. 'Could I have some cream for the Earl Grey?'

'No problem. I'll be right back.'

Steelie sipped her iced tea and settled back happily. 'So I call a meal at this time "linner", but guess what Matt calls it?'

Jayne didn't stop writing.

Steelie nudged her. 'You're not guessing!'

'Because I have a feeling you're going to tell me regardless.'

Steelie grinned. 'He calls it first dinner. Isn't that hilarious?'

'It's mildly amusing. Does he then have a second dinner?'

'He does! And I like that about him. He's solid.'

Jayne accepted a jug of creamer from the waitress and switched to her tea-making ritual.

Steelie examined the sheet:

Name	: Alexander Ayers
AKAs	: Alex Ayers
Date of Birth	: April 14, 1966
Age at the Time of Disappearance	: 23 years
Date Last Seen	: August 3, 1989
Sex	: Intersex
Sex on Missing Person Report	: Female (confirm this tomorrow)
Self-identified Gender	: Female
Height	: 5'7'
Weight	: Approx. 140 lbs

Ancestry	: Caucasoid
Hair Color	: Brown-blonde, known to highlight to lighter blonde
Hair Type	: Caucasoid, straight
Hair Length when Last Seen	: Approx. 17" from crown
Anomalies	: None known
Pathologies	: Healed fractures of distal right radius and proximal right ulna (age 14 years)
Dental	: See attached odontogram
Radiographs	: Medical and dental available from age 14 years (digitized)
DNA	: Familial DNA on file (buccal swab, first order sibling)
Nationality	: Australian
Location Last Seen	: Seattle, Washington
Notes	: @ age 14 yrs, cranium and mandible sex as female, pelvis sexes as male, postcranial elements present as gracile, male external genitalia per sibling

Steelie tapped the paper. 'I see you've got a parenthetical here that we need to get a look-see at the misper report. Why don't we have that on another to-do list as well? Like, get the misper report, see if we can get a print-out of the NCIC record now that Umar added the dental, find out if we can get a liaison to anyone in Seattle Missing Persons, etcetera.'

Jayne nodded and gave Steelie the pen. 'You know what would be good? Let's see if we can talk to the actual detective who handled Alex's missing person report.'

'What are the chances that someone from 1989 is still around now?'

'We can only ask. Maybe OC can give us an introduction to someone.'

Steelie was scornful. 'No cop is going to remember diddly squat. Alex was just another missing woman.'

Jayne looked at her. 'You're willfully pretending that missing person detectives don't have certain cases that get under their skin, just like homicide Ds do? They're still thinking about them after they retire.'

The waitress arrived with their meals and Steelie moved back to the other side of the booth.

As Jayne transferred some salad onto the plate with her lasagna, she said, 'Anyway, I thought you were all positive about police now.'

'I'm only positive about Matt,' Steelie said, forking up a mouthful of quiche.

'And Bud Reese and Theresa Sanchez and Scott and Eric and—'

'Fine!' Steelie smiled. 'You made your point.'

Toward the end of the meal, Jayne's cell phone rang. Steelie listened as Jayne confirmed for Graham that they were indeed safely in Seattle and would be going to the coroner's office in the morning.

The waitress came up to the table.

'Can I get you anything else? Dessert?'

When they said no, the waitress reached for their bill. 'And will this be on the room?'

Steelie couldn't help but snicker but stopped when Jayne looked at her curiously. 'Sorry. Inside joke.'

After signing the chit, Jayne said, 'I don't know about you but I'm ready for an early night.'

Steelie advised. 'Going to sleep early isn't the way to get through the days until you see Scott again.'

Jayne groaned like this was the tenth time Steelie had delivered this advice, when in fact it was the first. 'I'm not! I just want an early night.'

Steelie tried a different approach. 'Jayne, has it occurred to you that maybe Scott's back in LA, standing on your doorstep right now, wondering where *you* are?'

Jayne opened her mouth and then closed it. This clearly had *not* occurred to her. 'Um . . .' she said distractedly.

'It's Sunday night; they've gotta be back by now.'

Jayne pulled her cell phone out of her bag again and looked at it. 'He'd call if he came by my place and I wasn't there.'

'I don't know why you think he's going to call you when you're busy not calling him because you agreed to not call each other! Wait – did I say that right? It's too confusing. Just call him.'

Looking thoughtful, Jayne said, 'Even if he is back, this isn't a conversation I want to have on the phone.' Then, clearly trying to deflect the attention from her back onto Steelie, Jayne gave her a penetrating look. 'What difference does this make to you?'

Steelie thought about that as they walked back through the hotel's bar toward the lobby. 'I just hate to see good love go to waste.'

Jayne's eyes widened. 'Oh my God, who are you and what have you done with my friend Steelie?'

Steelie grinned. 'I'd forgotten how much fun it is to be so into someone that you're thinking about them all the time. You need Scott in your life, Jayne. Heck, *I* need him in your life.'

She saw the expression that passed fleetingly across Jayne's face. It was one of anguish. Steelie couldn't understand what it was doing there but she wanted it gone. She was on the verge of calling Scott Houston herself. Screw the MOU.

*

Scott was jogging in tandem with Eric, which was their usual habit as they'd found that it propelled each of them forward even when they were tired. The Bureau had booked them into an Anchorage hotel whose sprawling grounds included a tree-lined creek bordered by a paved path. It made for an ideal roundtrip run. It was during the return leg on a meandering uphill segment that AUSA Johnson came into Scott's head. Specifically, the way she'd said she was going to curb his tendency to 'jump the gun and be a hothead'. And while it was true that he did that a lot, the other, more problematic truth was that he'd been doing it more lately because Eugene King had a way of making him go to eleven at the slightest provocation.

It occurred to him that the way the AUSA had prepped him for the stand would actually serve as good advice for how he could talk with Jayne about King. Then Scott reflected that Jayne was the other reason he was going to eleven. He knew it was because he loved her and didn't want to lose her, but it wasn't just that: he felt like he needed her. The reality of that word 'need' hit Scott like a ton of bricks. He had to stop running. He bent over, hands to his thighs.

Eric, who'd gone on, came back and ran in place in front of him. 'If you're flagging now, you need to be running more. Want to hit the gym instead?'

The last thing Scott wanted was more weight on his chest. He'd rather drink – or smoke – but he wouldn't do either the night before going into court. He straightened up. 'Did you notice if the gym had a sauna?'

'Yeah, it does.'

'I'm going to head up there.'

'Ten-four.' Eric turned and continued up the hill at a run.

20

No one was using the hotel gym when Scott walked through. He readied himself for the sauna and found that its temperature was already moderate. He went over to the controls and notched them up. After a minute, he ladled up some water and threw it on the rocks. That produced a satisfying hiss. Sitting on the bench, he felt the warmth of the wood through his back and legs, but then, as he was the only one in there, he lay down on his back and closed his eyes. He realized later that that was his mistake.

Relaxing his body gave his brain the chance to throw on a record. Over and over, he heard Ty Collins saying, 'You didn't protect my daughter.' He finally answered just above a whisper: 'I know I didn't.' He'd known Ellie Collins, had talked with her, laughed with her, had given her rides home to get her off the street, warned her that there was a predator around. Scott remembered the day Ty had reported her missing. He remembered the dread he'd felt over the very likely possibility that a serial killer he and Eric hadn't yet caught had taken Ellie. And then King had linked Ellie's disappearance back to Scott, made him feel responsible.

Scott put his hands to his temples and massaged his forehead. He wanted new thoughts in his head. Even more, he wanted new blood in his veins, and the thought of that upset him because he knew this was shit he shouldn't let anywhere near Jayne, who had her own PTSD issues to deal with. The thought of adding pain into her life made Scott feel like something was breaking inside of him. Tears that had first threatened when he met the Alston parents – tears he had held back while talking to Ty Collins and Missy Belport – welled up. He finally let them flow. They rolled down his cheeks, mixing with the sweat to trickle into his ears, and now he was taking the intense heat of the sauna like a punishment. The idea of not being with Jayne until he'd dealt with this toxic stuff made life with her feel elusive, like he could lose her – not because of King, but because of himself, and the thought of *that* was so unbearable that he had to do deep breathing to stop more tears from coming.

The sauna door opened suddenly and Scott tilted his head back sharply to look. It was Eric, who from this vantage point was upside down. His partner had paused on the threshold, a towel around his waist. Scott turned his wet face to the wall, aware that his heaving chest had probably already betrayed him. He closed his eyes and listened as Eric shut the door, ladled some more water over the stones. Scott eventually glanced over. Eric was on the bench across the room. His eyes were half-closed against the heat but they were on Scott, dark and troubled, before he closed them fully and settled his back against the wall.

Scott regarded his partner, thinking about how Eric

had forged an uncomplicated existence after the negativity of his married life. He had divorced and then started life again, as though in a new skin. Scott wondered if he could do the same.

*

Eric didn't get in saunas enough. This was the perfect restorative after the run in the fresh air. He wasn't sure that the heat was working for Scott, though. Earlier, Eric had thought his partner had simply been tired, but when he walked into the sauna, he could see it was more than fatigue. It couldn't be down to the roleplay with AUSA Johnson, as bruising as that had been at times, because they were all good by the end. So, Eric deduced, it was probably the fact that Scott hadn't yet talked to Jayne.

Eric knew that Scott would want to nip the situation in the bud ASAP, but it had been almost a day since Eric had told him that something might be up with Jayne due to King. This brought Eric's mind to Jayne with the sudden realization that there had been two in the mix on the hillside the day of the landslip: King *and* Jayne. But he'd only been reviewing King's actions.

Eyes closed, Eric thought back: Jayne had actually been odd, right from when he'd helped her get up from the downhill slide. She'd been short with him, which was unusual for her. On the day, he'd put it down to the unpleasantness of the fall, but now he recalled the rigidity of her body, the impatience of her tone when she'd rejected his help. She'd been quiet up in the lab as well, thoughtful. Scott had said he'd noticed that Jayne had been acting oddly later, *after* Turner had ordered Thirty-Two One off the operation, but now Eric felt sure that it had begun earlier – several hours earlier. He opened his eyes.

Scott had a hand over his face but his chest was no longer doing the telltale deep breathing he'd been doing when Eric had first entered the sauna. He called over to him.

'Scott.'

'Yeah.' Scott sounded raspy and he cleared his throat.

'I'm pretty sure something did go down between Jayne and King on the day of the landslip.'

Scott didn't look over. 'I'm listening.'

'No one – me included – saw or heard anything but I remember that Jayne kinda bit my head off when I tried to help her up. And, on reflection, when we got to the road and even when she was working, she was preoccupied. I'd go so far as to say withdrawn.'

'Okay. Thanks for letting me know.' Scott sat up. 'Eric, you know your divorce?'

That caught Eric by surprise. This didn't have anything to do with Jayne. 'Well, it was *my* divorce so, yeah. Why?'

'I remember you saying Gabriela made you feel toxic. That's the word you used, right?'

'Yeah.'

Scott leaned his elbows on his knees. 'You don't feel that way anymore, do you?'

'Toxic? No.'

'But how did that happen? How'd you get your head straight?'

Eric joked, 'You mean besides hanging out with you

and Callista and thinking, "Thank Christ I'm not in a relationship anymore"?'

'I'm being serious.'

Eric thought for a moment. 'I don't know. After a while, I realized it wasn't me. I mean, it wasn't something, like, intrinsic to me that was toxic – it was the combination of Gaby and me. We wanted different things, as it turned out, so we were pulling in different directions. All the time.'

'But what if it had been intrinsic to you?'

Eric shrugged. 'Well, then it would still be good that we got divorced. So I wouldn't be making her put up with it too.'

Scott leaned back and was quiet for a moment. 'Yeah.'

Eric said, 'About Jayne—'

Scott waved dismissively. 'Don't give it any more thought, man. The shit didn't start on that hillside.'

Eric didn't know what Scott meant and he didn't get a chance to ask because Scott was on his feet and holding out his fist.

As they bumped knuckles, Scott said, 'Thanks, partner,' and then he was out the door.

Eric felt the stream of cooler air trail across his skin as the door closed with a soft thud. He resettled his shoulders against the wall and closed his eyes.

*

In his hotel room, Scott showered and turned on the television. He skimmed through program after program, switching channels without taking anything in. He watched people manipulate icing bags over layer cakes, repair siding to prevent rain damage, *Friends* being friendly no matter the misstep or mishap, lovers looking doe-eyed on an evening soap opera, slices of a 9/11 documentary jarring him each time he came back to that channel, until the late-night shows came on and he found that he wasn't laughing along with the audience because he wasn't actually listening. He turned off the television and lay back on the bed. Then he looked over at the hotel phone, remembering Eric's suggestion to call Jayne on that one. It was late; she'd be home.

Jayne's landline rang three times before the answering machine picked up. He knew she was probably screening the call because she didn't recognize the number so he spoke, trying to find the right words.

'Hey, it's me. I'm calling from a hotel in Alaska. Are you there?' He waited. Nothing. 'I'll give you a second in case you're far from the phone.' This was silly; he knew for a fact that she had three cordless handsets around the apartment and one of them was right next to the bed, which was where he was picturing her. She kept the volume high enough on her answering machine to hear it from any room, so he said, 'Please pick up. I really need . . .' He searched for the words. 'To tell you something.'

Nothing happened, which made him picture her listening to his voice coming out of the speaker and deciding not to answer – and *that* made him feel bad. As he drew breath to say something else, the answering machine beeped to signify it was no longer recording. Scott hesitated with the phone in his hand, thinking about calling back so he could leave the number for the hotel along with his room number, but then he replaced the receiver. The desire to yank the phone right off the table was great. But AUSA Johnson was still with him: hothead. 'Don't be one,' he said aloud, and he got all the way into the bed. He didn't sleep until he'd punched the pillow into the right shape. He told himself it wasn't that kind of punching.

DAY 8

Monday

21

Holding a battered Tupperware aloft, Olivia Caldwell led Jayne and Steelie to a table in the cafeteria of the King County Medical Examiner's office in Seattle. The room was lit by only half the fluorescent ceiling panels and was quiet now that the Nespresso coffee machine had finished providing them each with their preferred brew.

Opening the Tupperware to reveal homemade biscotti, Olivia said, 'How is the Agency? Missing the UN work yet?'

'No,' Jayne said. 'Well, we both missed the feel of the larger team in our first year but lately we've been doing some work with this group of Bureau evidence techs and it's good.'

'FBI techs in LA?'

'Yeah, a regional team that supports evidence collection before it gets out to Quantico or the lab in DC. They can process some evidence, digitize images so they can be analyzed remotely, things like that.'

Olivia nodded as she crunched through her biscuit. 'Quick and dirty stuff. That's smart. Saves evidence getting stuck in line in DC, like what usually happens to the material we send over. It sounds like you've worked with them more than once?'

Steelie said, 'We actually have an MOU with the Bureau now.'

'I'm impressed! Some guaranteed income for the Agency, no?'

'It was . . .' Steelie gave Jayne a look. 'You want to explain?'

Jayne had been stirring her coffee with her biscuit. 'Yeah. So the MOU's on hold at the moment.' She couldn't think of how to word the explanation.

Olivia knitted her brows. 'Because?'

Jayne looked at her speculatively. 'Do you remember me talking about Scott?'

Olivia gesticulated enthusiastically. 'Of course I do! He was that guy you met at Quantico who was the reason you said you wouldn't go out with my cousin Bryce, who, by the way, moved from LA to New York last year, so that wouldn't have been great, but anyway. That Scott?'

Jayne couldn't help but smile in agreement. Olivia was just the same as she'd been in college: a little loud, a lot enthusiastic and generous of spirit. But Jayne was also mentally adding Olivia to the list of people she felt like she was lying to by not mentioning the fact that she had reason to believe that Scott was married.

'Yayyy!' Olivia had been clapping her hands but faltered. 'Wait . . . not yay?'

'Not yay,' Jayne confirmed, 'because Scott's boss is concerned that our relationship might represent a conflict of interest for the MOU, so it's all under review right now.'

Steelie added, 'Which means our budget is under review, but yada.'

But Olivia was sitting back, grinning. 'You know what? I don't care about your goddamned budget. This is the best news I've had all year!'

She put her hand on Jayne's arm. 'Girl! We obviously can't get into details here . . .' She looked around the cafeteria, which had been filling up with other staff. 'But we have *got* to get into details.'

Jayne put her other hand over Olivia's. 'How's Keith? You didn't say when we talked.'

Olivia blew air up into her dark bangs. 'That's because Keith is happy with Kathleen. In Oregon.'

Jayne and Steelie both gaped at her.

Olivia shrugged. 'I know, right? He moves up here with me and then has the nerve to leave with his yoga instructor.'

'Yoga?' Steelie wrinkled her nose. 'How did he have time for yoga? I thought he was a mega-busy software engineer?'

'He stopped working due to stress. It seemed yoga was going to be the cure for his depression after he'd exhausted the aromatherapeutic stuff with glass cups put on his back, meditation, weird teas he had to make from dried flowers every day . . . you get the picture.' She pursed her lips.

'Good riddance then,' Steelie said supportively. 'He needed to put his downward dog on a leash and go.'

'Oh, he did and that was fun!' Olivia matched her sarcasm with a fake smile. 'But now I'm free! To work weekends and holidays!' Her tone walked a line between stand-up and strident.

Jayne gave her an understanding look. 'So you've been insanely busy partly by choice?'

'My corpses appreciate me. They don't even care that

I'm going gray.' She smiled but Jayne saw the sadness in her eyes.

Steelie pointed to her silver sideburns. 'Hey, I am way ahead of you on the gray hair.'

'But yours is in a cool place,' Olivia complained. 'Mine is just sprouting wherever. Like this one.' She pointed to the top of her head. 'I swear I got this one the day Keith told me about him and Yoga Guru Girl. Can you see it?'

Jayne laughed. 'No, we can't see it.'

Olivia blew her bangs up again and said, 'Okay, enough of Keith. Let's not keep the dead waiting any longer.'

Jayne and Steelie followed her past the main autopsy suite to a small room where a file box was sitting on a table. Olivia closed the door behind her, which muffled the noise of the morning schedule getting underway: forensic pathologists and autopsy technicians bringing out the first of the morning's case list of car accident victims, overdoses and homicides. The PA system was piped into this room as well and they could hear announcements that let staff know of the arrival of a detective at the visitor's door or of funeral home transport at the loading bays.

Olivia put her hand on top of the file box. 'Okay, here you go. Twenty folders. Steelie, as I mentioned to Jayne, some of the folders might represent more than one person. The organization of the folders doesn't need to concern you at this stage because if we get an ID off of any element, that'll put it onto a priority list for DNA matching with other material from the same site.'

'Got it,' Steelie said.

Jayne dug out her cell phone. 'OC, you said you needed us to turn in our phones?'

Olivia nodded. 'You can either leave them with me or we can get you a locker. Up to you.'

'With you works.' She handed Olivia her phone and Steelie followed suit.

Olivia said, 'Two phones, Steelie?'

'The big-ass one belongs to the FBI,' Steelie said.

'Even though your MOU's on hold?'

'I didn't have a safe place to leave it while we were out of town. You're a county employee: you should know how touchy the government gets about its toys. *Don't* forget to give it to me when we leave.'

'I'll have them in a drawer in my office, don't worry,' Olivia reassured. 'I'm doing posts until noon, so if you finish before then, just have one of the secretaries retrieve them for you and you can leave the files and your shortlist in this room. Door will lock behind you. Happy hunting.'

Jayne and Steelie split the folders, ten each, and began their review, their cheat sheets on Alex Ayers next to them. Although different bones of Alex's skeleton might display either male or female attributes, there were some unambiguous things about her. For example, she couldn't grow a new tooth where she'd already had one extracted. She wasn't a shark. So that ruled out five dental charts right off the bat. The remaining files weren't so simple and the anthropologists worked in silence, heads bent.

*

Eric and Scott emerged from the courtroom, walked a short distance away and waited for AUSA Johnson to come out. It was a few minutes, during which they watched others emerging – audience members who recognized them and looked over with interest, and people from neighboring courtrooms as other cases reached a closing point. The attorney finally pushed through the double doors, pulling her briefcase and accordion file folders, which she'd loaded onto a wheeled cart. She walked directly to them.

'Gentlemen. That went well, thank you.'

'The work you did with us yesterday was beneficial,' Eric said.

Scott added, 'I'd go as far as crucial.'

She looked at him. 'I want to compliment you on keeping a cool head during cross, Agent Houston.'

He nodded an acknowledgment. 'We're good to leave at this point?'

'Yes,' she said. 'I don't know if you caught it but we're moving on to other witnesses after the lunch break. And since you're not defense witnesses, we shouldn't see you back here.' She put her hand out in parting. 'Thanks again and safe travels back to LA.'

Eric shook her hand. 'We look forward to hearing that you secured the conviction.'

'Based on the jurors' attentiveness so far, it's looking good,' she said.

As Scott walked with Eric down the main staircase to rejoin their car, he checked his watch. Provided their flight was on time, he would be home in six hours. That included transit time to and from airports. He would shower and shave and then he'd be ringing Jayne's doorbell.

*

Joseph backed the car down his friend's driveway. He was so obliging, this guy; any time Joseph explained that he wanted to do something to surprise his wife or kids and needed a car to do it, his friend – unmarried and unsuspecting – offered up the key to his second vehicle. Joseph always apologized, saying that he intended to get another car but would probably wait until the kids were old enough to learn how to drive. His buddy would laugh and smile and hand over his key just as he had this time.

Now Joseph pulled the car into the gas station and executed the three-point turn needed to maneuver into the lane for the automatic car wash stall. He'd chosen this place because it took only one car at a time, parked, while the machine worked its way around the outside. He paid for a deluxe wash so he would have the maximum time. The machine said, 'Please pull forward.' Once in the stall, he waited for the machine to say, 'Your car wash is about to start; a pre-soak applicator is now being applied' and then he pulled the items out of his bag.

For the several minutes it took for the wash to go through the cycles, during which it was impossible for anyone to see into the car what with all the water flying around and the brushes and arms encircling the vehicle, Joseph applied the decals to the windows, dressed the dash with maps and old paper coffee cups and placed the business clothes onto the backseat. By the time the wash was done, he was done.

The machine said, 'Your car wash is complete. Thank you for using our car wash.' Joseph drove out of the stall in a vehicle that no longer looked like the featureless spare car of his friend. It was now the well-loved and well-traveled vehicle of someone else entirely. The only thing left was to come up alongside Lander and Hall.

22

In the small room adjacent to the autopsy suite of the King County Medical Examiner's office, Steelie tapped her pencil against her notepad. She said, 'I've got two files where the age is right but they refer to scars of parturition.'

Jayne looked up from where she was making notes. 'Those are controversial . . .'

'I know.' Steelie tilted her head. 'How about this: since Alex didn't have a uterus, I'll back-burner these two for now and go for remains where the anthro didn't think pitting in the pelvis meant the woman had carried a fetus or given birth.'

'Makes sense.'

When they had each completed one pass over their stack of files, they traded stacks in order to check each other's take on the strength of the possible match for Alex as well as provide some validation for their observations.

By the end of the second pass, they had flagged a total of three potential matches for Alex. One was a set of remains that had been found in the vicinity of where the Green River Serial Killer had left some of his victims' bodies but the bones had been determined to be male. Two were from remains determined to be female, both categorized as Caucasoid and within the height and age range for Alex, but they were found in other parts of the county. Because the determinations of age and stature were dependent on a prior sex determination of binary female/male, Jayne and Steelie's possible matches had a decent margin for error for a person with Alex's attributes.

It was just before noon when Olivia came to get them. She ushered them out into the hall. 'Any luck?'

'Maybe,' Steelie said brightly. 'We have a list of three possibles.'

'My boss can handle three,' Olivia said as she went into her office and sat down heavily behind her desk.

Jayne took a seat. 'How was the morning in the suite?'

'If it wasn't for having an awesome assistant like Umar and our fantastic techs, I'd wonder about getting through the afternoon.'

'That bad?'

'Multi-car accident. Five decedents spread across all the tables.'

'Oh, man,' Steelie said.

'I only had one of them. Then there was the accidental drowning. A newbie kayaker. Didn't know how to handle the wake of a so-called pleasure boat. Let me not go on.'

A knock came at the door but it opened almost simultaneously. Jayne turned to see a young man enter. His hair was a luxuriously wavy, almost curly type that Jayne imagined would produce a tremendous beard but his light-brown skin was clean-shaven. His attentive brown eyes were on Olivia as he held up a plastic bag that looked like take-out.

Olivia hailed him. 'Umar, what do I owe you? And meet Steelie and Jayne.'

He put the bag on the desk and turned to shake hands. 'The famous Lander and Hall,' he said. 'Nice to meet you.'

Jayne said, 'Thanks very much for adding the Ayers dental to NCIC.'

'No problem.' He turned back to Olivia. 'I used the five dollars you had left over from last time so it's just seven dollars.' He reached into the pocket of his white lab coat, pulled out a can of Coca-Cola and put it on the desk. 'And the machine still didn't have root beer.'

'I'm starting to get used to Coke at this point. Kinda like it.' Olivia was digging around in her purse. 'So, Jayne and Steelie have three possibles out of our backlog.'

Umar's eyebrows went up. 'That's exciting. I wonder if . . .' He looked questioningly at Olivia.

She held out the cash. 'If this afternoon goes well, I can finish up by myself and you can get started on their list. But only if it goes well.'

He smiled, took the money and headed for the door, saying goodbye to Jayne and Steelie as he went.

Olivia said, 'Umar studied forensic anthropology and only switched to pathology when he found out there are, like, no jobs. So he's loving this chance to follow up on the Ayers case. He's already asked me if I know when you're going to hire a third FA at Thirty-Two One.'

'From his lips to God's ears,' Jayne said.

'More like SSA Turner's ears, but whatever,' Steelie added as she and Jayne got up to leave.

Olivia came around to give them quick goodbye hugs. 'You'll hear from me direct if we don't get any matches. But if we *do* get an ID, my office automatically notifies

Missing Persons plus Homicide at Seattle PD if they're the originating agency on the misper report. Then we notify the family direct and then you two. The usual deal.'

Once Steelie was navigating their rental car back to their hotel, Jayne checked her phone for messages. There was one from Carol but before she could listen to it, the phone rang.

She alerted Steelie: 'Graham.'

When she greeted him, he sounded expectant. 'G'day, Jayne. I was hoping you could tell me what you found out this morning?'

Jayne didn't want to get his hopes up too high. 'Hi, Graham. It's very hard to say but we could hear something later today or tomorrow.'

She heard him suck in his breath. 'Well, Mum and I have been waiting all this time, I reckon we can wait another day. Listen. Remember I said that I met with my sister's bloke? Turns out he's still holdin' a candle for 'er; never married since then. And he told me he'd always thought Alex got lost when she went out to this nature reserve – some kind of beauty spot she told him reminded her of home.'

'He thinks she succumbed to the elements out there?'

'That's it.'

Jayne felt skeptical. 'Did he pass this information on to the police at the time? Because we were able to get a copy of the missing person report on Alex and there wasn't anything in there about possible hiking accidents.'

'He reported it *and* looked for her himself. No luck. But, look, after gettin' his take on things and him being so close to Alex, I can see how a hiking accident explains everything. He's offered to take all of us through the reserve today. I thought you could point out likely places my sister might've got into strife, maybe even spot her body?'

Jayne thought that was unlikely but not impossible – and she'd heard the hopeful lift in Graham's voice. She looked at her watch. They could do this, barring developments at the ME's office. 'That should be fine, Graham, but stand by a second.' She muted the phone and relayed the request to Steelie, expecting to be met with doubt.

But Steelie didn't question it. 'Fine by me.'

Jayne looked at her for a second and decided that Steelie hadn't really engaged with the idea of an afternoon of hiking because her mind was on something else, namely Matthew West.

Jayne resumed her call with Graham. He explained that Riley would drive him to the nature reserve so they could all meet there and he gave her the location.

'Oh, Jayne,' Graham said. 'One more thing. I haven't mentioned anything to Riley about Alex being born both female and male. Out of respect for her wishes. You won't . . .?'

'No, we won't. We wouldn't anyway but I'm glad that we're confirming this.'

'Good on ya, Jayne. See you there.'

Jayne hung up and dialed Carol as she said to Steelie, 'Graham just said "gudonya".'

Steelie smiled. 'I love his accent.'

Jayne spoke into the phone. 'Hi, Carol. I haven't heard your message yet. Anything up?'

'Oh, I was just checking in on you two,' Carol said. 'We've received dental X-rays for the new case from San

Diego. There was a note inside from the father asking if we would be good enough to send a copy to San Diego Missing Persons once they're digitized.'

Jayne nodded. 'Okay, Steelie will do that when we're back tomorrow.'

'You think you'll come in?'

'It's a morning flight and it's direct so we'll have time to come in for a few hours in the afternoon.'

'Well, let me know when you've landed at Burbank. It'll be good to have you two back on home turf again.'

Jayne updated Carol on their movements for the afternoon, giving her the name and location of the nature reserve they were heading to outside Seattle. She added, 'There's a chance King County will call as soon as this afternoon with news about Alex. If they can't get either me or Steelie for some reason, they know to call you and leave a detailed message.'

'I'll be here.'

'But you *can* leave for lunch, Carol. We left you the petty cash expressly for that reason.'

'I know but I brought lunch!'

'Oh, alright, fine then. We're going to get lunch ourselves. Talk to you later.'

As Jayne hung up, Steelie pulled into the parking lot of a place that looked like a food court.

Steelie said, 'Sandwiches? We can get them to go.'

'Let's get some for Graham and Alex's boyfriend as well. Just in case.'

When they pulled into the nature reserve's large dirt parking area forty minutes later, they saw Graham leaning against the side of a Saturn station wagon with a lanky, good-looking man in his mid-forties or even as much as fifty who Jayne took to be Riley. She had to remind herself that he would have been in his late twenties when Alex knew him. He was wearing what seemed to be a Seattle uniform of plaid shirt, cargo pants and a backpack.

Steelie parked alongside them although there were no other cars around; she could have parked anywhere. From the lot, they could see that the reserve sloped upwards and the mixture of deciduous and evergreen trees eventually gave way to rocky peaks.

Graham made the introductions. Riley was friendly but he had a lot of questions.

As everyone strapped on their backpacks, he said, 'Wouldn't the coroner have identified Alex by now if they had her body?'

'It can be complex,' Jayne said. She was going to honor Graham's wishes and refrain from expounding on issues relating to people who could fall through the cracks of postmortem systems because their remains could check more than one box for sex.

'Because that's the reason I've always thought she's out here somewhere.' Riley gestured behind him. 'She loved this place.'

Graham said, 'I've been telling Riley that you might have new ways to identify Alex whenever she's found.'

Riley started toward the trailhead. 'Doesn't the coroner have forensic anthropologists like you?'

'They do,' Steelie confirmed. 'But they can only try to make IDs against police missing person reports, which are skewed toward finding people who are still alive. Different foci; mixed results.'

Jayne added, 'What our organization does is spend a bit more time building a forensic interpretation of the missing person's life with the goal of identifying them if they're later found dead.'

'Hm!' Riley said. 'Interesting! And is there a lot of call for your kind of work?'

'I'd say so. Nationwide, unidentified bodies number a conservative 40,000.'

Riley whistled.

Steelie said, 'And there's the war dead that forensic scientists are still identifying, going back to the Korean War, and then the ones who no one is even trying to identify. The list goes on.'

Graham exclaimed, 'Strewth!'

Trying to make things more convivial, Jayne said, 'What do you do, Riley?'

'I manage a coffee and tea bar. What else, in Seattle?' He smiled. 'But I'd love to treat you all to a drink there after this – anything from the menu. I'd like to toast Alex in my own small way.'

*

Carol was wrapping up her lunch leftovers and going through the mail that had just been delivered to the Agency when the phone rang. She recognized the area code as that of Seattle and answered, expecting it to be the King County Medical Examiner's office.

Instead, she heard: 'This is Detective Resden, Seattle

Police Department, calling for . . . let's see . . . Jayne Hall or Steelie Lander.'

'Both Ms. Hall and Ms. Lander are out of the office but I can get a message to them.'

The detective sounded unconcerned. 'If you could just have them call me back on this number.'

Carol noted the number and called Jayne. There was no answer. In fact, the cell rang and rang before going to voicemail, so she knew that Jayne hadn't simply been on the other line. If she had been, Carol's call would've gone straight to voicemail. She left a message and called Steelie. The same situation.

In her voicemail for Steelie, Carol said she assumed there was limited cell phone service at the nature reserve, as though that made everything okay. But after she hung up, Carol realized that being out of contact was very much not okay, especially if anything were to happen, like an accident. Or worse. If there was one thing she'd learned in her short time with Jayne and Steelie, it was that their work brought them into contact with the unsavory and the unexpected. They crossed paths with people at the edges and hiding in the dark, just like the cops Carol herself used to counsel. But those officers had badges and guns. What did Jayne and Steelie have besides their wits?

23

Following Riley up the increasingly steep path, Graham said, 'I'm glad I'm wearing my Blunnies.'

'Ah, yes!' Riley called back over his shoulder. 'The legendary Blundstone boots. Alex was always talking about how you lived in them. She told me about a – what was it? A herdsman? In your Blunnies one time.'

'A huntsman,' Graham corrected. 'It's a deadly spider!'

'That's the one! A huntsman! But Alex said it *wasn't* poisonous.'

'Mate, it's so big, it scares you to death.'

Everyone laughed at Graham's joke, but then Graham stopped short. Riley hadn't noticed and was still striding off but Jayne and Steelie were behind Graham. Jayne put a hand to his back to comfort him and he wiped his face.

When Riley realized they'd stopped, he came back, his face showing concern. 'Are you okay?' When Graham couldn't readily reply, Riley looked to Jayne for explanation.

She shook her head.

He seemed to get it then. 'I'm sorry. I shouldn't have just started reminiscing about Alex like that.'

Graham sniffed and pulled his sunglasses down in front of his eyes. 'Mate, don't apologize. I just had a moment there when I thought, I can't wait to tell Alex what a piss-up time I had with her bloke. Then I remembered we were out here looking for her body.'

'I'm really sorry. About everything,' Riley said softly.

Graham sniffed. 'To be honest, I break down like this about m'sister once a week.'

Riley pursed his lips. 'I was the same at first. And then, one year, I was out here, doing a search, and I just felt like Alex was here. And as much as it hurts that she's gone, the fact that she loved this place has made it easier to bear. I don't know if that will help you the way it did me.'

Graham produced a weak smile. 'I can always hope.'

Steelie said, 'Maybe you should eat the sandwich we brought you now? We can wait.'

'A sanger would go down a treat, but I can walk and eat; do it on the farm every day.' He put his shoulders back. 'Let's keep going, if you girls don't mind?'

*

When Carol couldn't reach Jayne or Steelie after trying several more times, she decided to call the Seattle detective back. After all, she'd been told to expect a call from the medical examiner's office, not the police. It was bothering her that she didn't know what the call had been about. She wanted to assess its importance. She wanted to do something. So she dialed the number and identified herself.

'Detective, it occurred to me that I should let you know that Jayne and Steelie are in fact in Seattle but I haven't been able to reach them by phone.'

'Are you concerned for their safety for some reason?'

Carol was familiar with this kind of law-enforcement-speak, where the police officer puts the onus on the caller to either declare an emergency or risk revealing their pre-existing paranoia. She said firmly, 'It is out of character but I wasn't sure if the location was the issue.'

'What's the location?'

Carol gave the name of the nature reserve.

The detective assured, 'I wouldn't worry. There's no cell reception in most of that park.'

Carol felt relief. 'Ah, I see. Thank you. Before you go, I wanted to ask if you were trying to reach them in relation to Alex or Graham Ayers? Are you from Homicide?'

'Yes?' The detective's tone was wary now.

Carol felt sure that it would be important for the detective to be in touch with Jayne and Steelie sooner rather than later and it was up to her to connect the dots. 'Well, both scientists are with Alex Ayers' brother, Graham, and Alex's boyfriend, Riley, who was taking them to the reserve to—'

'Just a moment,' Detective Resden interrupted roughly, but her voice became muffled as she called out to someone while apparently covering her mouthpiece.

Carol could just make out that there were raised voices and a sense of urgency. She automatically stood up when she heard the tail end of the detective's sentence: '. . .and get the Park Service on it *now*.'

Then Resden's voice was back with her. Carol could tell that the detective was on foot and moving fast. She was talking fast, too. 'Carol, you said? Here's the situation. You may or may not be aware that about an hour ago we got a positive ID on Alex Ayers from the King County ME's office. The ID reactivated the status of a person of interest on what had been a cold case. That person is a possible threat to your colleagues.'

Carol felt her heart pumping painfully in her chest. 'Oh my goodness.' She grabbed the edge of her desk because her knees felt weak.

Resden said, 'We are deploying as we speak and we have Park Service sending out a drone to locate them, hopefully faster. Let me give you an additional phone number you can use to get a message to me in case you hear from your colleagues.'

Carol sat down to transcribe the number but her hand was shaking so much that her writing was barely legible. Through the phone, she heard a siren start up. The detective directed someone to '*Drive*,' before addressing Carol again.

'I need their cell phone numbers, any details on their appearance and clothing, if they have a rental car and any other information you have that will help us locate them.'

After Carol had wracked her brain for everything she could think of, the detective rang off.

Carol couldn't believe that she was sitting in the calm reception room at the Agency with Fitzgerald the aloe tree sitting placidly in the corner. Her hands were still shaking. She got up and put the 'Closed' sign on the door. Then she paced, feeling anxious and helpless, until she had an idea. She leaned over the counter to her desk and pulled up the Post-it of emergency numbers Jayne had left for her before flying to Atlanta for the FBI mobile operation. She ignored the numbers for Jayne and Steelie's respective parents and ran her finger down to Scott's information. She dialed. He didn't answer and she left a rather frantic and garbled message asking him to call her back as soon as he could. Then she called Eric. She had to leave a message again but this time she was more coherent. Calls made, she took a deep breath and exhaled as slowly as she could. She was trained in how to stay calm, but it was taking a conscious effort to do so now.

*

Just before the Alaska Airlines flight attendant notified the passengers that they could turn on their cell phones as they taxied into the airport in Seattle, Scott powered his back up. He saw he'd missed a call from Agency 32/1 – Eric said the same – and they listened to their voicemails. Scott cut his off before it was complete and started dialing Carol, indicating to Eric that he was going to conference him in. Eric clicked over and they heard Carol's voice.

'I'm so relieved to hear from you, Scott. I'm so sorry to call—'

'What's going on, Carol?' He didn't want the embroidery, not when she was panicking like this.

Her words tumbled out. 'Jayne and Steelie are in Seattle with a client – they're actually with him and his sister's boyfriend – oh, it's too hard to explain but I've had a call from Seattle PD and they consider them to be in danger from a suspect and the problem is that they're in a place outside the city where there's no cell phone coverage and I can't reach them—'

While Carol had been talking, Scott had started to feel

uncomfortably restrained. Then he realized he was trying to catapult himself out of his seat while his seatbelt was still buckled. He got up, pulled his bag down one-handed from the overhead compartment and almost dropped it onto the head of the passenger in the row ahead of him. It wasn't his turn to disembark but he started moving toward the front of the airplane, willing people to move faster as he listened to Carol. He looked back for Eric. His partner was right behind him, phone to his ear but his eyes on Scott. He looked concerned but determined.

Scott put his phone to his chest and said to Eric, 'We're gonna need airport police and any federals they have here.'

Eric nodded and clicked out of their conference call. 'I'll see if we can track the BlackBerry Turner gave them.'

'Carol.' Scott gently but firmly cut through her cascade of words. 'What is the name of the officer from Seattle PD and which division are they in?'

Carol's voice was shaky. 'Detective Resden, Homicide. But she said that the Park Service would be helping too, with a drone.'

Scott was now walking behind Eric, who was moving fast through the terminal while saying in a loud voice, 'Move aside, please, federal agents,' as he pushed past members of the public, leaving an open wake for Scott to walk through unhindered.

'Good,' Scott said to Carol, already feeling reassured that others were treating this like the emergency he felt it was, despite not having all the details. 'Park Service is federal and they'll be on the scene quicker. When did Resden call you?'

'She first called about an hour ago but it was just fifteen minutes ago that I told her that Jayne and Steelie were at the park.'

Scott glanced at his watch. 'And when did you last hear from them?'

'It's probably been two hours since they started driving over but I don't even know how long it was supposed to take for them to get there!' She sounded like she was about to cry.

'Okay, listen, Carol.' Scott heard his calming tones like they were coming from outside his body. 'Eric and I just deplaned in Seattle on a layover—'

'You're in *Seattle*?'

'We're here.' Now his words were calming him. He glanced up at the sign above the door through which Eric had just disappeared. It read *Sea-Tac Air Support*. He took his first deep breath since Carol's call.

'I'll reach Resden and we'll get Seattle PD to take us to wherever this park is, but I'll be back in touch. Okay? I have to go now.' He holstered his phone and pushed through the door.

24

Now that Jayne and Steelie were in the part of the nature reserve that Riley had described as Alex's favorite hiking area, they were looking more carefully at the surroundings, using a forensic scientific interpretation of slopes, surfaces and crevices. The possible sites for accidents had been off to one side of a path that was narrowing as boulders started to outnumber trees. So far, Jayne and Steelie had found plenty of signs that birds, small animals and insects moved around the reserve but there were no signs of old bones, lost shoes or nearly disintegrated clothing. The place they were now moving into had more potential though, at the base of a large rock that Riley had described as having a table-like summit where Alex liked to stop for her nutrition breaks.

As Jayne and Steelie climbed downhill into the brush near the base of the rock, Riley waited with Graham up on the path. They could just hear Riley talking about what Alex had admired about the place. While Jayne probed the bushes, Steelie craned her neck to look up the short cliff face.

She spoke quietly so only Jayne would hear. 'I don't think a fall from up there would be fatal. Unless you landed headfirst.'

'You could easily break a leg, though.'

'Sure, but provided your mouth still worked, you could yell for help.'

'No one was looking for Alex at the time to hear her.'

Steelie gestured up the hill. 'Riley was.'

'True. Oh, look at this.' Jayne used her leg to push back one side of a shrub so Steelie could get closer.

'Aha. Definitely bony,' Steelie confirmed, sounding markedly interested.

Jayne started to feel excited because what they could see of the bone was also large enough to have come from a human. She handed Steelie a chopstick from the outer pocket of her backpack. 'Expose a bit more.'

As she took the chopstick, Steelie said, 'Thank you for letting me be the one who got to do the honors.'

She scraped the soil away from the bone. 'It's got curvature that could be femoral head, sized right for human. And even if it isn't Alex, it's someone. *Oh shit!*' The chopstick had functioned like a fulcrum and propelled the bone into the air, because it wasn't the sturdy head of a human femur. It was the lightweight skull of a non-human animal, which, having landed on top of the shrub, was clearly not fully round either.

Steelie was wiping her face and spluttering.

Jayne picked up the skull and turned it around. 'Well, that's that.'

'Fine for you to say,' Steelie muttered. 'I have a face full of dirt.'

'Been there.' Jayne settled the bone back under the shrub.

While Steelie looked for a kerchief in her backpack, Jayne completed the search of the area. She didn't find anything.

When they climbed back up to the path, Graham looked anxious. Behind him, Riley looked like he was trying to see if the anthropologists were carrying something.

Graham put a hand out to help lift Steelie up the last part. 'I heard one of you shout. You found something?'

'No, sorry,' Steelie said.

Jayne felt awkward. Were they sorry they hadn't found his sister or was it a good thing because it meant maybe she hadn't died out here in this wilderness? When she got close enough, she said, 'We're willing to carry on until we lose the light.'

As Graham and Steelie started up the path, Riley extended his hand to Jayne.

She waved him off while getting her last foothold among the rocks. 'Thanks but I'm probably heavier than you!'

'Don't be silly.' He easily lifted her up and deposited her onto the path.

Jayne gasped; he'd made her feel light as a feather.

He made a show of taking his hands off her body. 'Not used to being manhandled, I'm guessing – liberated California woman like yourself? But we men are still good for some things.' He gave her a naughty grin and headed up after the others.

Rooted to the spot, Jayne thought, *What just happened?* That had felt completely out of step with Riley's Saturn-driving-Pacific-Northwest-baristo-ness. Then she realized that she was the one who'd taken all those disparate elements and made them add up to 'Sensitive New Age Guy'. But no SNAG had ever made her feel like this. As she followed a few paces behind Riley, she tried to figure out what the feeling was. And then she hit upon it. He'd made her feel female. And, given that she *was* female, why had that felt so upsetting?

*

Scott switched his phone's screen from the list of GPS coordinates to map mode. Jayne and Steelie, or their Bureau BlackBerry anyway, was on the move again and it didn't seem to matter what airspeed this Robinson 44 was flying at, he wasn't getting as close to them as he wanted to be. He looked out of the helicopter window. It was skimming the top of yet another forest. *Seattle, what the fuck?* He was still wondering how long this chopper ride would take and where they'd be able to land and just what the hell was happening to Jayne, when the trees abruptly disappeared. They had reached a clearing and the pilot was slowly spinning the chopper around as he landed it. During the revolution, Eric tapped Scott on the shoulder. He looked over and followed where Eric was pointing out the window on his side. A reassuringly large cluster of law enforcement and government vehicles, including ATVs and a dog handler's van, were well-hidden, parked under the trees. Further into the forest, Scott could just make out the caps and hats of the personnel that went with all the vehicles.

The pilot's voice came through their helmets. 'I have another call-out so my rotors will remain powered. Keep it low all the way out. Beyond where you think.'

'Roger,' Eric said into his microphone, unbuckling his harness and reaching for the door lock system.

'Thank you, sir,' Scott said.

The pilot turned his head and nodded. 'Copy.'

Scott ran in a crouch behind Eric, only coming up to full height once they heard the helicopter lifting off. Scott looked back at it, feeling anxious because there was a chance they might need a chopper for a medical evacuation if this operation went sideways. Which brought his mind back to Detective Hannah Resden. She had sounded capable and efficient when he'd called her but there was a big difference between the phone and the field.

He caught up with Eric and was gratified to see that a woman with Resden's commanding voice had the attention of the large group of people standing around a table where a laminated map took up most of the surface. Even though she was wearing a bulky bulletproof vest, it was clear she was a petite woman despite the big voice. Her tousled dark hair was cut into a short back and sides that put a square jaw and high cheekbones on show. Also on show, Scott realized as he got closer, were a pair of intelligent dark eyes. She was making assignments as she handed out walky-talkies with call sign labels taped onto them. She looked up as Eric walked over, hand outstretched.

'Special Agent Eric Ramos, FBI.'

She took his hand. 'Detective Hannah Resden, Seattle PD.' She switched her glance to Scott.

He liked her demeanor first and her strong grip next. 'SA Scott Houston, FBI. What do you have for us, Detective?'

She spoke rapidly. 'First I need your latest GPS coordinates for the target BlackBerry.'

Scott put his own BlackBerry in the center of the table

to display the GPS coordinate list. Immediately, two US Park Service security staff leaned in and transferred the new location coordinates to the map on the table. That made him feel good; like he'd done something to get to Jayne.

One of the Park Service people looked up at Resden. 'That broadly tallies with our heat sensor from the drone; they're moving and stopping in a northeasterly direction with increasing altitude.'

'Okay,' she said. 'Let me bring the agents up to speed. We've got heat readings for four individuals. We obviously don't know exactly who's holding that phone—'

'It's Jayne's – Ms. Hall's – Ms.—' Scott stumbled over his words but Resden was holding up her hand to stop him speaking anyway. He closed his mouth.

She said, 'In case the phone is no longer with Misses Hall or Lander but is being used by the perp to lure us away from them, we have a team that will split off to address that location.'

Scott almost spoke over her. 'You said "no longer". Does that mean you got confirmation earlier that the women were with the phone?'

'We did—'

'Visual?'

When she nodded, Scott got in what he really wanted to know. 'Ambulatory?'

'They were alive, Agent Houston. But we can't assume the phone is still with them.'

Scott inhaled sharply. The less nice way of saying that was 'We can't assume they're still alive.' He rubbed his lips hard. He wanted – needed – to take over this operation. But none of the people standing around the table were his people; no one was going to listen to him. All he would be doing was acting like a hothead. A rebellious voice in his head said, *Maybe that's just me! I* am *a hothead and I'm going to own it*. He glanced at Eric, who gave him a stare that Scott read easily: *Resden's good, so calm the fuck down.*

But it was as though Resden had picked up on Scott's agitation. She was ready to move out. 'From here and using ATVs, it will only take two minutes to get close to their location, but then we go in on foot to avoid making noise. We want to get eyes on the situation before we move in. Since our targets are mobile, we need you feeding us any GPS info live, Agent Houston.'

She handed him an earpiece and a portable radio and then held out the same gear to Eric. 'Every move they make, you radio everyone. Likewise, Parks, if your heat readings show movement, radio everyone because those will be coming through a hair faster than GPS.'

Scott liked that Resden knew that satellite data was slightly delayed. Eric was right; she was good. But he wished he could get a look at the Park Service visuals. He wanted to see Jayne and Steelie walking on their own two feet for himself.

Resden was giving last instructions. 'Remember what I said at the top. This is a rescue operation but we believe a suspect capable of lethal force is at large in the reserve. We want him alive but not at the cost of any of our asses. Keep your eyes peeled, your voices low and your Kevlar on.'

People immediately began moving toward the ATVs, checking their gear and holstering radios.

Looking at Eric and Scott, Resden said, 'I've got protective gear for you.' As they followed her to her vehicle, she said, 'What are you holding?'

'Glock 22s,' Eric said.

She nodded. When they got to a cruiser, she popped the trunk. Eric and Scott both reared back slightly: it looked like a publicity photo from a gun buy-back event. The only thing not immediately visible in Resden's arsenal was a rocket-propelled grenade launcher.

She brought out rifles and bulletproof vests for the agents.

Scott strapped in and said, 'Detective, you said you were requesting a helicopter?'

She snorted derisively as she slammed the trunk closed. 'I did and the brass told me to call back when I actually had an emergency. That's the problem with being from Homicide. They expect my vics to be dead.' She headed toward the ATVs.

Scott cursed under his breath, muted Resden's team radio and made a call on his Bureau phone.

*

'There's going to be a place up ahead where we have to kind of squeeze between two large boulders,' Riley said to the others, pointing. 'It looks tight but if you carry your backpack in your hand and kind of do one foot at a time, it's doable. Or you could turn sideways like I'm going to.'

Jayne watched Riley slip through the gap. *Typical male pelvis*, she thought. Once through, he was out of sight because the path curved uphill again but Jayne could hear him calling to her with words of encouragement. She indicated to Steelie and Graham that she'd go next, but as she approached the gap in the rocks, she wasn't sure she was slim enough to get through. She realized with a start that if Alex used to go through here with Riley, she'd been thinner than in the last photo Graham had of her.

Jayne took off her backpack, wedged her right foot into the space and put her hands onto the faces of the boulders on either side. They were incredibly smooth and met at the ground so tightly that only the smallest blades of grass were growing there. She hoisted herself up, trying to figure out if she should get her left foot into the wedge as well or try to step through, twisting her hips as Riley had, when something whizzed past her and impacted the rock face to her right.

From behind her, Steelie called up with a note of concern. 'What was that?'

Frowning, Jayne examined the rock face next to her. There was a divot in it. *Funny how that looks like a projectile hit it*. Then something else hit the rock and ricocheted behind her. This time, Graham called out in alarm.

'Some bush pig's takin' the piss! That's a bleedin' bullet!'

Jayne couldn't compute. She hadn't heard a weapon being fired. But she hastily reversed out of the wedge, almost falling, and looked to where Graham was pointing. It was definitely a misshapen bullet. She'd seen enough of them in mass grave sites to know. Her panic was instantaneous and she made eye contact with Steelie, who was already crouching, eyes darting this way and that. Jayne grabbed her backpack and started pushing Graham and Steelie back while yelling, 'Run! Back, back!'

The three of them moved fast. Then Jayne realized that they were leaving Riley behind. She yelled out, hoping he would hear her. 'Riley! Take cover! Someone's shooting!'

Jayne felt her pack bouncing up and down on her back as she ran, slipping on loose pebbles, afraid to look behind her but knowing she should check on Riley. She forced herself to look back.

Riley *was* behind them but he wasn't running. His feet were planted as he drew some kind of weapon level with his eyes. Jayne saw his head tilt to an odd angle and his mouth grimace into a thin line. He was aiming.

Jayne screamed, 'Down, get down, zigzag!' as she darted left. Steelie and Graham scattered to different places as something hissed through the air space where they'd just been. Still running at full tilt, Jayne's lungs were screaming and her throat was burning, but they were still alive. The trees around them barely had lower branches, they were just trunks going all the way up to heaven, it seemed, with a carpet of needles below and nowhere to hide. She chanced another look back for Riley. He was gone from her line of sight but she knew he'd be back.

Up ahead, Steelie suddenly changed course and yelled, 'Follow me!'

Jayne immediately saw what Steelie was planning. A cluster of bushes had grown together to form a thicket but it was tall enough and wide enough for them to hide in. If they could *get in*. Steelie dove into it, exclaiming as she pushed resistant vegetation aside. Graham was right behind her, trying to help by pushing his backpack in front of him, and then Jayne was pushing her way in, getting slapped in the face by flexible branches as they rebounded off Graham. Closing her eyes, Jayne propelled herself forward blindly, but then someone strong pulled her to the ground. As she went down, she was faced with the sickening reality that Riley had been one step ahead of them the whole time. He clamped a hand over her mouth just before she could scream.

25

Jayne pulled hard at the fingers over her mouth, knowing that she was in the fight of her life, trying to get sound to carry beyond the enclosing hand. Face down as she was, she couldn't see Steelie or Graham and didn't know why they weren't screaming. What had Riley done to them? She tried to turn over and then Riley helped her, which was confusing. She felt alarm. What was he playing at?

She managed to twist and look up. But it wasn't Riley. It was Scott. Her head was actually in his lap. *I've died*, was her first thought. *I'm dreaming*, was her next. But then Scott lifted his hand from her mouth and held a finger to his own lips to indicate that she needed to stay quiet. Only then did Jayne take in the fact that he was wearing a flak jacket and holding a rifle in his other hand. She felt tears springing to her eyes as she made sense of it. He'd come to rescue her. She didn't know how he'd found her or if he'd be going back to his wife after this, but he was here now. She struggled to stifle the sob of relief that suddenly rose up in her throat. He squeezed her hand and then indicated that she should get behind him. As he helped her to her knees, she saw that Steelie and Graham were already huddled deeper in the vegetation behind Scott, looking stressed and disheveled, still breathing as though they were running.

As Jayne hunched past Scott, she heard him murmur something. She turned around to face him, Steelie and Graham just behind her, and saw that he was talking into his earpiece. Then he signaled them with his hands but Jayne didn't know what the signals meant. The next thing she knew, Scott was silently sliding the rifle into the vegetation facing the direction that they had come from a minute earlier.

Jayne stared, trying to see what Scott could see. And then she heard the noise. It was the unhurried step of a person who wasn't concerned about the crunching pine cones and snapping twigs. In fact, the person was whistling. The sound was odd and out of place, the sort of thing that would make a deer stop in its tracks to listen before darting away. *Riley?*

Jayne saw him through the shrubbery.

Riley, walking with an unusual rifle in front of him, its long barrel pointed toward the ground as he loaded ammunition. Jayne didn't understand why Scott wasn't just shooting him. Then she saw Eric plus many people in different uniforms advancing silently from behind Riley at different angles, weapons drawn. But when were they going to take him down? Jayne couldn't stand it. They were going to get shot before anyone did anything! Riley lifted the rifle, did that odd tilt with his head again and aimed right at the bush where they'd taken cover. Jayne was shaking uncontrollably, but suddenly Eric launched and took Riley down to the ground in a tackle. There was a flurry of noise and shouting and Jayne couldn't see what was happening. Then she heard Eric's voice: 'Suspect is down!'

Scott lowered his rifle and Jayne heard Graham sob. *Our client!* She turned around to check on him. His hands were over his face, sunglasses scratched and askew on the front of his shirt, hair almost as thick with vegetation as the thicket around them. Steelie's hair was just as bad but Jayne couldn't understand why she was just lying back on the vegetation, looking off to the side at nothing. Then Jayne saw the blood. Steelie's shirt was soaked through and it was still coming.

Jayne scrambled toward Steelie in a panic, trying to see her face. Steelie's mouth was open but her eyes were actually closed. She looked drained and lifeless.

Jayne screamed with unintelligible noise that burned her throat as it came out.

Scott came over and bodily moved her out of the way. He pulled up Steelie's shirt to find the wound and grimaced at the ragged flesh around the left side of her torso. Steelie's eyes stayed closed and her limbs were motionless. Scott shouted toward the sky, 'We need a medic!'

He held his fingers to Steelie's neck and then her wrist.

Jayne tried to speak. 'Is she . . . can you feel her pulse?'

But Scott was speaking into his earpiece. 'Resden, we're gonna need that bird.'

A helicopter? Jayne felt tears leaking from her eyes.

A dark-haired woman with a police badge clipped to her bullet-proof vest came crashing through the shrubbery, holding a red bag with a white cross on it. She glanced at Jayne and Graham and then crouched next to Scott. While they wrapped some kind of bandage around Steelie's inert body, there was the noise of a chainsaw chopping through vegetation and the thicket opened up next to them as a park ranger was pruning off a section with quick, efficient movements. When the ranger turned off the chainsaw, she shoved barriers into the gap to keep the opening clear. Another ranger ran up with a flimsy portable stretcher and he sent it toward the policewoman.

Scott took over. 'Jayne and – what's your name?'

Graham tried to speak but only a croak came out.

'Graham. Our client,' Jayne managed to say. 'From Australia,' she added, feeling idiotic.

'Jayne and Graham,' Scott said. 'We'll need your help to lift Steelie's head and shoulders onto the stretcher while we get her feet on board over here. We're going to lift her on my count and get her out of these bushes. Then other people will carry her to the chopper. Jayne: you will go with her. Do you understand?'

She nodded and helped Graham to lift Steelie onto the stretcher, trying not to panic over the blood and the way Steelie's eyes were now half-open but unseeing. Once they had fixed the stretcher's straps over Steelie's light frame, they hunched their way out of the shrubbery, already able to hear the rotor noise of the approaching helicopter.

As soon as they were under the canopy of trees again, other people came and took over the stretcher from her and Graham while Scott stayed at the front, communicating with the policewoman while at a very fast walk. Jayne looked for Riley but didn't see him.

They followed everyone to the edge of a clearing up ahead where, sure enough, a large helicopter was landing with a huge amount of noise and wind, blades of grass flattening this way and that under the pressure. Even before the chopper had fully touched down, a door opened to emit someone in a flight suit with a first aid bag who ran in a crouch to meet the stretcher. Jayne stayed with Graham because she didn't know when she should approach.

It was only a minute before Scott called out to her, shouting over the rotor noise.

She started to run over and then remembered the rental car. Running back to Graham, she held out the keys. 'Someone might need these!'

He looked bewildered for a moment but then relieved, like it was good to have a task he could complete. He gave her a thumbs-up sign and she squeezed his arm.

She ran back toward the helicopter, her eyes on Scott. He was just turning from watching the paramedics load Steelie on board.

Jayne swallowed some saliva so she could try to make sound. She successfully shouted this time, 'Could you call Matt and tell him about Steelie, please?'

He nodded and squeezed her shoulder.

Eric ran up and shouted to her. 'We'll take care of your client! Don't worry!'

The person in the flight suit took her arm then, handing her a headset and indicating that she needed to put it on and get on board. She took a seat alongside the paramedic, who was hooking Steelie up to some kind of medical machine and an intravenous drip. Scott was talking but Jayne couldn't hear over the chopper blades and through the headset, and then he was leaving while someone clipped her into her safety harness. As the helicopter lifted off the ground, the side door was still open and Jayne watched Scott become ever smaller. He was running back into the forested area, Eric at his side, and she felt tears of relief and regret begin to overflow.

26

Jayne sat as though stuck to the chair outside Steelie's room in the hospital's post-operative recovery ward. It was quiet here, but down the hall at the nurse's station, there was a hum of activity. Jayne felt tired, knew she was covered in dirt and there were probably still leaves in her hair. The past several hours felt like they had taken several days, between the helicopter ride, watching Steelie being rushed into the operating room, and then having to wait in a windowless area where cell phone use was prohibited. She'd lost her connection to daylight or sense of time – even to people. Until she'd been ushered to this hallway.

Here, she could power up her phone but not yet visit Steelie, who was still under the effects of the anesthesia. Seeing all the missed calls from Carol, Jayne had called her first and discovered that Carol, in typical emergency-efficiency mode, had already rescheduled Jayne and Steelie's flights and contacted their respective parents, all because she had been updated by Scott.

Scott, Jayne mulled. Sitting in this unfamiliar place, in an unfamiliar city, after facing her own mortality, Jayne felt as though she was getting a long view across space and time on their relationship. She saw how their five-year slow burn had ignited that summer into something that was almost too good to be true. Then she saw how Gene's comment on the hillside in San Antonio had sown a seed of doubt that had bloomed grotesquely in her mind.

She saw something else, too: Scott not in relation to her, but in relation to his job. She had a vague recollection that Bureau agents were subject to a morality clause. It was something she'd heard newly minted agents talking about while she and Steelie had been at Quantico. Something about how agents could jeopardize their job if they were married but had an affair, that even something like that could be used be used by foreign agents or criminals to blackmail FBI agents for access to federal investigations.

Which then made Jayne think back to the *way* SSA Turner had asked Scott if he was having a relationship with her. Had Turner's question represented more than just a conflict issue for the MOU? Like, Turner knew Scott's relationship with her was extramarital and therefore a disciplinary issue or a firing offense? Jayne immediately imagined Scott *not* getting divorced and returning to Callista. She squeezed her eyelids shut to try to banish that image.

She opened them when she heard the elevator doors down the hall. A well-dressed man in his thirties stepped out, hurriedly walked away to the right and then turned around, his expression one of concern. It was Matthew West.

Jayne almost cried with happiness. His was the first familiar face Jayne had seen in hours. She felt like running to meet him, like something from a film. He strode quickly over to her but she almost fell into his arms when she stood unsteadily. They hugged each other beyond any familiarity they'd ever had and then Jayne started crying, not just about Steelie but about Scott, and Scott and Callista, and Matt was patting her on the back, saying, 'Sh, sh, sh, sh, sh' like she was a baby and that made her cry even harder.

*

When the Seattle police officer offered Scott a chair in the listening post adjacent to the interrogation room, Scott shook his head in a mute acknowledgment. He wouldn't be able to sit down while listening to Detective Resden pull the confession out of Riley Joseph. Well, 'pull' was too strong a word. Joseph was talking. He was calm, too calm. Or maybe that was just his face. Almost expressionless even as he spoke. A few scratches from being face-down on some pine needles, hair a little mussed, but that was it.

'What'd I miss?' Scott asked Eric, nodding toward the two-way glass.

Eric stood up from his chair, a file in his hand. 'They only got him in here from processing a few minutes ago. He's said he wants to make a confession on the promise that certain details will be kept out of the media, for the sake of his family. Resden's doing the paperwork now.'

He gestured at Scott's BlackBerry. 'How'd it go with Turner?'

Scott tried to find the right word to characterize the debriefing their boss had just put him through. 'It was . . . thorough.'

'Well, obviously, 'cause it's Turner. So?'

'He's at the i-dotting and t-crossing stage of looking into the conflict-of-interest stuff. Made it clear it wasn't over until he said it was. But he did say he wouldn't have facilitated the medevac helicopter for Steelie if he wasn't confident that we're still in our lane with the MOU. Speaking of Steelie, what have you heard?'

'She's still in surgery but everyone's optimistic.'

'Jayne called?' Scott knew he hadn't missed any calls from her but it would have been a good sign if she'd called Eric.

Eric shook his head. 'Resden's getting updates direct from the hospital.'

Scott peered through the glass at Riley Joseph, remembering him advancing on them with his rifle. 'So what's the deal with this guy?'

Eric waved a sheaf of papers he'd been holding in a folder. 'Resden gave me some pretty interesting reading.'

Scott glanced at the folder label. 'Alex Ayers? Is that his AKA?'

'No. Alex Ayers is Joseph's girlfriend. Or she was – almost twenty years ago. She went missing. Seattle PD liked Joseph for her disappearance but they weren't too hot and heavy about it because there was no sign of a struggle, an abduction, or, like, a body. No case for suspicious missing. In fact,' he pointed to the folder. 'She'd overstayed on a visitor visa from Australia and there was no movement on her passport. So the misper unit figured she'd gone to ground, moved cities.'

'Okay . . .' Scott tried to picture the man in the interrogation room being anyone's boyfriend. A few hours ago, he'd been hunting humans. Now he was coolly reading a police form like it was a newspaper.

'Fast forward to now,' Eric continued. 'Ayers' brother comes to Jayne and Steelie for help in finding her because the family had started thinking she'd been killed during the Green River situation. And today, unbeknownst to Thirty-Two One, they ID'd her.'

Scott looked at Eric intently. 'Homicide?'

'Presumably. But that's not the main thing: Jayne and Steelie ID'd her as Alex*ander* Ayers.'

Scott's brain shuffled these facts like a deck of cards. 'Oh, she was transgender or a cross-dresser or something?'

'No, intersex. Born both male and female but with enough of a penis for her parents to assign her a male identity. When she grew up, though, she was more into her female self.'

Scott looked back at Joseph, who was now signing some papers. 'Fine. But if Alexander was male, that meant he was in a same-sex relationship with our shooter, right? So what?'

Eric gave him a rueful smile, opened the folder and pointed at some photos paperclipped to the back flap. Scott saw a man who was unmistakably Riley Joseph in a small clutch of people yelling in opposition to the leading edge of a Seattle Pride march, judging from the banner. Joseph's arm was around a woman standing next to him. They were flourishing a flag that depicted the international symbols for male and female interlinked and encircled by a heart. Joseph was also clearly yelling at the moment the photo was taken, his mouth open right in the face of someone on the other side of the Pride banner.

Eric said, 'There's a bunch more photos but they're along the same lines. Going back to 1989.'

Scott grunted, 'He wouldn't be the first homophobic gay man.'

'Uh, yeah, he's a homophobic straight man, per his own rantings. That woman,' Eric tapped the woman linked with Joseph in the photo, 'is his wife.'

Scott reshuffled his mental cards again. 'He's straight, and murdered someone because . . . why?'

'Resden's take, per the file,' Eric fanned the air with the sheaf of papers, 'is that Joseph didn't know Alex was intersex – until he did.'

Scott drew breath to speak but Eric shook an index finger in the negative and indicated the two-way glass. A second detective had just joined Resden, carrying a file he placed in front of her along with some transparent plastic bags. Resden looked through the bags and then held one of them up and slightly behind her, apparently for the benefit of anyone in the viewing room. The bag held a small cardboard box with a label on it.

Eric read it out. 'Explosive ammo?'

'It is,' Scott confirmed. 'But unopened. See the seal?'

Eric nodded and activated the speaker that would allow them to hear the people in the interview room.

Resden had placed the bag with the others and begun speaking. 'Mr. Joseph, now that we have the preliminaries completed, I am confirming that the recording still continues under the same waiver of your right to an attorney that you signed earlier. When did your relationship with Alex Ayers begin?'

'First, as I said already, I'd prefer you to address me as Joseph O'Reilly.' His voice was melodious and his tone said he was at a job interview and he was pretty sure they wanted him for the position.

Resden rifled through some papers in the file and then examined a sheet. 'You haven't changed your name legally, though, have you? Because when we ran your fingerprints, you came back as Riley Joseph. So, I'm thinking you've never gone through the process of . . . y'know, actually changing your name.'

'Well, no, I didn't do it legally. But I've thought of myself as Joseph O'Reilly for the better part of twenty years.'

'Since 1989, by any chance?'

He gave her a thin smile. 'Yes, since about then.'

'Okey-doke,' Resden returned the paper to the file. 'Now that we've established that you're still Riley Joseph, we'll recommence. When did your relationship with Alex Ayers begin, Mr. Joseph?'

The suspect looked annoyed but then reset his expression. 'I was never in a relationship with an Alex Ayers.'

Resden pulled out another document, like she'd expected him to say this and was ready with a rebuttal. 'She told her family in a letter from 1989 that she was in a relationship with you. She called it, quote-unquote, serious.'

'That would have been part of his lies. I was conned by an Alexander Ayers. I was a mark. The victim, in fact.'

Resden sounded curious. 'Conned into what?'

Joseph looked incredulous that he had to explain this. 'Into a homosexual liaison, of course.'

'So, you *did* have a relationship with Alex Ayers.'

'You can keep calling him Alex if you want, but let the record show that his name was Alexander.' He jutted his chin toward the recording equipment. 'Let the record also show that he had proof of his manhood.'

Resden tilted her head in consideration. 'How do you know that? Did Alex show you this proof in the course of your relationship?'

Joseph gave a small laugh. 'You don't have to trick me into this, Detective. I'll tell you all about it. This was a righteous kill.'

Scott heard Eric mutter an expletive.

Resden said, 'Then why didn't you take credit for it back when you killed her? Why'd you try to make her death look like she was a victim of the Green River killer?'

'Because I know how you people think. You won't see it as righteous. Just like you don't see Green River as righteous.' He smiled. 'I have proof of the righteousness of it: my two children. If I had confessed to killing Alexander, I never would have gotten married and never had my kids. Two lives. Two good lives for one shitty death. I think you'll find that the math works.'

Scott saw Resden give her colleague a look and the colleague, a man, took over. 'Okay, Joseph. Tell me how this righteous kill went down. I'm listening.'

Joseph closed his eyes briefly and inhaled. When he exhaled and opened his eyes, he pointedly looked only at the male detective. 'You know by now that Alexander Ayers was nothing but a dime-a-dozen illegal alien, a guy who couldn't hack it in his home country, who came out here to leach off of an American man. But I didn't know that at first. I thought I'd met a nice girl, a bit of a hottie actually, with that Aussie accent, who was surprisingly naïve about men and just working hard at a little job, living with another girl. I had no idea she was an illegal. And no idea what she had between her legs.' Joseph made a look of disgust.

'No idea. At all.' The detective's tone suggested he understood how easily this could have happened.

Joseph clearly felt encouraged. His face became animated, he spoke faster, his tone plaintive. 'None! Especially since she had a perky set of tits on her. I liked the look of those but never touched them. I'm not that kind of guy when I'm dating. I'm chivalrous. I take the girl out. I pay the bill. We did dinners, kayaking, strolls in the park hand in hand. Like that. Everything was going great and I was looking for a wife, especially a working woman who knows that she's supposed to hand her pay packet over to the man of the house.'

The detective was nodding like this all made sense to him. Scott had noticed that neither detective was calling attention to the fact that Joseph was switching Alex's sex from male to female depending on which part of his story he was telling.

Joseph was still talking. 'That's what I liked about Alex: she wasn't afraid of work even though I could tell she wanted to get married. So, after an appropriate interval, I bought a little ring – not an engagement ring but a promise ring. Enough to get her sweet, let me touch her tits, maybe even take her to bed, get a little taste of what I'd be getting for the rest of my life. And would you believe it, the bitch let me put that ring on her!'

He was ogling the detective like he would understand his outrage, but it was Resden who spoke. 'Is that when it happened, Riley? When you gave her the ring?'

He looked at her like he'd seen a ghost. 'How'd you know?'

'I guess I understand how upset you'd be if she took the ring but then didn't give you anything for it.'

His eyes widened with surprise. 'Yes! That's right! I had to spend my money on the ring and she lets me put it on her finger, tears of happiness and the whole deal, and just when I'm about ready to get mine, she says, all quiet, "Riley . . .?"'

Joseph's voice had gone high and into some accent that was semi-Australian and semi-Irish. '"I need to tell you something. I was born intersex."'

His own voice returned. 'That's what she said. "Intersex". Had no idea what she was on about but I had sex on the brain so I caught on pretty fast. She kept talking but words don't matter; it's the equipment. So I got a hold of those tits – figured they were fake, but no, they were real. They were definitely attached. That was good. I liked them, in fact. But under her skirt . . .' Joseph stopped. He looked nauseated.

When he'd swallowed and regained some composure, he sounded confident, boastful. 'He might be alive today if he'd worn pants 'cause he'd have had more time to fight me off. But with a skirt, boy, did I get my hand under there so fast he didn't have time to stop me, and that's when I found the junk in the trunk. And right when my hand got on it, he screamed. That guy sounded like a girl right to the end.'

Joseph closed his eyes as he continued to speak, more slowly now, as though he was watching a movie in his mind. 'I took that blond hair, wrapped it tight around my hand and snapped his head right back.'

His film reel had apparently got to the end because he opened his eyes and looked at the two detectives mildly. 'Didn't take long.'

The silence between Eric and Scott in the viewing room was mirrored by the silence in the interview room. It was Resden who broke it.

'And the ring?'

'I took that back, of course. Pulled it right off his dead finger.'

Resden was nodding. 'Do you still have it? Maybe kept it as a trophy?'

Joseph arched an eyebrow. 'I'm beginning to think you really do understand me, Detective. Yes, I still have it. I gave it to my now-wife as an engagement ring – *after* I made sure she was all woman. I learned my lesson there.'

Resden looked like she'd drawn breath to speak and then paused to change direction. 'What did you do with the body?'

Joseph smiled again, back in interview mode. 'The first time or the second time?'

'Both times.'

'First time, I buried the body outside of town. You guys never found it. All that missing person stuff didn't get you any closer. Anyway, I'd taken his passport, hairbrush, toothbrush, all the stuff that could identify him. That had the added benefit of making it look like he'd left to move to another city. But when his roommate ended up being a Green River victim, I moved him out to near where the roomie was found, let it be picked up as another Green River victim. His body was already just a bunch of skinny little bones. There was no sign of his masculinity. I knew you'd never identify him.'

'But we did.'

Joseph started. 'You did?'

Resden nodded. 'Uh-huh.'

He scrutinized her for a moment. Then he chuckled and shook his head. '*You* didn't. Lander and Hall did. Right?'

Scott stiffened. He could not get used to these pieces of shit saying Steelie and Jayne's names.

Joseph had brightened. 'Must make you feel like a stellar detective: they accomplished in one day what none of you could do in sixteen years.'

Resden ignored the dig. 'Let's get back to your attack on the scientists. You don't deny that you attacked them today?'

Joseph's eyes were amused. 'Attack? I was trying to *kill* them. And not just them, but Alexander's idiot brother as well – before they could get to the coroner's office and potentially identify Alexander Ayers. I knew his body had been found where I'd left it. The brother had told me that these scientists could use whatever records he'd given them to match to the bones. Said it didn't matter anymore that no one had ever found the passport or the other stuff. And then there was the brother's DNA. He said he had an appointment to give blood so the coroner could use that for a match now that he was here in America. The brother was a walking time bomb for me. So were Lander and Hall.'

'What were you intending to do?'

'After I killed them? Bury them where they fell.' He shrugged.

'And you were going to, what, just walk away?'

'Worked for me before.' He leered at her.

'Okay.' Resden closed her notebook and placed it on top of the files as she spoke into the recording device to state that a break would be taken.

When she had turned off the machine and was readying to leave the room, Joseph suddenly said, 'I admit some curiosity about how you found me out there in the nature area, Detective. Like you knew right where I was.'

Resden looked down at him. 'Mr. Joseph, you've been on *my* gaydar for quite some time. You just didn't know it.'

He looked at her in shock as she left the room.

A moment later, she entered the observation room. She nodded grimly to Scott and Eric. 'Got all that?'

'We did,' Eric said as he handed back her file on Alex Ayers. 'Thanks for getting us in here.'

'It's the least I could do after dropping the ball on the medevac chopper.'

Scott shook his head. 'Team effort.'

'Thanks.' She gave him a grateful look. 'Been wanting to ask you, who exactly was it that I called on the number you gave me? Because that helicopter got there like it was already on its way.'

Scott rocked his hand from side to side. 'Our boss has friends in all the right places.'

Eric pointed at him. 'Of course, now you owe him.'

'There is that,' Scott admitted. He looked back at Resden. 'Thanks for making that call without asking questions.'

Resden waved this off. 'Don't have to ask me twice on something like that. I have pull, but not that much pull. Kinda liked it.'

Scott smiled at this and then checked his BlackBerry.

She looked at his phone. 'I received word that Ms. Lander's post-op. You should get over there.'

He glanced over at the interrogation room. 'You're done with the suspect for today?'

'Nope. I've got a little plan.' She tapped her temple. 'Wanna hear it?'

'Absolutely.'

'He just revealed that he gave the ring he took off Ayers' finger to his wife? Well, she's coming into the station – one of my guys is bringing her in while the evidence techs start the search of their house and car – and I'm gonna get my hands on that ring. Have it checked for Alex Ayers' DNA.'

Eric raised his eyebrows at her. 'It's been sixteen years.'

'Yeah, but prongs holding little rocks – and I'm betting it is a *little* rock – have a tendency to retain microscopic traces.' She shrugged happily in reply to his look of skepticism. 'Hey, I'm feeling lucky. Wouldn't mind sealing that confession with some hard evidence.'

Scott liked Resden's style. And he liked that he could

leave this in her hands so he could get to Jayne. 'Copy that. Let us know?'

As they left the room together, Resden stopped without warning and made a little noise, like, *Oof*. The agents turned to look at her. Digging in her pocket, she pulled out a set of car keys dangling from a rental car company keychain. She held them up. 'My guys have the scientists' car parked in our lot. Feel free to take it now or later. Whatever you need.'

Scott didn't want to deal with the car right now. He wanted to get to Jayne and talk to her before she tanked from fatigue. And while he was hesitating, Eric took the keys.

27

It had taken Jayne some time to calm down enough to stop crying and it was only then that she realized that Matt was trying to keep her at arm's length. Embarrassed, she pulled back, but it turned out he'd only been maneuvering a small pack of tissues out of his blazer's inner pocket.

'Here,' he said, holding it so that she could pull a tissue free.

She wiped her eyes and blew her nose and then took another tissue, which was when she saw his face. It was full of tension. 'Oh, Matt! I'm sorry, crying like this and not telling you the one thing you need to know: Steelie's going to be okay!'

He immediately looked relieved. 'She's in there?' He gestured to the room across from them where the glass panel in the door was obscured by an interior blind.

'She is. Oh, your jacket . . .' Jayne couldn't believe how wet she'd made it.

He looked down at it and then took it off, laying it on the chair near them. 'Don't worry about it. All that matters is that you guys are okay. Here, sit down.'

Jayne resumed her seat and Matt took the one next to her.

He seemed to be taking in her appearance. 'Do you want help to get the . . . what is this? Pine needles? Out of your hair?'

'It's a lost cause until I can shower. Listen, Steelie's surgery went well. The bullet just missed her ribs.'

'Jesus! I'm really glad you had Scott call me. I definitely want to see her. If she wants to see me.'

'Well, I have a feeling she will want to see you first.'

Matt ran a finger around the side of his collar. 'Has she said anything about me? In particular, I mean?'

Jayne looked at him. He was a nice person. Warm. Modest. Down to earth. She liked him. 'Matt, you took her to dinner in Vegas. You blew her mind.'

He beamed.

A fresh tissue to her nose, Jayne realized that she could do with Matt what she'd never done with Scott. She could consider it practice. She said, tentatively, 'You are single, right? No wives or girlfriends – or boyfriends – in the background?'

His smile dropped instantly and he looked shocked. 'No. I mean, yes, I'm single and no one's in any kind of background. Why? Does Steelie think . . .?'

This hadn't gone as Jayne expected and she didn't want him to think Steelie didn't trust him. She cut him off. 'No! It's me. I recently learned that it makes sense to ask some basic questions before you . . .' Tears threatened again.

Matt scooted closer to her and pulled her to him, putting her head on his shoulder.

She tried to talk through her tears. 'I can't mess up your shirt as well as your jacket.' But he just held onto her more tightly.

After a minute, he said, 'Hey, when we're back in LA

and all this feels like some bad fuckin' dream, you guys can buy me a new shirt. You might have to pool your money, though, because my stuff's expensive.'

Jayne pulled back so she could look at his shirt and also see his expression, which was amused. They both burst out laughing and Jayne felt like an immense weight had been lifted from her shoulders. At that moment, Scott and Eric emerged from the elevator down the hall. Scott's expression changed from curiosity to confusion or maybe disapproval. Jayne knew that her laughter would look incongruous under the circumstances and her smile fell away. She could see the question in Scott's eyes, but before he reached her, Matt stood up and did a guy-style back-slapper hug with him while they shook hands.

This gave Eric a chance to crouch in front of Jayne. 'Doing okay?'

She nodded. 'Are you guys okay?'

'Us?' Eric glanced back at Scott. 'Of course.'

A nurse passed by, glanced at them and went into Steelie's room.

Scott took the chair next to Jayne and gave her a perfunctory rub on the back while he looked at the door where the nurse had gone. 'Steelie not out from under yet?'

Jayne was struggling to read Scott's body language. It would fit for a married man trying to comfort his mistress in public. She shook her head in answer to his question.

Eric jerked a thumb toward Steelie's door. 'We need to be glad it wasn't exploding bullets.'

Matt exclaimed in disbelief.

'Yep. The shooter had 'em, just hadn't loaded 'em yet.'

Matt looked concerned. 'He's not a cop, is he?'

'No,' said Eric. 'That's the one complication this situation *doesn't* have.'

Jayne managed to talk but she talked to Eric. 'Graham's okay?'

Eric said, 'Thanks for reminding me. He's fine, tucked up in his hotel, but asked if you could meet him at the medical examiner's office tomorrow morning because, dun dun dunnn, his sister's been identified. Thanks to you and Steelie.'

'Oh wow.' Jayne tried to digest this and then tried to fit it into what happened at the park. Before she could formulate her next question, the blind moved from the window in Steelie's door and the nurse emerged, leaving the door ajar.

'Ms. Lander can have visitors now – one at a time.' She took in the badges on Eric and Scott's belts. 'And I mean it. Your badges have no power here.'

Jayne gestured at Matt to go in first. He gave her a grateful look, went in and closed the door behind him.

Eric followed and looked through the window. 'Steelie looks good, considering. And – whoa! I can see that it's full steam ahead with Matt.'

Jayne felt Scott's eyes on her. He said, 'How about I take you to your hotel so you can decompress? Steelie's in good hands. And then we can talk – about everything.'

Jayne glanced at Eric to see if he was okay with this.

He shooed them both. 'Go on. Get outta here.'

Jayne took a deep breath, then accepted Scott's outstretched hand and got to her feet.

*

Scott stood just behind Jayne at the entrance of the restaurant at her hotel, absorbing her appearance. She looked completely revitalized by the shower she'd taken in her room while he'd checked in and got a room for himself, Eric and Matt. She was wearing his favorite sweater of hers, a lightweight cashmere crewneck that stopped just short of the beauty mark on her neck and was a shade of slate blue that was beautiful against her coloring. But her jeans were a pair he'd not seen before. The dark denim hugged her body so closely, he could see the outline of her hotel room key in the right rear pocket. The hostess arrived and Scott readied himself for the conversation to come.

They walked through the hotel's large and busy bar to a quiet dining area where snug booths were gently lit by sconces. Jayne took the side that allowed a view back the way they'd come. It was the side that Scott would usually take because he liked to watch entrances and exits, but he knew that Jayne liked to do the same; it mitigated anxiety that could crop up if she heard or saw something that she registered as out of place. She'd been better lately but . . . triggers were triggers. Being shot at earlier in the day definitely counted as a potential trigger.

He picked up a menu and glanced at her over the top. She was looking down at her own menu. Her eyelashes were dark with mascara – she looked up at him but it was a fleeting glance. He tried to focus on the words on the page.

When the waitress arrived, Jayne ordered a non-alcoholic cocktail and the pork chop dinner, which Scott had thought of ordering himself but instead he'd gone with the shrimp pasta. He asked for a whisky.

Looking at Jayne, he started with, 'About what happened today . . . how are you doing?'

She finally looked at him properly. 'I'm actually doing okay. Something about going with Steelie to the hospital seems to have stopped me from getting . . .' She trailed off and looked down.

'Stuck?'

She nodded. 'Yes. And I wanted to thank you. For today. For being there.'

Scott decided that it had to be whatever King had said to Jayne that was making her speak to him like he was just an acquaintance. The waitress brought their drinks and Scott took a large swig of his. It hit him in the chest and then it spread.

Jayne said, 'I still don't know why you and Eric were even in Seattle.'

This was easier ground and he took it. 'We were on a layover from Anchorage.'

'Oh! I thought you'd gone back to LA after the recovery operation.'

'Turner had other plans for us.'

She looked stricken. 'So he did take you off the assignment after San Antonio.'

'No. Just made me switch places with Nate.' Scott figured she'd know this was a joke.

But her eyes only widened in disbelief. 'Nate, the *driver*?'

'I'm kidding. That is to say, my boss would've *loved* to have turned me into a driver but the trailer's too valuable for that.' Scott smiled, trying to get her to do the same.

Jayne only said, 'Oh,' and sipped her drink, taking a deep interest in the twinkling crystalline rim of her glass.

Since Jayne hadn't taken up his attempt at levity, Scott gave up on that. He took a drink and got serious. 'Turner flipped Eric up to lead the recovery and put me on liaison back to Atlanta Missings, helping Angie. Just took me out of the chain of evidence while he kept the operation going.'

'Is it finished now?'

'The recovery is. And Jayne, we found the rest of Mrs. Patterson.'

He'd been hoping for the chance to tell her this. Jayne and Steelie had been the key to making an ID from two dismembered arms on the side of a Los Angeles freeway that summer, and it had been this woman's arms. Mrs. Patterson: King's last victim and the one whose remains had led to his downfall.

Jayne had stopped playing with her glass and was staring at him. 'I didn't expect that. That's . . . incredible.' She was starting to smile as she took in the news.

He enjoyed having her gaze on him. 'Not just that. We got DNA from all of the other families.'

Her smile turned to a look of wonder.

He drove it home. 'That's because of you, Jayne. You and Steelie.'

Tears came to her eyes so quickly, Scott wasn't ready. He tried to give her his napkin, apologizing, but she was shaking her head and wiping the tears away.

'I'm happy,' she said. 'I don't know where the tears are coming from.'

Scott had a pretty good idea that they were coming because she'd stared death in the face that afternoon.

He said, 'What I was leading up to is that Turner has a lot of reasons to make sure the Bureau still has an MOU with Thirty-Two One.'

He paused while the waitress delivered their meal.

'Is he done with his investigation?' Jayne asked.

'Not quite.' He ground pepper onto his food. 'Closing a bunch of cases, from whatever jurisdiction, is a big result from an MOU he only inked a few weeks ago.'

Jayne was cutting into her pork chop. 'I've been expecting him to pull it.'

'I don't think he will.' Scott took a bite of pasta. 'Eric and I pointed out to him on Wednesday that the MOU was his idea – not mine – and it doesn't have a conflict-of-interest clause in it. If he wants to add that clause, he can draw it up again.'

They ate in silence for a moment.

Scott swallowed. 'That being said, he'll want this to be clean, especially with perps like King trying to make something out of whatever it was you and I were . . . doing with each other.'

Jayne went straight back to staring at her plate and he was tired of it.

He leaned toward her as much as the table would allow. 'Jayne. Turner I can deal with. The MOU I can deal with. But I know King said something to you.'

She looked up, startled. 'How did you know?'

Scott felt his anger rising – King was in this! But then remembered AUSA Johnson. *Don't jump the gun*. He sat back, counted *one, two* and then said, 'I didn't know for sure until just now. I didn't even guess. It was Eric – or Steelie – who did that. I'm just the schmuck sitting here wondering why you didn't say anything.'

He waited for a response but one didn't come.

He leaned in again. 'Jayne, you can barely look at me. And if it's because of something that piece of shit said, I need to know what it was so I can deal with it.'

He watched her put down her fork, the mouthful still on the tines. She said quietly, 'I tried to dismiss it but I haven't been able to.'

'Haven't been able to dismiss what?'

'Gene said to ask you about . . .' She looked strained. 'Callista.'

Of all the things she could have said, he'd never expected that and he had to put his own fork down. He rubbed a finger over his lips, aware that his eyes were scanning the ceiling, racing around the walls, skating over the illuminated green EXIT signs while his brain catalogued what – or how much – King knew about him and Callista. Her name hadn't come up when they were interrogating King. Was it like a lot of the guy's known surveillance records: photos, notes, newspaper clippings? Or was video or audio secreted somewhere in his house or the storage unit that the investigation hadn't uncovered? Scott could picture video or, at the very least, photos. Callista and her goddamned open curtains and exhibitionism – and him not fighting the battle over the curtains most of the time because there were other, bigger battles to be fought.

Then it dawned on Scott that nothing King had recorded or seen or *known* mattered. Everything he'd done in his life before this moment was on him. It was in him, too, and that was the real problem, not King. He brought his gaze back to Jayne. There was a mixture of sadness and curiosity on her face but she was waiting for him. Her full attention was on him as she waited. The moment felt profound. He was so moved, he wanted to go to her side of the booth, to hold her and be held by her, to take his time, to tell her everything. The moment had come and he was ready.

As he began to stand, Matt and Eric arrived, sliding into the booth without even stopping their own conversation let alone taking stock of Jayne and Scott.

28

Scott immediately looked at Jayne in consternation, but she conveyed to him with a smile that she found Matt and Eric's easy assumptions funny, not frustrating. Scott tried to relax. He could tell that Eric, who was right next to him, was belatedly aware that he and Matt might have interrupted something because he raised an interrogative eyebrow, but Scott just shook his head. He could wait if Jayne could.

But Matt was clearly oblivious as he got comfy next to Jayne. 'That locks good.' He was pointing at her plate.

'It is,' she said but she looked down at her pork chop like she'd forgotten it was there.

The waitress had followed Matt and Eric to the table with menus. They asked her to wait while they scanned the options quickly. Matt ordered surf and turf while Eric went for the shrimp pasta. They dismissed her with their drinks order, asking her to re-up whatever Jayne and Scott had been drinking.

Jayne smiled at Eric. 'You're getting the same thing Scott did.'

He glanced at Scott's plate and rolled his eyes good-naturedly. 'We spend way too much time together.'

Scott handed Eric a room key and then passed another one across the table to Matt. 'You're with us. 318. Unless you decided to head back tonight after all?'

Matt pocketed the key. 'I'm keeping it to the early-bird flight in the morning. Thanks.'

The waitress arrived, opened the beer bottles and decanted into tall glasses.

Matt took a long drink and then compressed his lips to clear the beer that had settled on his top lip. He turned toward Jayne, putting his arm across the back of the booth behind her to get an easier angle to talk. 'So, Steelie's doing as well as can be expected. Said to tell you she'll be discharged in two or three days. And they've let her have her phone. She doesn't have a charger but you're under orders from her to not come back with that tonight.'

'I'm so glad you spent time with her. I'll take her charger with me when I finish at the coroner's office in the morning.'

As Scott finished his meal, he noticed Matt and Jayne smiling at each other, a dot of pink in Jayne's cheeks.

Matt was saying, 'So, Jayne, why was someone shooting at you? Steelie had no idea.'

Jayne grimaced. 'I can only guess at that.'

'You don't have to,' Scott offered. 'We heard his confession.'

Jayne looked back at him in surprise. 'You did?'

Scott held his tongue as the waitress delivered food still sizzling on the plates.

Eric thanked her and took over from Scott. 'Seattle PD let us listen in.' He started to summarize the story told by Riley Joseph AKA Joseph O'Reilly, but Matt interrupted by gesticulating with his fork.

Matt said, 'The vic in '89—'

'Alex,' Jayne supplied.

Matt nodded. 'Alex was both male and female? Like, transsexual?'

'Intersex,' Scott said. He had sat back with his drink. 'Born both male and female, as Jayne and Steelie already learned from her brother, right?'

She nodded but looked surprised he knew this. 'Yes, but her parents selected a sex for her when she was still a baby, as many parents do. In her case, they went with male.' She looked from Scott to Eric, her expression thoughtful. 'Did Riley say that he'd known Alex was intersex?'

Eric shook his head. 'He didn't know until she told him. And he translated that as him being in a relationship with another man. He wasn't okay with that so he killed her, allegedly. He tried to prevent you from identifying her so no one would know he'd had a same-sex relationship.'

'Plus killed someone,' Scott added.

Matt looked at Jayne. 'So what was the deal with the coroner's office? They had her body but had her listed as male?'

She opened her hands wide. 'I don't know. This all went down while Steelie and I were at the nature reserve running . . .' She trailed off.

Scott spoke so she didn't have to finish that sentence. 'The detective said that the bones Thirty-Two One suggested might belong to Alex were ones the coroner's office had down as male. Including a pelvis.'

Matt stated flatly, 'So it was a SNAFU.'

Jayne shook her head. 'Actually, it's Systems Normal.

Even if an anthropologist observes the same combination of bony features Steelie and I did on X-ray, they're still forced to choose a single sex to get the Doe record into NCIC. They can't put in, say, "female skull, male pelvis".'

'Like with Stilson at UCLA?' Matt was looking questioningly at Jayne. 'He was mixed race but the coroner had to pick one race for NCIC.'

Scott thought Jayne looked inordinately glad that Matt had made the link with the case they'd all worked on together the previous month.

She was addressing Matt directly now and looked excited. 'Exactly like with Jared Stilson! In fact, any time the missing person report requires someone to "pick between" race or sex labels and then NCIC requires the medical examiner to do the same, we've introduced an opportunity for error. It gets even worse when remains are decomposed or skeletonized. Picking between labels just doesn't make sense when dealing with humans.'

She paused when the waitress came up to the table to check on everyone. When Eric and Matt ordered more beer, Scott asked her to bring him one too. Jayne said she was okay for a drink and continued, warming to the subject.

'In this case, the missing person report said "female". It was put in by someone who only knew Alex to be a woman. But it seems the coroner's office went with the apparently male pelvis—'

'Wait, why?' Eric interjected.

Jayne started making shapes with her hands, trying to show them something Scott felt he probably needed a textbook to understand. 'Well, an adult female pelvis is structured to allow for the carrying of a fetus. It's so different from a male pelvis that if you have a skeleton with a male pelvis on the autopsy table, it's going to be more determinative of sex than any female characteristics on another sexually dimorphic part of the skeleton, like the skull. Et voila, John Doe misses his match with his female missing person report in NCIC. And in Alex's case, the one person who could've provided the information that she might have male *as well* as female – Riley – made sure no one knew.' She sat back.

Scott was contemplative. 'Until Alex's brother arrived and blew the lid off. With your help.'

Eric popped up in his seat, like he'd just had an idea. 'Yeah, yeah – what Scott just said: *your* help. But this can't be the first time this has come up! What's the fix?'

'Just a second,' Matt said scornfully. 'Can this really come up this often? How many intersex people are there?'

'Does it matter?' Jayne challenged. 'To quote your man Harry Bosch: "Everybody counts or nobody counts."'

Matt reared back with a smile of admiration. 'Touché.' He held his hand out to her, palm up. 'Gimme five.'

She laughed and slapped his hand. 'I wasn't trying to be mean! I was trying to say that it's not just about intersex people, right? It's about the ability of coroners who don't have a forensic anthropologist on hand – which is many, if not *most* of them – to accurately estimate sex or other characteristics from bone. I've heard of coroners who've identified a skeleton as male because it's wearing pants.'

'You're shitting me!' Matt exclaimed.

Jayne's eyes widened. 'I'm not! If someone's not trained

in human osteology and forensic anthropology, then they don't know what they don't know.'

Eric said, 'Bringing me back to my even more pressing question, then. What's the fix?'

'Well, since you're asking,' Jayne said with a smile. 'Steelie and I believe that instead of trying to make IDs using culturally flexible labels like race or even sex – which are themselves already encompassing highly variable characteristics – we should prioritize something that's actually unique to one human. At least for long-term unidentified bodies.'

'Unique. Like . . .?' Eric said.

'Like their dental characteristics or dental work.' Jayne let that simple concept just hang out there.

Eric took the bait. 'As you had the coroner's office do with Stilson.'

She grinned. 'Indeed. And we should harness computers and software to deal with the increased number of records that would need to be compared.'

'A big increase?'

'NCIC would need to compare, like, 100,000 records at any given time instead of, say, half that – but the comparisons would be more valid and we would . . . well, we'd get more dead people home.' She shrugged one shoulder, as though to undermine this lofty statement, but she was blushing deeply.

Scott knew that Jayne had become embarrassed about being so fervent, but he loved that part of her and always had.

Matt had been quiet for a while, apparently digesting

Jayne's take on the world, but now spoke as he lifted his glass from one ring of condensation on the table to another, matching up the circles. 'I've been in Homicide a long time and I still don't understand people. So you find out that the person you're in a relationship with is a little different on the inside than you thought. You're gonna kill them over it?'

Jayne looked at him for a beat. 'Not everything is on the inside, Matt.'

Scott watched Matt's eyes widen slightly. He knew him well enough to know exactly where his mind had gone.

But Matt rallied. 'Still. If ya love someone, ya work stuff out. Or you break up. You don't kill 'em.'

The waitress delivered the beers but Matt told her to keep the glasses so she opened the bottles and left them at the end of the table.

Eric slid a bottle toward Scott as he spoke. 'I don't think people like the perp today actually love anyone. Maybe themselves. At the most.' He pointed at the table with his forefinger. 'You want to know what I noticed when I took Riley Joseph to the ground? He wasn't even sweating. He knew it was going to be like shooting fish in a barrel to take the three of you out. That's the way people like him work. They don't want a fair fight.' Eric had sounded bitter.

Jayne made an appreciative gesture toward Eric. 'Yes! That's a perfect way to describe it. It wasn't a fair fight. It often isn't, between a man and a woman.'

Matt said, 'Wait, now you're calling this intersex person a woman!' He was shaking his head like the world was upside down.

Jayne held her hands out defensively. 'Based on what her brother told us, during life Alex skewed toward female averages in terms of size and weight. That makes a difference in a fight with an average-sized North American male.'

Matt grabbed a bread roll and started to slather it with butter. 'I don't know how I'd feel if it turned out I'd been dating a guy.'

She turned toward him in astonishment. 'Five seconds ago, you said you'd work stuff out! And she wasn't "a guy": she had both male and female attributes.'

Through a mouthful of bread, Matt said, 'Yeah, well, I'm picturing one male "attribute" in particular.'

Jayne rolled her eyes. 'And now we're all picturing it, thank you very much. Anyway!' She sounded like she was trying to get the conversation out of the locker room. 'I agree with what I *think* you were saying before, Matt: if two people love each other, then gender labels or even ideas about what sex someone is shouldn't matter.'

Matt turned in his seat to focus on her, clearly enjoying himself. 'So. Jayne. You would kiss another woman?'

She didn't hesitate. 'Of course. Why wouldn't I?'

Even as Scott heard Matt follow up with absolutely standard girl-on-girl fantasy questions, and even as he wondered why Jayne appeared amused by Matt's transparency, a fleeting memory of kissing – was that possible? Kissing? – *Eric* came to him. The memory was hazy but his sensory memory wasn't. It was something about the beer bottle he was drinking from . . . The scent? The taste? And then he remembered the taste of this very beer with . . . yes, the feel of Eric's lips.

Slowly, Scott lowered the bottle and rotated it to look at the label. He was pretty sure it was what Eric had been drinking at the bar in New Mexico, a beer Scott didn't usually drink. And now it was all coming back to him: the bar, the smoking, the chick in the cut-offs and Eric. Eric, who had stopped him from doing something stupid in the aftermath of having had to talk with Collins and Belport. No: of having been talked *to* by Ty Collins, who'd always made it clear that he considered Scott to be a total failure in his job because he hadn't protected his daughter. Scott remembered being in the bar and feeling intensely grateful to Eric for stopping him from being a failure in his life as well. It had been an overwhelming and not exactly brotherly love for his partner at that moment.

Scott ran his memory forward and couldn't remember anything else from that night. Regardless, he could add the sexual assault of his partner to the list of his toxic shit. God knew what Eric had been thinking since then. Scott was suddenly hyper-aware of Eric's shoulder next to his, of the fact that their legs had actually touched under the table multiple times during the meal in a way that would normally be, well, totally normal given that there was barely enough space for the two of them in the booth.

He glanced sideways at his partner. Eric was chuckling at the banter between Jayne and Matt as he finished his meal. Nothing in his behavior now or in the past few days had signaled that Eric thought something was amiss. But Scott knew that it didn't matter if Eric had somehow excused the whole thing; it was up to him to deal with this and to deal with it now.

He indicated that he needed to get up, but once he and Eric were both standing, Scott indicated with his head for Eric to follow him. Eric looked puzzled but complied. Scott went to the hallway near the restrooms and halted next to a demilune table holding a vase of flowers below a wall-mounted mirror.

He faced Eric. 'I'm not absolutely sure about the details but . . .' He cleared his throat as he looked around to ensure no one was within earshot. 'Did I lay one on you when we were at that bar in New Mexico?'

Eric raised an eyebrow. 'You did.'

Scott worked hard to keep eye contact. 'I – I'm sorry. I don't know what I was thinking.'

'Probably because you were drunk.'

'Right.' Scott passed a hand over his face.

'To be honest, I didn't think you'd remember.' Eric sounded intrigued.

'I only just did,' Scott explained, but now he was starting to wonder why *Eric* hadn't said anything. Or if he ever would have.

But Eric was grinning. 'Is this why you gave me that "Oh, shit" look a few minutes ago when Matt was talking about dating a guy?'

Scott's annoyance with himself increased; he hadn't realized he'd been that obvious. 'I hope he didn't see that.'

'Uh, I think Matt's too busy quizzing Jayne to notice what you're doing.'

Scott glanced distractedly back toward the dining room. He needed to talk with Jayne too. But first, this. 'I can't remember anything after the bar. Did I do anything else?'

Someone came out of the men's room and looked startled to see people right outside the door but then continued toward the dining room.

Eric spoke quietly. 'So you don't remember sleeping the night in my arms, all cozied up?'

Scott tried to picture this. 'I slept in your . . .?' The picture widened. 'Did the Critters see . . .?' Then Eric's demeanor cut through his imaginings. 'Oh. I get it.'

Eric was chortling like he'd been holding it in. 'You only slept on me in the car, man, but that was too good to pass up!'

Scott shook his head but he was relieved. 'I'm glad you're having fun. But seriously, you're . . .' He forced the words out. 'Within your rights to report it – to report me.'

Eric was instantly serious. 'Scott, we weren't working. I took you off-site so you could blow off some steam, so I'm not reporting anything, okay?' He crossed his arms with a kind of finality.

'Okay.' Scott suddenly felt exhausted and didn't know how he was going to find the energy to talk to Jayne tonight as well.

He drew himself level with Eric, pulling his shoulders back. 'Are we good, partner?'

Eric put his fist out for a bump. 'We're good.'

They returned to the table, where Matt's arm was again on the back of the booth as he and Jayne talked while sharing a piece of cheesecake topped by a large dollop of whipped cream. There was a second slice on a plate on the other side of the table, with two forks nestled against each other on a bed of fresh napkins.

Matt looked up. 'We weren't sure if you guys wanted dessert, but if you don't eat it, we will.'

Scott hesitated. He couldn't see getting back into that little booth and sharing a dessert with Eric right this second. Even the utensils seemed to have overtones and it needed a night, or maybe a week, to clear that out. He caught Jayne's eye. 'Could we maybe finish our conversation?'

Matt moved with some difficulty out of the booth so he could let Jayne out, apologizing for having interrupted anything earlier.

'No, it was okay,' Jayne said when she got to her feet. 'I'm glad you came.'

'Thanks. Me too,' Matt said and they embraced.

Scott watched as Jayne turned to kiss Eric on the cheek and then he caught Eric's eye. 'Put all the meals on our room?'

'You got it,' Eric said, already pulling the plate of cheesecake toward him and removing the second fork without hesitation.

29

Jayne made her way to the hotel's lobby elevators with Scott walking next to her. She felt jittery but also relieved to be alone with him again. It was time to find out if this was the end or the beginning. She looked at him. He looked tired.

She said, 'I thought we could go to mine and Steelie's room. Save us getting interrupted by Matt and Eric in a bit?'

Scott nodded and they got in the elevator. Jayne pressed the button for the seventh floor and they looked at each other's reflections in the polished brass of the elevator doors. The carpeted hallway on her floor was silent, the beep of her electronic door key the only sound when they entered the room. Jayne turned on a lamp but left the curtains open to the view of Downtown Seattle.

She said, 'Mini bar?'

'Abso-fuckin-lutely,' Scott said, crossing to the fridge and opening the door to peruse the contents.

Jayne joined him. The bottle of white wine immediately appealed to her, even though she usually avoided alcohol because even a light buzz made her anxious that she wasn't being vigilant against, well gunshots or landmines. But next to Scott in this hotel room, she thought a glass of wine could work like a sign to herself to let go. She picked up the bottle. 'Want to share this with me?'

His eyebrows went up slightly. 'I'd love to. And . . .' He selected one of the miniature liquor bottles from the shelf in the door. Then he took a second one.

While Jayne poured the wine into the two stem glasses on the sideboard, Scott poured his liquor into a tumbler. They sat on the plush armchairs by the window, only a tiny drinks table between them. They were close enough to each other that they could hold hands if they were to reach out, but neither of them did.

Scott finished his tumbler contents in short order and moved on to the wine. Then he leaned forward, his elbows on his knees. 'So, I'm just going to jump right in. Callista is who I was with in Atlanta.'

Jayne felt like her systems were shutting down. Gene hadn't made Callista up. This woman was out there, wearing a ring Scott had given her.

Let go. She said, 'And was it over before you left? Before we got together?'

'For me it was.' He sounded like he was trying hard to be honest.

The effort in Scott's voice made Jayne take another, larger taste of the wine. 'When we were all in Atlanta this summer . . . did you see her again?'

'Not while you and Steelie were there, but I did see her later.' He rushed on, as though to soften this statement. 'After we arrested Eugene King, Eric and I were on the interrogations, dealing with evidence coming in from the crime scene at King's house, and Turner was making noises about wanting an MOU. We were working twelve- or fourteen-hour days. There was a lot of news coverage.

Callista saw it. She called me. Asked me to pick up some of my . . . things. From when I was last there. April, May. The spring, anyway.'

Jayne couldn't keep eye contact. Scott was recounting a time when the two of them had only ever kissed, yet the idea of him being intimate with his wife still felt like a betrayal. Jayne looked down into her glass and saw that the surface of the liquid was rippled. She was trembling. Keeping her gaze on her glass, she forged ahead. 'Did something happen? When you saw her?'

'She wanted it to but I'd figured that's where it was going when she called. I'd already told her to just throw the stuff away but . . . whatever. She didn't.'

Jayne looked up to see if he looked as annoyed as he sounded. He didn't. He looked embarrassed as he sipped his wine.

She said, 'But you went over anyway.' She hadn't meant to sound accusatory – why couldn't a husband go see his estranged wife? But she couldn't take it back.

Scott put down his glass and spread his hands like he was trying to clear the air. 'I went over to make it clear that it was over for me, no matter what she said or did.'

An image came into Jayne's mind of the totally unknown but definitely svelte and absolutely lithesome Callista Houston letting a linen . . . no, silk robe fall open as she draped herself onto Scott in the foyer of their . . . mansion in a bid to save their marriage.

Scott said, 'Jayne . . . I'm sorry I didn't tell you about her.' He sounded earnest, his voice softer and quieter than it had been.

She couldn't look at him yet. Unable to tell if she felt sad or angry, or with whom, she didn't know what to say.

Scott seemed determined to explain himself. 'Ever since you and I met, I've wanted – thought I wanted – I've had this idea, this hope – of being with you. I thought it wouldn't just be a distraction from horrific things I'd seen or the things I was feeling. I could be in it with you because you've seen what I've seen. But I realize now that I'm carrying a lot of other negative stuff that I shouldn't bring into your life. Do you know what I mean?' He made a noise of exasperation. 'Christ, I feel like I'm running my mouth like a fucking fool tonight.'

She heard him move suddenly and looked up. He'd gone to stand a few feet away at the window, his hands clasped on top of his head, elbows jutting out. He appeared to be looking out at the night sky, which was visible where his form blocked the room's lamplight.

Jayne looked at his back. She did know, exactly, what he meant. It was what she'd felt for him over the years. But his negative thoughts were not the point right now. The point was his marriage. She stood up to join him and instantly felt the effects of the alcohol, like her brain was still back in the chair. She steadied herself, then put her glass on the table. She was going to let go, once and for all.

Coming to stand next to him, she stared unseeing at the cityscape outside. 'Scott, you know I have my own negative stuff from my work. Plenty of it. I can negative back-chat myself endlessly, about the bodies we didn't identify, the bodies we never found, about the families still waiting. Whatever you felt was inside of you from your work didn't scare me. You didn't have to go and make yourself "whole" for us to be together. You only needed to be, y'know . . .' She exhaled. 'Not already married.'

Scott's arms fell from his head and he turned toward her in astonishment. 'Married? Jesus, Jayne, I'm not *married*.'

She frowned. 'But Gene said Callista had your ring.'

Now Scott was frowning. He looked as though he was reviewing something in his mind. Then he said, with new, and total, understanding, 'Not mine. Hers. *She* was married.'

Jayne felt stunned. 'Wait, *what*?'

'Separated,' Scott said. 'Or getting separated. Whatever. Some complicated bullshit I never had the patience to listen to.'

Jayne turned and sank down onto the deep window ledge. Callista *was* married but to someone else.

She became aware that Scott was watching her. He spoke like he was forcing a word out at a time. 'So you're not . . . turned off by me being kind of . . . damaged?'

Jayne almost burst out laughing but spluttered instead. 'Scott! You're the one who helped me to see that I should get help for the PTSD that I'd spent years hiding from you! Why would I be worried about you dealing with the same thing? If anything, I'm relieved you're not perfect!'

He looked at her in confusion and she loved that he was waiting for her to explain it all to him.

She put her hand to his face and stroked his cheek. 'To answer you another way: I'm very turned *on* by you not being married, the way Gene had me believe you were.'

He put his hand over hers and held it there. 'King knew what buttons to push to make you feel jealous, to mess you up, to mess *us* up. That was his goal. But it's all just feelings.' He took her hand from his face and held it. 'I mean, I feel jealous of every guy you've been with – or even look at.'

She was skeptical. 'Seriously?'

'Yes.' He was just barely keeping a grin at bay. 'Please stop hugging Matthew West.'

Smiling, she said, 'His arms are definitely going to be around Steelie for the foreseeable.'

Scott chuckled and interlaced their fingers, stroking her thumb with his.

She said, 'Why is this so hard, Scott? Me and you?'

He tilted his head to the side and gave her a speculative look, as though he was trying to understand her point of view. 'I don't think it's that hard. But maybe it's feeling weird because the MOU is mixed up in it? I think Turner coming out to San Antonio made it feel like our relationship was somehow part of the MOU.'

Jayne finally felt a delicious clarity. She squeezed his fingers tightly. 'You know what? I don't care if Turner pulls the MOU. I really don't, if it's a matter of choosing.'

He smiled at her happily and kissed her hand. 'Me too. But I don't want to have to choose.'

Jayne did laugh now, throwing her head back.

'What?' Scott's tone was innocent but he'd moved in front of her and was parting her legs.

She pulled him close. 'Eric did tell me once that you like to have it all.'

'Now, why does everyone say that like it's a bad thing?' His voice had gone low and slow as he brushed the tip of her nose with his. 'And speaking of having it all . . . why don't *we* get married?'

Jayne felt heat spreading across her face and a smile coming to her lips, only for it to falter on disbelief, then strengthen again on excitement. She couldn't speak.

Scott was searching her face, seemingly trying to read whatever he saw there. 'You think it sounds crazy. But I've been thinking about it a lot and we've basically wasted five years already.'

He started to run his hands up and down her thighs. 'Look, you just said that your biggest fear is me not being available for you so . . . let's take care of that. Let's take care of that totally.' He kissed her at the base of her throat. 'And forever.'

He moved to kiss her neck and Jayne felt like every nerve ending in her body was tingling as she looked down at the top of his head. She ran her hands up his arms, her palms rising and falling over the contours of his deltoids where they were flexed under his shirtsleeves, across the twist in his clavicles, up along his neck until her hands were on the back of his head. She grasped his hair between her fingers and pulled back gently. Scott's eyes immediately flicked to hers, pupils dilating, the flecks of hazel almost lost in the green, and then he was looking at her lips, leaning in to reach her mouth with his.

Jayne felt his anticipation was as much for them to be together right this second as it was for them to be together 'forever' as he'd put it. That word was ridiculous, but heavens, was it wonderful. In fact, she felt like she'd finally pulled the handle on the slot machine and the winnings were raining down on her. *Ding, ding, ding, ding, ding, ding, ding!* She smiled at the thought.

'Alright,' she said. 'Let's get—'

But her last word was lost under the sound Scott made as he kissed her, pulling her off the ledge and onto him.

DAY 9

Tuesday

30

Steelie opened her eyes to see Jayne and Olivia sitting across her hospital room in visitors' chairs that they'd pulled close together as they talked. Even though Steelie felt utterly tired out, the pain medication was masking actual pain, allowing her to appreciate how good it was to have two old friends here, watching over her as she'd slept.

She could tell Olivia was asking Jayne about Matt. Steelie closed her eyes, pretending to still be asleep, and listened as Jayne talked about what a sweet guy he was, and thoughtful, but also kind of stubborn like Steelie; how he looked mainstream but there something unexpected about him, which made him intriguing.

Olivia said, 'You make him sound like an onion – a sweet Vidalia onion but layered nonetheless.'

Jayne giggled. 'But isn't that perfect for Steelie? She likes people who surprise her.'

'And who make her eyes water when she peels back the layers? Is he cute?'

'Yes. And he gives good hugs.' Jayne sounded almost nostalgic and Steelie realized some bonding must have taken place between her disparate people while she'd been hopped up on pain meds.

Olivia was saying, 'Hugs? I thought you were going to say something else.'

Steelie had to suppress a laugh. It wasn't easy and she almost farted. She could tell that Jayne had playfully smacked Olivia's hand.

'OC!' But this was total mock outrage on Jayne's part. 'You haven't changed. And anyway, how would I know anything about how he is in bed?'

Olivia was unrepentant. 'Girl, you have to ask! What's the point of being best friends if you can't ask about this stuff?' She let out a peal of laughter. 'And I can't believe you didn't tell me that The Onion was here last night. I could have come over to get a hug. Let him make *my* eyes water. Ha!'

'You are so naughty. Tell me, how often are you getting down to Irvine to see your parents? You should come visit us next—'

A loud cracking noise jarred the room. Steelie opened her eyes to catch sight of the door to her room bouncing back from the rubber doorstop on the wall straight into the palm of a woman taking up the doorway. Steelie had no idea who she was. The skin on her face was reddened on the cheeks but almost white around her mouth. She was screaming at them.

'*Bitches! You're all bitches! Why couldn't you leave it alone? What difference did it make to you?*'

Bolting from their chairs, Jayne and Olivia moved protectively in front of Steelie.

Olivia used a commanding and loud tone: 'Ma'am, you need to leave!'

But the woman kept shouting. '*Do any of you bitches have husbands?*'

Jayne yelled, 'Security!'

The woman started to reach into her coat.

Steelie felt like she needed to get to her feet but her IV needle was pulling at the skin on the back of her hand and she didn't know how to disconnect it to get free. Then she realized that Jayne and Olivia were charging across the room. They reached the woman just as hospital security arrived, all of them trying to pull the woman's arm out of her coat as she screamed and let her knees buckle to the ground. When they succeeded in wrenching her arm out, in her hand was not a weapon but a pair of wallet-sized photographs. Then she was being pulled out into the hall, wailing, '*Why couldn't you have just left it alone?*'

Steelie recognized the nurse who rushed into the room, closing the door behind her and pulling the blind over the window. 'My God, I'm so sorry.' She didn't stop moving and came directly to Steelie. 'Ms. Lander, are you alright?'

Steelie felt sick and confused, like, *if this is the world, let me go back on the meds*. But she tried to take stock of the feeling around her wound and everything down there felt the same. So she said, 'I think so.'

The nurse was focused on the IV equipment and getting out the blood pressure cuff. She attached it to Steelie's arm as though getting her vitals would fix everything.

Jayne came over, her brow furrowed, but she didn't say anything, only patted Steelie's other hand.

Steelie tried to look around the nurse to see the whole room. 'Where's OC?'

'Gone to find out what that was about.'

That made Steelie feel better. Olivia would come back

with answers. The nurse was asking her to stay still so she tried to do that.

Taking off the pressure cuff, the nurse said, 'Good. Your BP's only slightly elevated. I'm just going to take your temp – oh, your IV stent needs re-setting. Let's get that taken care of.'

When the nurse left, Olivia walked in. She mimicked wiping sweat from her forehead. 'Okay, I got the woman's name: a Mrs. Joseph. I'm guessing she wasn't someone you cut off in traffic?'

Jayne sighed and shook her head.

Steelie wasn't enlightened. 'Is anyone going to tell me what's going on?'

'Don't look at me,' Olivia said.

Jayne looked reluctant. 'I wasn't planning on giving you the update until you'd been awake for more than five minutes.'

'Consider me awoken,' Steelie said drily.

Jayne said, 'Okay. So, I think that must have been Riley's wife.'

Steelie put two and two together and did not come up with four. She spelled it out slowly. 'Riley, as in the guy who shot at us but claimed he'd been holding a candle for Alex?'

Olivia had her hand raised like she was in class. 'Alex, as in my Jane-John Doe?'

Before Jayne could explain, a cell phone on the table started to ring. OC moved fastest, picked it up and then handed it to Jayne. 'It's yours.'

Steelie watched as Jayne greeted a detective whose name

sounded like Resden, answered a bunch of questions about Steelie's condition and then listened for a while.

When Jayne hung up, she said, 'That was Seattle PD, confirming that Riley's wife bolted out of her initial meeting with him in Holding. Didn't even use the allotted time. They think Riley told her that you were probably flown to this hospital yesterday, Steelie, because the police certainly didn't tell him.' She put her phone in her pocket. 'Anyway, she won't be coming back. Unless she wants to land up in jail too.'

Steelie was wondering about what the woman had been trying to show them. 'What was in her hands?'

Olivia said, 'Pictures of their children: a boy and a girl. She was trying to show them to everyone in the hall too. Kind of sad, actually. When you get past the whole "you bitches" part.'

Steelie looked back to Jayne. 'So Riley from the park was actually married with kids. Did he kill Alex?'

Jayne drew up a chair. 'Here's what I know.'

Steelie listened passively as Jayne told them what she'd learned about Alex's death. She felt herself digesting the fact that Alex had taken the chance of her life on Riley of all people. She grew colder and colder before she realized that the reason she felt cold was that the IV fluid was making its way through her system.

Steelie pulled her thoughts together. 'I feel sorry for Riley's kids. I even feel sorta sorry for his wife. But what kind of mom would want Alex's mom to not have her missing child found? I mean . . .' She didn't have the strength to carry on with the argument like she normally would.

She jutted her chin toward Jayne. 'Can you pull up my blankie? And maybe get me another one? I'm cold.'

As Steelie drifted off, feeling blankets being laid on her, she heard Jayne talking with Olivia. 'When you tell Umar that working for Agency 32/1 means getting hunted down by murderers and their angry spouses, he might re-think his letter of interest.'

OC had started munching on something and spoke with her mouth full. 'You kidding? He'll fast-track it.'

When Steelie woke again, she felt better. Jayne was the only one sitting next to her. Eating her Jell-O, in fact.

'If it's Jell-O you want,' Steelie said weakly, 'you could always hang out with my mom.'

'That's why I'm eating yours: you had your fill during your formative years.' Jayne finished scraping the shallow plastic bowl clean and smiled at her as she put it down on the meal tray.

Steelie squinted her eyes. 'I can see about twenty-eight of your thirty-two shiny teeth. Let me take a guess on why you're giving me the full Julia Roberts.' Steelie considered Jayne's face. 'You and Scott talked and you've patched up whatever went wrong last week.'

'Mm-hm.'

'There must be more because now thirty teeth are on show. Either put me out of my suspense or get me some sunglasses, Julia.'

'We got engaged.' Jayne sat back with a broad grin on her face.

'Oh my gosh.' Steelie actually felt the skin on her cheeks stretching, unaccustomed as she was to smiling this wide in the past twenty-four hours. She reached for Jayne's hand. 'This is . . . amazing.'

Jayne leaned in and clasped her hand. 'Isn't it?'

'I'm so happy, Jayne. I barely know what to say! Tell me everything. Like, which one of you went down on one knee?'

Jayne made a dismissive noise. 'Can you see *me* asking *him* to get married?'

'Yeah, you could talk yourself out of that idea in a heartbeat. I will rephrase, your Honor: how did he get you to say yes?'

'Well, on the one hand, he got me with logic.'

Steelie huffed. 'So romantic.'

Jayne laughed again. 'And yet . . .?'

'Okay, logic is a good way to your heart. You like logic and reasoning.'

'Whereas you like argument. And, before you protest, I didn't say "arguing".'

'Hey, I'm not arguing!' Steelie grinned. 'So, what else did he bring to the party besides logic?'

'It's hard to describe. He made me feel like . . . like I'm the person he's always wanted to be with. Almost needed to be with.'

They both fell quiet.

Steelie felt an unexpected surge of emotion. 'Hit me with a tissue?'

Jayne brought the box over and took a tissue for herself at the same time. She started dabbing her eyes.

'Jesus,' Steelie said as she wiped her face. 'Look at us. At least I can blame my pain meds for making me emotional. I have *no* idea what your excuse is.' She scrunched up the tissue. 'Told your parents yet?'

'No – and I'm glad you brought that up. You're going to have to act surprised when Scott and I tell you this news at some point in the near future.'

'What is this, high school?'

Jayne said, 'I know. Apparently, he wants to wait to tell Eric until the spousal background check is underway at the Bureau. But I *had* to tell you.'

'Heck yes you did. I need time to find my maid-of-honor culottes. Or maybe I could do a skort?'

Jayne's uproarious laughter made Steelie laugh and that's how she found out that laughing hurt. For now.

*

When Jayne walked into her hotel room later, she was immediately struck by the armchairs near the window. They were in the same position she and Scott had left them in when they'd had their conversation the night before. She missed him intensely even though she'd woken up with him that morning. She presumed he and Eric had made it to LA safely on their rebooked flights but she reached for her cell phone to call him. It began to ring before she could dial.

She looked at the readout and wondered, not for the first time, if there was some kind of telepathic connection between her and Scott.

'Hey,' she said, the way they'd greeted each other

from the days when every conversation they'd had was by telephone.

'Hey yourself,' Scott said, keeping to tradition. 'How are you? Are you back at the hotel?'

'I am.' She liked that he was picturing where she was at this time of day, even when she was in another city.

'How's Steelie doing?'

She liked that he thought of Steelie, too. 'Better. I think half of her grogginess is because the anesthetics aren't totally flushed out of her system yet.'

'What's the hospital saying about when she can leave?'

'The doctor said probably Thursday, but . . .' She curled up in the armchair Scott had sat in. 'Since she has to get on a plane to get home, they'll give her a brace to protect the wound. She can take it off once she's home.'

'Are you planning to stay over at her place?'

'She's already lined up a nurse.'

'Oh.' He sounded like he was looking at something else but asking questions he was mildly curious about now that he knew Steelie was going to be coming home soon. 'Her mom?'

She smiled, anticipating Scott's reaction to this tidbit. 'Her Matt.'

Scott sounded like he almost dropped the phone. 'Whoa! Really? Actually, on second thought, he'll be a happy camper. He's a total homebody.'

This was news to Jayne. *Maybe that's why I get on with Matt so easily.* 'Like me,' she said.

'Yeah,' Scott said like he'd seen that coming. 'You two are going to get along great.'

Jayne got a nice image of her, Scott, Steelie and Matt doing things together. *But what about Eric?*

Scott had cleared his throat. 'So, you know what you said about not wanting an engagement ring?'

Jayne had sensed that he'd bring this up again. 'I know you don't agree.'

'I didn't say that. I just hadn't thought about any of that stuff before, about mining and, like, inequality.'

'But you want to buy one anyway.'

'At this point, I'd be uncomfortable doing that. But what would you say if I had a ring made from stones that are already in my family?'

Jayne felt her heart expand. Why hadn't this occurred to her? 'That would be lovely!' She hadn't been able to keep her voice from trembling.

Scott made a soft, exultant noise.

Jayne gathered herself. 'Are the stones from a ring or a bracelet . . . ?'

'Oh no,' Scott warned laughingly. 'I'm not telling you anything more about it. Now that I've got the green light, the rest is going to be a surprise. Plus, it might take a little time to get it made.'

Jayne felt so happy, she wondered why she'd told Scott that she didn't want an engagement ring. She could tell by how she was feeling that she *did* want a ring. It had really been about how to make it happen. She'd been blind to the how, so she'd shut it all down. But Scott wasn't like that. Presented with the problem, he'd found a solution. She loved him for this. 'Thank you so much, Scott. I love your idea.'

His voice softened. 'Jayne, I gotcha, alright? And I'm glad you like this idea because I, well, I would really like to give you something . . . tangible.' He paused. 'Can you chat a bit longer or are you too wiped?'

She had just crossed to the bed, the conversation having taken her places that made her feel like she needed to lie down. 'I'm actually taking you to bed with me.'

'Don't tease me like that.'

She laughed, enchanted that he found her that enticing.

'Seriously,' he said, 'don't, because I'm sitting here looking at the Bureau background check form we'll need for you and it's longer than I expected. But if we start on it now and keep chipping away at it, I can submit it before the week is out.'

'Sounds good.' Jayne pulled the duvet over her and arranged the pillows into a comfortable position. 'I'm all yours.'

'So, I know you're a dual citizen but it's asking if you have an actual US birth certificate or the certificate of a US Citizen Born Abroad, from a consulate. Do you know what they're talking about?'

'I do and I have both.'

'Great. I think we'll only need to submit the birth certificate for this form. I'll find out.'

He went on to a series of questions about where her parents were born and their citizenship. Jayne heard him moving papers around and she pulled the covers up further as she answered as many of the questions as she could off the top of her head like this. She was enjoying the feeling of being part of something with another person. She felt unusually comfortable and safe and closed her eyes. The next thing she knew, she was holding hands in a circle with Scott and Callista. Whenever one of them moved, the other two were pulled in that direction; if they all moved, it could either be a dance or a struggle.

'Jayne . . . Jay-ayne . . .'

She heard Scott's voice as though he were far away. Then she realized her cell phone had fallen from her hand and was next to her on the pillow. She picked it up. 'I'm so sorry, I drifted off.'

'I could tell but I didn't want to hang up on you.'

Half-asleep, half-awake, Jayne murmured, 'Scott, how old's Callista?'

'Callista? Uh . . . forty-four.'

Jayne realized that her imaginings of someone younger than her had been off-base. 'And why did she want to keep things going with you even though she knew you wanted to end it?'

There was a pause before Scott answered. 'She wanted a baby.'

'Oh.' Jayne digested that. 'Well, at forty-four, I'd probably be thinking about children too – if I wanted them and hadn't had any yet.'

'Jayne, she didn't want children. She wanted "a baby". That's how she put it, like it wouldn't grow up.'

'And you didn't want a baby.'

'No.'

'And children?'

There was a longer pause. 'She should have been having them with her husband,' he said. 'And I hope to hell she is.'

Even in her sleepy state, Jayne was aware that Scott had chosen to answer that as though she'd only been asking about Callista's choices and not his own, but it didn't bother her. She felt like nothing could bother her now.

Three Days Later

Friday

31

Scott sat across from Supervisory Special Agent Craig Turner, looking intermittently at the folder Turner was paging through and at the reflective sheen on the surface of Turner's vast glass-topped mahogany desk. Scott smoothed a hand over his tie and changed to looking out of the large windows where they met at the corner of the room. Here in Westwood, the marine layer was finally lifting, the sunlight coming through weakly, but Scott could discern that out by the ocean side of Santa Monica, the fog blanket was just beginning to break up. It was promising to be a beautiful day in Los Angeles. He glanced at his boss. Turner was the deciding factor as to whether the beauty in Scott's day would extend beyond the weather.

Turner closed the folder and put down his pen. 'That is all in order, Agent Houston.'

Scott nodded briefly. He knew it was all in order because he'd spent four days completing it and then he'd checked, double-checked and triple-checked it. Anyway, Turner only needed to approve the first two pages, not the rest of it.

Turner said, 'Since Ms. Hall was already backgrounded for the MOU, there shouldn't be any issues, however, I won't be able to ask them to forgo this background just because that one was completed so recently.'

'I'm not asking for any shortcuts, sir.'

Turner looked at him. 'I know you're not. *I* was considering it, however.'

Scott didn't know what to say to that so waited for Turner to speak again.

Turner said, 'That brings me to the next topic: the MOU.'

'Sir.'

'I have completed the look-back at the agreement with Agency 32/1. There is no conflict issue and no exposure in terms of the cases. I will be re-issuing their adjunct badges forthwith.'

Before Scott could remark on this, Turner held up a hand. 'I have also established that you have not displayed a lack of candor or engaged in nepotism in regards to the MOU, as was alleged by King.'

Scott just barely avoided interrupting his boss. 'It's confirmed that the tip came from King, sir?'

Turner gave him a shrewd look. 'I see you're aware that there was a tip. Yes. I had it traced and it was King but that didn't alter the fact that it was a tip that required a response. I pulled it off the conveyor belt before it got to OPR.'

Scott inhaled sharply. The Office of Professional Responsibility probably wouldn't have let him stay on the operation, not even as Angie's caddie, while they did their internal affairs investigation.

Turner indicated Scott's documents on the desk. 'In light of this official notification of your intent to marry Ms. Hall, I will be required to redraft the MOU and send it out to bid as a contract.'

'Understood,' Scott said but his mind was leaping ahead with the potential implications of a bid process. He could not envision working on Thirty-Two One type cases with any outside organization other than Thirty-Two One.

'I don't believe you've taken in the import of what I'm saying, SA Houston.' Turner stood up and went over to the window.

Scott had never seen his boss take in the view. And it turned out he wasn't this time either.

He'd turned his back on the windows and was regarding Scott. 'I did my own checking before I proffered the MOU to Agency 32/1. Are you aware that they're the only outfit in the country that does what they do?'

Scott felt he *should* have known that but he wasn't sure he had. Or maybe it was just Turner. The guy always made him feel like he was missing something. He shook his head.

Turner gave him an understanding nod. 'Would you agree, therefore, that it is highly unlikely, if not impossible, for Thirty-Two One to face significant competition from other bidders?'

Scott said, 'I would,' beginning to grasp Turner's point.

Turner talked as he walked back to his desk. 'Thirty-Two One was instrumental not only in producing IDs on the King case but also in leveraging families to provide DNA. That's in addition to them generating goodwill between the Bureau and multiple constituents.' He grasped the back of his chair as he addressed Scott directly. 'I have every intention of keeping them in our arsenal, so make sure your fiancée gets that bid in once the RFP goes out.'

Scott gave a business-like nod, but he felt relieved and oddly warm toward the Ice Man.

Turner appeared satisfied with Scott's nod and continued. 'While you and Eric were still on the recovery operation, I had Atlanta PD's Head of Missing Persons, Head of Homicide and their Chief calling me, all smiles. Some big fish in Phoenix and various guppies in New Mexico also thanked us for not just finding remains in their jurisdiction but taking them away with us as well.'

Scott smirked, then reined it in.

Turner finally took his seat again. 'San Antonio is a different story, however.'

'Oh?' Scott was immediately on edge.

'Stand by.' Turner used his desk phone. 'SA Ramos. Please join me and your partner in my office.'

He hung up and looked at Scott. 'Is your engagement public at this time?'

'No, sir,' Scott said. 'It will be soon.'

Turner stood and leaned over his desk, hand outstretched. 'In that case, Scott, let me be among the first to congratulate you.'

Caught unawares, Scott jerked forward out of his chair only to have his hand crushed the way Turner liked to do it. 'Thank you.' He couldn't bring himself to call Turner 'Craig'.

They sat in silence for a moment, waiting for Eric, and then Turner added, 'Ms. Hall is an impressive woman. I trust you will be very happily married.'

Feeling out of his depth in this unprecedented personal conversation with the Ice Man, Scott managed a few words. 'I think my ability to make her happy is more the . . .' He trailed off, not wanting to inadvertently reveal, to Turner of *all* people, his fear that his toxic past could taint Jayne someday. The man would probably send him on a combo Internal Affairs-Psych Debrief 'holiday' at Quantico.

But Turner was giving him an avuncular look and an approving smile. 'Then be sure you put as much effort into your marriage as you put into your job.'

Scott exhaled. He wasn't sure he could get used to having conversations like this with the Ice Man. He wouldn't be able to keep calling him the Ice Man behind his back, for one thing.

Fortunately, a knock came at the door.

Eric came in, nodded at Scott and said to Turner, 'You needed to see me, sir?'

'Take a seat, Agent Ramos.'

Eric sat down in the chair next to Scott, his back ramrod straight.

'San Antonio,' Turner said. 'The young woman whose body you came across. Indigenous and trafficked.'

'Sir,' Scott acknowledged.

'They found more.'

Eric and Scott glanced at each other but it was Eric who addressed their boss. 'At the truck stop?'

Turner nodded. 'Yes, but don't worry that you didn't find it yourselves. It was beyond your search area. Now, San Antonio PD is complaining because they've got multiple bodies and they can't ID some of them. They're already getting word from neighboring states of criminal activity related to the trafficking of these young people through their jurisdictions. It's a shit sandwich.'

'Are we eating it?' Scott asked.

'We are. When San Antonio requested federal assistance, DC did a connect-the-dots and saw that our office had involvement with the truck stop at the start, so now the case is ours.'

Turner pushed a thick file across the desk. 'Get Lance to copy that for you. There's some electronic material already coming your way. I will not be having you go mobile again; recovery is done with these remains. But there is going to be an identification issue, liaising with Canadian authorities, possibly others.'

He tapped the file. 'You can see where I'm going. I will want Thirty-Two One on-boarded so we can streamline this, get family engagement to kick-start IDs and move on to getting leads on who's responsible for the abductions, the trafficking, the homicides.'

Eric said, 'Thirty-Two One makes sense, sir, but what about the MOU? Is it still on hold or . . .?'

Turner glanced fleetingly at Scott. 'No. I will be lifting the hold and will take care of communicating with Ms. Hall and Ms. Lander soon. In the meantime, get stuck in to this material. There's a lot of it.'

He picked up his desk phone and then looked at the agents as though he didn't know why they were still there. Fingers hovering over the keypad, he said, 'You're dismissed.'

*

Jayne pushed Steelie in the borrowed wheelchair out the doors of Terminal 1 at LAX over to Tom Bradley

International, maneuvering around people getting out of cars and checking in bags curbside. As they approached Bradley, Jayne spotted Graham. He was back in the *Holden* T-shirt he'd worn the first day he came to the Agency. He was clutching his duffel bag and looking anxious. He hailed them the moment he saw them.

His anxiety was explained immediately. 'They gave you an earbashing because I didn't come in person, didn't they? I have to go m'self? See Alex in her coffin?'

'No, no,' Steelie soothed. 'Everything's set. Airport staff is used to family representatives being involved with something like this.'

He scratched his head roughly. 'Lotsa people check their relatives in as baggage, do they?'

Jayne didn't try to negate his feelings. 'It's not easy for anyone. This is why Steelie and I are here today. For you, for Alex.'

She gave him the documents she and Steelie had finalized with the baggage staff in Terminal 1. 'This is yours for when you get to Melbourne. It's the same container you arranged for Alex with the funeral home in Seattle but it won't come out on a baggage claim carousel. You'll need to talk to a baggage handler there at Melbourne Airport. They'll have it to the side for you.'

Steelie added, 'And if you don't want to even see the container, just wait for the person from the funeral home that your mother set up. They'll find you and take care of everything with the baggage folks.'

'Thank you.' Graham folded the documents into his carry-on bag. 'I feel like a wuss. If looking for Alex had been left to me, my mum would have lost me too because I'd have been dead in some park in Washington state.' He shuddered and the tip of his nose went red.

Steelie said gently, 'Graham—'

He stopped her. 'Hang on. You ladies didn't just find Alex, you saved us heaps of money, because I'd been prepared to stay in Seattle for a couple of weeks or more. What that means is, we've got some dosh left over from when we sold the land to pay for all this. Mum's decided . . .' His eyes started to water. 'She's decided to donate it to the school where Alex went, get them to make a music and arts program named after her. They've agreed.' He gave them a bright smile but had to wipe his eyes with the back of his hand.

Steelie smiled up at Jayne and Jayne squeezed Steelie's shoulder.

Graham laughed sheepishly. 'Sorry. I've been a bit weepy since that bloke tried to top us. And he didn't even wing me like he did you, Steelie.'

Steelie was chirpy. 'Oh, I *threw* myself in the path of the bullet just so I could get some hospital food. They won't let you come in and get three squares a day if you don't get winged first.'

Graham smiled gratefully at her joke and Steelie gestured at the terminal building. 'I think you've got time to check out Duty Free before they call your flight.'

'Right-o.' He picked up his duffel bag. 'I can't believe I'm actually taking Alex home to Wangaratta. Which reminds me: my mum says if you're ever Down Under, you've got a place to stay with us. And she means it. She'll make you a pav.'

Jayne hesitated because she didn't know what that was.

Graham stared at them, wide-eyed. 'Pavlova? Crikey, if you've never had a pav, you gotta have my mum's. Lotsa fresh cream, lotsa berries from the garden, meringue – aw, my mouth's waterin' just thinkin' about it!'

Steelie grinned. 'So's mine.'

He suddenly hugged Jayne tightly. Then he kissed Steelie on the cheek and went without another word.

Jayne leaned on the back of Steelie's wheelchair as they watched him go to the first security barrier. Graham turned to wave at them and they waved back until he disappeared into the pedestrian tunnel.

Steelie said, 'All that talk of pav, whatever that is, has made me want to stop at that bakery on the other side of La Tijera.'

Jayne was feeling good that Graham was safely on his way back to Australia. 'Yeah, let's get brownies.'

Steelie added, 'If we get coffee too, then it won't matter if we hit traffic on the way back to the office.'

Jayne started pushing the wheelchair. 'You're not going to the office. You're going home to rest. This was a special dispensation.'

Steelie started grumbling but Jayne didn't think her heart was really in it. She was sure of that a few minutes later as she helped Steelie into the Jeep Cherokee. Despite taking the transfer slowly, Steelie's quiet but frequent gasps told Jayne that her friend really needed more rest.

*

When they left the bakery, Steelie enjoyed sipping her coffee and taking some bites of brownie, all possible because she wasn't driving. She liked Jayne's new ride. Its height gave great visibility as Jayne took the carpool lane on the 105 Freeway, using its graceful, curving ascent to transition onto the northbound Harbor Freeway.

The northward turn took them out of the foggy marine layer that was still breaking up over the airport's ocean side. Steelie looked into the distance and confirmed what she'd guessed: the skyscrapers of Downtown Los Angeles were already bathed in sunlight. That meant that it would be sunny at Parker Center. She wondered if Matt was at his desk or out running down a lead on some case. She liked knowing that she'd find out later.

She glanced at Jayne. 'Have you been thinking about Seattle?'

Jayne swallowed her coffee. 'What happened to us or what happened to Alex?'

'Both, I guess.'

'Off and on.' Jayne tracked a passing car. 'You?'

Steelie winced as she adjusted her seatbelt. ''Twas a bit of a close call. For both of us.'

Jayne noddded. 'Agreed. So, what do we do? Close the Agency? Try and make change another way? Work for the coroner's office after all?'

This had crossed Steelie's mind – briefly – when she'd been diving into a bush to save their lives. But she'd had a lot of time to think since then. 'Closing the Agency is the nuclear option. I think we have other options.'

'You sound like you've been thinking about this.'

'Being laid up in a hospital bed does that to me.'

'It didn't in Atlanta, after Gene.'

Steelie shrugged. 'That was different. I already knew Gene was an ass, so when he started acting like one, I wasn't that surprised. Made me more angry than anything else. But getting shot by someone I thought was harmless . . .?' She had to blow out her breath to reduce the tension building in her body.

Jayne reached out and squeezed her arm. 'I was really scared we were going to lose you, Steelie.'

'That's how I felt after you sank to the bottom of the reservoir in your truck.'

She saw Jayne shiver as she returned her hand to the steering wheel, gripping it a little too hard. Steelie realized that this wasn't the time to be talking about being run off the road.

She tried for a peppier tone. 'So, what do you think about us having a rule that we don't go into the field unless it's an MOU job?'

Jayne looked surprised and interested. 'Okayyy.' She glanced at Steelie. 'But what if there's no MOU by the time Turner is done taking a hard look at it?'

Steelie shook her head. 'He won't. We just got them a bunch of results, right? Scott told you they're on track to get every one of Gene's victims ID'd? Turner'll make sure he has an MOU so he can get more of the same. We give *him* options.'

'I don't know.' Jayne sounded doubtful. 'Gene has a way of . . . wreaking havoc from within.' She looked behind her as she exited from the carpool lane before it came to an end. 'I've been wanting to tell you something about him.'

'So you're finally going to let me in on this,' Steelie

said, trying to turn in her seat to face Jayne. 'Is it from the landslip day?'

'Yeah.'

'I knew it!' Steelie slapped her knee and then regretted moving so abruptly. 'I *knew* something happened. What did Gene do?'

'He didn't actually do anything. He said – God, this sounds so awful – he *said*, or I understood him to say, that Scott was married.'

'Oh!' Steelie's mind rejected this and then . . . didn't. Crap like this could happen. But Scott and Jayne were now engaged so he couldn't be married. At least, not since last week. 'Okay, I can see why that could have put you into a tailspin at the time. You didn't ask Scott about it right away?'

Jayne made an exasperated noise. 'Turner arrived and we were out of there!'

Steelie had forgotten that part. 'Oh, yeah. Not much time or even the right timing for that kind of conversation.'

'Not just that, Steelie: Gene gave me a name and I figured he could only have learned it by doing surveillance on Scott like he'd done on me.'

Now Steelie understood why Jayne had been so thrown, leaving aside the fact that Gene always threw her. 'So you thought it was legit.'

'Exactly! I immediately started hoping Scott was actually separated or divorcing – like, soon to be available. Then I worried that he was just plain old married. I got so upset that I kind of . . . turned inward.'

Steelie drummed her fingers on the windowsill and looked outside. They were passing Downtown. She glimpsed her parents' condo adjacent to the Disney Concert Hall where the silvered, curving exterior was reflecting light in every direction. She was pretty sure that what Jayne had been doing was called catastrophizing. It was part of her PTSD and it was affecting her relationship with Scott.

Steelie asked, 'What name did Gene say?'

'Callista,' Jayne said.

'And when you eventually talked with Scott, you asked him about her by name?'

'I did. Their relationship ended just before he moved to LA.'

'Hm. Gene had the right name but the wrong situation.'

'Yeah, she and Scott had dated – while she was separated from her husband. It did seem to catch Scott off guard when I asked him about her.'

Steelie dismissed this. 'No one likes talking about their exes. Anyway, you had to have known Scott had been around the block a time or two before you got involved. I don't know why you're blushing; so had you.'

Jayne exclaimed, 'But none of my relationships were serious!'

'Who said Scott's were? Gene? As we say in court: "fruit from the tainted tree". Fuhgeddaboudit.'

She paused, then said, 'Jayne, it's always seemed to me that you and Scott were waiting for the other one to make the first move. I remember those days at Quantico. You were drawn to each other. But I get why you didn't tell me about what Gene said until you'd talked to Scott.'

Jayne exited the freeway and headed for San Fernando Road. 'I didn't want you to think badly of him. Or me.'

'Look, I know Scott in my own right and have my own perceptions of him. As for you . . . never.'

Steelie wanted to add, *But I think it's time for trauma therapy.* She realized she was holding her tongue because maybe she needed to take her own advice on this, the way she was thinking of hiding inside the Agency's four walls. In this moment, though, she wanted to make sure Jayne knew she supported her and her choice to be with Scott.

So she said, 'However, you *will* go down in my estimation if you make me wear a dress to your wedding.'

Jayne chuckled as she approached the Agency. She pointed at the copies of Graham's documents. 'I'm going to lock these in the safe before I take you home.'

Steelie nodded. 'Oh, and Matt is hoping you, Scott and Eric can come over to help with my backyard after work today.'

Jayne came down on her like a ton of bricks as she pulled the car into their lot. 'Please tell me you're not doing yard work.'

'I'm not! But Matt is. And he'll order in if you want to stay for dinner.'

'Okay,' Jayne relented. She picked up the documents. 'Be right back.'

As Jayne opened her car door, a black Chevrolet Suburban with a US Government J-plate turned into the parking lot at a fast clip and reversed neatly to face her, engine and headlights still on.

32

Standing by the rear bumper of her car, Jayne watched SSA Turner emerge from the back seat of the Suburban. He walked toward her, his long legs making short work of the distance between them.

She greeted him. 'SSA Turner. Would you like to come in? I can open up.'

He glanced at the building. 'There's no need for that. Is Ms. Lander with you?'

'In the car.' Jayne gestured at her Jeep. 'She's recovering from an injury. Well, you'll have heard.'

'I've done more than that. I'm glad you agreed to get on the chopper with her.'

'Oh! Were you—'

Before Jayne could confirm that Turner had been the one to get Steelie medevac'd after Riley shot her, Steelie opened the passenger door. She didn't get out.

SSA Turner came to her door. 'How are you feeling, Ms. Lander?'

'The wind's a bit out of my sails, to be perfectly frank.'

'I can see that. I trust you will be back on your feet soon, to mix metaphors.' He made an expression that could have passed for a smile. 'Not least because I am returning these to you and Ms. Hall.'

He held out Jayne and Steelie's FBI adjunct badges.

'These are temporary. A new form of agreement is being drawn up. You will be notified about it in due course. However, between now and then, you will remain available to the Bureau for any and all activities agreed upon in the extant Memorandum.'

Steelie gave Jayne a self-satisfied look as she took her badge. Jayne's badge felt good in her hand. It felt like options, like Steelie had said. She thanked Turner.

He nodded. 'I also wanted to thank you in person for your contributions in Atlanta and on the mobile recovery operation last week. The team made it clear that the successful outcome was largely due to your involvement.' He put his hand on Steelie's door. 'Rest up, Ms. Lander.'

'Oh, I will,' she said.

Turner closed the door for her. Then he turned to Jayne. 'Walk with me.'

Feeling curious, Jayne accompanied him over to the Suburban. The driver came to open the door but Turner shook his head in the negative. He turned to Jayne. 'Ms. Hall, Scott has notified me of your engagement. Congratulations.' He did that smile-like thing again.

Jayne felt embarrassed. She didn't know why this man always had that effect on her. 'Thank you.'

He'd already stopped smiling. 'Have you set a date for the wedding?'

'I – we – no.'

'I ask about the date because I don't want a conflict with something else on the calendar for SA Houston. Please keep me informed.' He got into the Suburban, then added, 'Not before your own family, of course, but a close second.'

He closed his door and Jayne was left watching the enormous vehicle bulk its way out of the driveway.

Steelie called to Jayne. 'What was *that* all about?'

Jayne walked over slowly. She spoke with a tone of wonderment. 'He seemed to be congratulating me on the engagement. And asking when the wedding will be.'

Steelie snorted. 'I would have loved to have heard that.' She took on a Turner-like tone of voice. 'Due to the forthwith personal entanglement between you, Civilian, and one of my people, I hereby notify you that I will be in your head and on your six, twenty-four-seven, in order to preserve and protect the Bureau's mission and indeed its property: namely, Scott Houston, Special Agent Number 34927-dash-007.'

Jayne laughed. 'It was a bit like that. But I'm warming to him.'

*

Eric let himself in the side gate to Steelie's backyard and saw her sitting on an outdoor loveseat shaded by a cantilevered umbrella. She waved without raising her arm above her shoulder.

'Eric!' she called out. 'Thanks for coming. I'd give you a beer but I just got into a good position. Help yourself.' She jutted her chin toward a cooler on the table.

He got a beer and sat next to her, noticing that she had a cushion behind her and another in front for additional support. Clinking his bottle against hers, he said, 'So, how you doing?'

She tilted her head to the side in consideration. 'I've felt better. But being home and feeling crappy beats being in hospital feeling crappy. Even if I did like being waited on hand and foot.'

'From what I hear, Matt makes a decent nurse.'

'It is really weird what things you "hear", Eric,' she said with a smile. 'I thought guys didn't talk to each other.'

He chuckled.

Just then, Matt emerged from the backyard shed carrying various gardening tools. He looked hot and dusty. One of the smaller tools fell from his grip, then another. He straightened up and squinted over at them. Eric raised his beer in salutation.

Matt yelled over, 'You were supposed to be coming over to help.'

'I thought it was to help drink the beer,' Eric called back. He frowned at Steelie with mock concern. 'No?'

'Ha ha,' she said with a thin smile.

Matt rolled his eyes and carried the tools to the far end of the yard. Eric heard the latch on the driveway gate click upwards. When he saw Jayne and Scott walking in, carrying a large cooler between them, he stood up to get them drinks.

'You're not dressed for yard work either,' Steelie said, sounding aggrieved.

Her comment made Eric look at them a second time, having not taken in their clothes. Scott was in jeans but it was true that he was wearing a nice button-down shirt, its sleeves rolled partway up his arms. Jayne was wearing a T-shirt with a skirt; Eric realized he'd only ever seen her in pants before – or Tyvek.

Scott was taking in the scene: banked garden beds taking shape on both sides of the yard, a solar fountain at the end, pots of lavender and young trees in position for later planting.

He said, 'Looks to me like Matty has it under control. And you're looking good, Steelie.' He came over to fist-bump Eric and accept a beer.

But Jayne had stopped in her tracks. 'This looks fantastic. Matt did all this?'

'I'd done a bunch over the past few weeks,' Steelie said. 'But Matt's moved it forward and he's added a few things. Like the baby trees you all were supposed to be planting this evening.'

'And the seating,' Jayne enthused as she sat down on the loveseat across from Steelie. 'This wasn't your exact plan but we can sit out here already. I love it. Look at this rug! The colors are great.'

Eric had poured a sparkling apple cider for Jayne and handed it to her.

'Thank you, Eric. Sorry, I hadn't even said hi, I was so distracted by the yard.' They kissed each other on the cheek.

Eric went to stand next to Scott again, both of them nursing their beers as they looked around. Eric said, 'It is a huge improvement.'

'Huge.' Scott added.

Steelie gave them a look. 'You don't need to emphasize the *huge* so much.'

Scott laughed and gestured to Jayne to join him in going to greet Matt.

Eric took his seat next to Steelie again.

She patted his arm. 'I wanted to thank you for everything

in Seattle. Jayne told me you were the one who actually tackled Riley.'

He shook his head. He didn't feel the need for thanks. 'Just doing our jobs.'

'You say that and yet it was way outside anything you had on the books.'

'True, but as soon as we knew you needed assistance, we were there. That's our job. It helped that we could track you with GPS.'

Steelie shook her head in disbelief. 'I can't believe I ever complained about having to carry that Bureau BlackBerry.'

He chuckled. 'You're allowed to complain, Steelie.'

She swallowed some beer. 'I admire what you do, Eric. How you and Scott think, how you work with each other, teaming with the Critters . . . all of it.'

He figured Steelie was still feeling raw from being used for target practice, so he said, 'I admire what *you* do.' He paused. 'Y'know, after you and Jayne left the recovery operation, I tried to help out at the sites a couple of times.'

He smiled at Steelie's shocked expression.

Eyes wide, she pointed at the ground like there were bones in front of them. 'Actual hands-on stuff?'

He nodded. 'Yep. And partway through, I realized there was a reason I'd trained to be an investigative agent, not a criminalist.'

He suddenly pictured the dried-out scalp with the hair holes and couldn't even take a sip of beer.

Steelie said, 'You're thinking of something in particular, aren't you?'

'A scalp,' he admitted. He'd never say that word the same way again.

Steelie made a face. 'Ooo, nasty. Decomp'd?'

'Uh-huh.'

Steelie sucked her teeth. 'Yeah, those holes will getcha every time. Sorry.'

He gave a rueful laugh. Of course she knew all about it. He said, 'It was bizarre, Steelie. I couldn't turn off my regular eyesight and see that scalp as . . . what? A clue? However you'd have seen it.'

'I'd have seen it the same way you did but then I'd push through to see it as a chance to get someone identified or at least recovered. I've done a lot of pushing through, Eric.'

He was astonished and could only look at her, waiting for her to explain.

She drank and then she spoke, more quietly. 'From the first time I ever went to a coroner's office in grad school to every time I've exhumed some clandestine grave, I've had to push myself to do my job, not just sit down and fucking cry.' Her voice wavered and she looked away.

Eric didn't know what to say for a minute. 'Man, Steelie.' He tried to find words to express his deep surprise at this revelation without making it sound like he'd thought she was just . . . Teflon. 'But you're always so peppy. Punchy, even. About your work, anyway.'

She glanced at him between wipes of her eyes. 'I *am* peppy about it. I love it. But the work has a tail and sometimes the tail wags. More and more often for some; a little less for others. But it wags.'

He could only squeeze her hand. She held his tightly and

looked out to where the others were starting to walk back. Then they let each other go.

Jayne and Scott were still complimenting all the work that had been done to transform the backyard. Matt was taking off his gloves and looking pleased as he went for a beer. Eric got up so Matt would be able to sit next to Steelie.

Steelie called out to Jayne. 'Did you already tell Scott about Turner?'

Jayne shook her head.

Eric swallowed his beer. 'What about him?'

'Your boss paid us a visit,' Jayne said.

'Today?' Scott sounded suddenly alert. He looked like the answer really mattered.

'Uh-huh,' Steelie said. 'Gave us our MOU badges back. Said a new MOU is coming? Not sure why, though.'

Scott answered distractedly. 'Yeah . . .' He put his finger to his lips in thought, then said, 'Actually, I can update you on this. The new MOU will be a contract that'll go through a bid process.'

Steelie immediately started peppering him with questions. He held up a hand. 'If you'd let me finish? Turner expects – *wants* – to see a bid from Agency 32/1.'

Eric was thinking this through. 'But why does Thirty-Two One need to bid when it's been determined there's no conflict with the existing agreement?'

'Because . . .' Scott's face reddened as looked at Jayne. 'Jayne and I are getting married.'

Eric felt a drop in his stomach like he was in an elevator that suddenly went down. He heard the outbursts of enthusiasm from Matt and Steelie, saw Matt jump up to slap Scott on the back while Jayne bent to hug Steelie, and then Jayne was turning to him. He hugged her and made the right noises and then Scott was in front of him, pulling him into a hug. Unbidden, Eric's brain recorded every detail of the embrace before it took him to the bar in New Mexico and the feeling of Scott's lips on his. He felt a brief confusion of time and place but Scott's expression as they moved apart was clarity itself: *What's up?*

With effort, Eric energized his voice. 'You and Jayne. I'll drink to that!'

'Yeah!' Matt whooped. 'Got any champagne, Steelie?'

Scott waved him off. 'We brought some.'

Eric held the glasses for Scott and handed them out automatically while everyone but him talked at once. He couldn't understand the time warp he'd just been in or why it had happened. Finally, Scott approached Jayne with the cider.

Matt pointed at the bottle and then at Jayne. 'Wait, you're pregnant?'

Jayne almost dropped her glass and Scott poured cider onto the rug. He said, 'Shit! Jesus. What?' as he turned on Matt.

Matt gestured expressively at the Martinelli's bottle. It was a moment before everyone but Matt started to laugh, very loudly. Eric managed a chuckle.

'Matt?' Steelie's voice eventually cut through the noise. 'Jayne doesn't drink.'

'In general,' Scott added, mopping up the spill at Jayne's feet.

Eric saw Scott drop his little half-grin on Jayne and his stomach fell down the elevator shaft again. He moved away, to stand with Matt.

Matt was muttering, 'Sorry, I saw the apple juice and I thought—'

'Yeah, Matt,' Steelie said as she glanced at him in amusement. 'We know what you thought. But,' she lifted her glass, 'mazel tov on the engagement, guys.'

Eric chanced a look at his partner, almost afraid of what would happen this time. But nothing happened. He just saw Scott. In fact, he'd never seen his friend this happy – the same for Jayne. With relief came understanding: the thing with Scott – Eric still couldn't think of it as a kiss – had sparked something in him. It was something that had always been there but had quietly gone dormant in the wake of his divorce. It felt like a small, flickering flame somewhere inside him.

And in that moment, Eric knew he was going to give it some oxygen – he was going to give *himself* some oxygen. He didn't know the where, the when, the how or the who, but the flame had been rekindled. For that alone, he raised his glass high and gave his partner a full-throated roar of approval. Scott immediately looked at him, then lifted his own glass and toasted Eric. Jayne tracked this exchange, met Eric's eyes and smiled. Then she blew him a kiss in a heartfelt, jubilant flourish that made Eric laugh aloud.

Matt grumbled, 'Are you people gonna drink this stuff or are you just gonna stand around, grinning at each other?'

Steelie hid her glass. 'Oh, were we supposed to wait?'

Afterword

Although this book is fiction, the Green River Serial Killer case is real. Since the first victim's body was found in 1982, the medical examiner's office in King County, Washington, has continued to try to identify the victims, while law enforcement has tried to locate other women who are still missing. These efforts continue today and King County requests help from anyone who may have information that could bring these women home.

To see clay facial reconstructions of some of the unidentified women and photographs of some of the missing women, please visit:

https://kingcounty.gov/depts/sheriff/about-us/enforcement/investigations/green-river.aspx

Acknowledgments

Heartfelt thanks to my editor Amy Baxter for applying her editorial skills to this book with enthusiasm and precision. Thanks also to my publisher Helen Huthwaite for a wonderful collaboration across continents.

My literary and film agents Carla Briner-Mercier and Anna Soler-Pont truly represent me and I thank them for the connections they make. I deeply appreciate everyone at Pontas Agency and give special thanks to Clara Rosell for her ever-presence.

The late Dr. Walter Birkby first prepared me for presenting evidence at trial when I was a graduate student in his forensic anthropology program. Walt taught me the science within its context, a combination that continues to galvanize me.

Another of Walt's students and a friend of mine, the late Dr. Katherine ('KT') Taylor, went on to the King County Medical Examiner's Office in the state of Washington. I acknowledge KT's work, as well as the work of my colleague and mentor, the late Dr. William Haglund, to identify victims of the Green River killings on behalf of King County.

In honor of my great-uncle Alan (Abraham) Koff who was the mayor of Lordsburg in times past, I set part of this book in that small New Mexico town. However, the

Ocotillo bar and other scenes there are as fictional as my 'FBI mobile operation'.

Credit for Steelie's phrase, "a face as long as Ventura Boulevard," goes to my Studio City acting coach when I was a teenager; while credit for "Everybody counts or nobody counts" goes to the author Michael Connelly.

Warmest thanks to Anne and Sam, as always and for everything.

I thank my family for embracing my endeavors and I thank Jon for embracing me.